TICK TOCK

THE TICK TOCK DUET

JANE HARVEY-BERRICK

HARVEY
BERRICK
PUBLISHING

CONTENTS

TICK TOCK

The Tick Tock Duet

Copyright © 2021 Jane Harvey-Berrick

Military advice by Justin Bell QGM

Cover design by Sybil Wilson / Pop Kitty Design
Photographer: GG Gold / Model: Gergo Jonas

To Justin Bell QGM, and the men and women who walk toward danger.
E. xplosive
O. rdnance
D. isposal

TICK TOCK

A NOTE ABOUT THIS BOOK

This hasn't been an easy book to write for lots of different reasons—it's important to me, so getting the research right has been tricky.

But I have close friends from the EOD community, and close friends from the Muslim community, who have helped and guided me through.

They have guided and advised, but ultimately it's my book, so any mistakes are mine and mine alone.

The aim is to be respectful to both communities, and to tell a story of love and compassion in a very dark place.

There may be 'triggers' for some people in the story, so please be advised.

In the end, it's a love story, not a hate story, and I hope that's the part that remains with you.

But also huge thanks to my lovely team who've helped me shape this story: Madeena Mohana Wali, Dzana, Selma and Sejla Ibrahimpasic who advised on Islamic customs.

I should also mention that *TICK TOCK* and *BOMBSHELL* are written in British English and spelling rather than American English, so some of the slang used is mentioned in the Glossary at the back.

PROLOGUE

WE'RE BORN ALONE AND WE DIE ALONE.

I've never been afraid of dying. It's living that scares the hell out of me.

But in the bomb suit, I am utterly alone.

There is no today, no yesterday, no tomorrow.

Just here, right now.

There is no God, no Devil, no good, no evil.

Just me. And the sound of my breathing, loud and rhythmic.

Just me. And this bomb.

A bomb is a device that is designed to kill, maim or harass.

I'm not afraid. I don't have time to be afraid.

The sun burns down, the light is a white haze, sweat runs into my eyes. The longer I'm out here, kneeling in the dust, the more vulnerable the team watching my back.

I can't be quick. I have to be certain.

Because if I'm wrong, I die.

I am an EOD operator.

Explosives

Ordnance

Disposal.

Bomb disposal.
I am the Tick Tock man.

CHAPTER ONE

JAMES

I raised my SA80 rifle and aimed at the man's chest. *Got him!*

From 20 yards, I couldn't miss. But then again, neither could he.

He was driving an old Jeep, so battered that it looked as though string and chewing gum held it together. He revved the engine threateningly and I ducked behind a lamppost so he wouldn't be able to run me over. I couldn't see the driver's hands. What was he doing with his hands? He could be reaching for a weapon, or he could be arming a device that would blow a hole through the world.

Shit just got serious.

I gestured with the rifle, my voice harsh and gritty—a command.

"Raise your hands and place them on the steering wheel."

He didn't move, he just stared at me, his eyes narrowed with hatred.

"Raise your hands *now!*"

Still nothing.

The soldier next to me started to twitch.

"Staff! He's not doing anything! Does he even speak fucking English?"

He'd got a strong Geordie accent, so it sounded like, *Stav! Ees not dooin' ennyfink! Doos ee even spook fookin Eenglish?*

"I don't know. Do you?"

He gave me a quick, nervous grin. But my joke had helped him to relax. Or maybe he'd just stepped back from the edge of a big mistake.

I took a pace forward, pointing my SA80 at the insurgent.

"Hands where I can see them!"

Even if he didn't speak English, my meaning was clear.

But I was distracted by the soldier next to me who was jigging from foot to foot like he wanted to piss his pants.

I glanced toward him.

"Calm down, it's alright…"

Suddenly, there was a loud bang, a flash of light from the Jeep, and a cloud of dust and blue smoke flared upward.

I lowered my rifle and swore.

"Staff Sergeant Spears!" bellowed Captain Elderman, shaking his head. "If that had been a real device, you and your men would be very fucking dead right now. You should have made sure his hands were in sight. It's a good thing this is a training exercise in Wiltshire and not a real life situation in Ifuckingdontcareistan. I expected better of you, Spears. See me in my office later."

Then he strode away.

The Jeep driver grinned, tossed a V-sign with his fingers, racing off in a cloud of dust, the exhaust rattling asthmatically.

"Sorry, Staff," said my Lance Corporal, his expression crestfallen. "I fooked it oop."

"You, me, both," I sighed.

We joined the rest of the Troop and trudged back to the bus that would take us from the training ground to the barracks.

The pack on my back weighed 110 pounds: 50lb of basic Army shit; 60lb of EOD kit. It was 31°C and I was sweating my 'nads off. English summers weren't supposed to be this hot.

It was sheer relief to climb onto the bus and crawl to a seat at the back where I could dump my pack and drink some tepid water from my flask.

I looked around at my team that I'd been attached to, all from REME—the Corps of Royal Electrical and Mechanical Engineers. They were good lads, but young and inexperienced. At 29, I was the oldest. Next stop thirty. When did I get so old?

I leaned back against the seat and closed my eyes, letting the weariness take me. Within minutes, I was falling asleep. That was something you learned in this job: catch some ZZZs while you can. Hours in your sleeping bag can be few and far between on a deployment in a hostile environment. Over the years, I'd trained myself to sleep anywhere: in a hammock, up a tree, in a tank, or lying on a slab of concrete. Time and opportunity was all I needed.

Although a nice soft bed with a nice soft woman in it wouldn be even better, but I took what I could get.

When the bus arrived back at base, I was jolted awake.

Military bases are all essentially the same: red brick housing for families, low concrete barracks for unmarried personnel, ugly buildings, boring offices, hangars for planes or transport, tarmac parade grounds—grey, functional, depressing.

The Ministry Of Defence kept promising to tart up the living quarters, but I hadn't seen any signs of it lately. At least we all had single rooms now, except for recruits who hadn't passed basic.

Back at the Armoury, we returned our weapons, and the ammunition was carefully counted. No one wanted ammo to find its way into the wrong hands.

"Well done, lads," I said, grinning despite my tiredness and our joint failure. "Not a bad op today—we were tight ... right up until we had a weapons-grade fuck up. Think about how it could have been improved so next time we'll be on it."

"Yes, Staff," came the muttered replies.

The smile slid from my face as I turned and headed toward the building housing the REME officers.

Not all officers are wankers. By the law of averages you occasionally come across one that you don't want to shoot. Elderman was alright, not that I knew him well. I'd only been attached here for three weeks —barely enough time to find my way around base.

If I'd been overseas on ops, I'd have used the time to unofficially requisition some better kit for my men. There was always something they needed that the bastard of a Quartermaster wanted to keep tidied away in his nice, neat stores. Raiding his supplies could be a useful training exercise for my team. Unofficially, of course. But on a home base, it would be viewed as highly unprofessional and probably career ending—amassing spares on ops was viewed differently.

Totally against regulations. But that was the thing about the men who were in my trade: ATs, Ammunition Technicians—bomb disposal officers—we made lousy soldiers, but we made great ATs.

Our minds worked differently from most soldiers—we were trained specifically for that reason. We had to see three steps beyond everyone else. We were taught to analyze, taught to think. And that made us independent—which most officers hated.

We were the opposite of fighter pilots: they tell everyone who will listen that they're a pilot and that speed is life. I didn't tell anyone what I did, and speed is death.

Captain Elderman accepted my salute briskly and waved me into a chair.

"Fuck up today, Staff. Not your finest hour."

"No, sir."

He'd seen what happened, I didn't need to apologise for it.

The Captain leaned back in his chair, tapping a cheap plastic biro against the scarred desk.

"I've had an unusual request come across my desk and someone at Division HQ thinks that you're the man for the job."

I stared at him warily. In my experience, a volunteer was someone who hadn't understood the question.

"It seems our friends across the pond need some help—someone with your skill-set, as it turns out. Working with their own EOD teams —some sort of training exercise. You need to report to RAF Croughton tomorrow. Apparently the Yanks are so keen to have you, they're sending transport to pick you up. Be packed and ready by 0700."

I wasn't expecting that—a training exercise with American military?

Could be interesting: Americans trained hard. Fifteen years ago, they said they wanted to be world leaders in EOD within ten years, and maybe in terms of equipment, support, numbers and capability they had it all going for them. In the British Army, we'd been trained for decades by learning how to neutralize everything the IRA could throw at us. There was a different background of knowledge to draw on, which was just as well, because we definitely weren't funded to the same level.

"Yes, sir. How long am I going for?"

He frowned and looked at the paperwork.

"Doesn't say. Best expect to be away for a few weeks."

"Yes, sir."

I took the orders that he handed to me and flicked through them as I headed back to my room, growing more and more confused.

The orders simply said when and where I'd be picked up: nothing about the training exercise, how long I'd be away, what I'd be doing, which regiment I'd be working with, or who'd requested me. Weirdly, the only contact was an email address that went to an office I'd never heard of at the MOD HQ in London.

It didn't seem as though Elderman had been told anything more than was in my orders.

It wasn't completely unusual to do training exercises with our opposite number in the U.S. Army; I'd even trained with Navy SEALs, and EOD teams in the U.S. Marine Corps—but this was definitely different.

For one thing, it looked as though I'd be travelling by myself rather than with the Unit I was attached to; and for another thing, there was nothing to say where I was heading. Besides, the logistics of these sorts of joint exercises always took months to plan. I should have heard something about it before now.

I pulled out my phone and Googled RAF Croughton:

"*Royal Air Force Croughton houses the 422nd Air Base Group whose function is to provide installation support, services, force protection, and worldwide communications across the entire spectrum of operations. The group is located in the UK and supports NATO, U.S. European Command, U.S. Central Command, Air Force Special Operations Command, U.S. Department of State operations and Ministry of Defence operations. The group sustains more than 450 C2 circuits and supports 25% of all European Theater to continental United States (CONUS) communications.*"

In other words, spook work.

There was a story behind this deployment, I just didn't know what it was. Because it sounded like the sort of thing that would usually be undertaken by the Special Forces ATOs. But since I'd been dumped in a dead end unit after the incident in Afghanistan, it gave me a chance to escape to something more exciting—and possibly save my career.

So there was nothing for me to do but pack my bags. Since I'd only been in Wiltshire for three weeks, I hadn't exactly made myself at home and I'd travelled light in the first place. Packing wasn't an issue: where to store my Ducati Sport 1000 was. I didn't trust those clumsy bastards in transport, the Royal Logistics Corps, not to damage it.

But as I was leaving in 12 hours, I didn't have a lot of choice either.

I decided to shoot a text to my mate Noddy, reminding him that he owed me, and asking him to look after my wheels until I got back.

He agreed, but also wound me up by threatening to ride it while I was away. Noddy had been in my platoon but left the Army five years ago, and now he weighed 300 pounds and had as much balance as a lame hippo: if he tried to ride my bike, they'd be taking him to A&E and my bike to the knackers' yard.

For a moment, I thought about texting Vanessa, but then remembered that we'd broken up a month ago because she didn't like being in a long distance relationship. She hated me being sent away all the time, bitching and moaning about cancelled dates and missed birthdays; complaining when she found ants in her kitchen and I wasn't there to sort it out. What the hell did she think the Army was? A holiday camp where you could come and go as you liked?

The Army was my home—the only one I had, so I did what I was told—mostly—and went where they sent me.

I tried not to think about what I was going to do when I'd served my 22 years. Returning to civilian life at 40 didn't hold any appeal for me. A few people stayed on after they'd done their full stint, but not many.

I shook my head: I still had 11 years before I had to face that horror story.

I settled down on my hard bunk with my hands behind my head and wondered what the Army had in store for me this time.

CHAPTER TWO

AMIRA

Grief gripped me, making it hard to breathe, hard to think.

My lungs struggled to draw in the warm Californian air, and my whole body was clenched so tight, my bones might shatter from the pressure.

Zada leaned against me, her sobs loud and hopeless; our mother was incoherent, wailing as tears tracked down her cheeks. Only our father sat tall, his pride keeping him upright.

"Your brother will yield entry into Paradise on the Day of Judgement," he said, his voice hoarse with pain.

I couldn't cry—I was too angry to cry.

My brother.

My baby brother who wasn't supposed to die at 26.

My little brother who died in Syria. Killed in a U.S. air raid while he was volunteering at a hospital in Raqqa, a city strangled by Daesh and battered by years of fierce, violent fighting. Whether it was an accident, or whether the U.S. government had believed the hospital was harbouring rebel forces, no one could agree.

The newspaper reports from Syria showed harrowing pictures of bombed out streets, children numb with loss, staring blank-eyed at the cameras, and we all had compassion fatigue, wearied by war thousands of miles away.

But not my brother. Not my sweet, generous, caring brother.

Thinking of Karam crushed beneath the collapsed hospital walls brought a new wave of rage rushing over me. I was hot, I was cold, I was filled with fury. Assaulted by every emotion, I forced myself to concentrate on my family. My family needed me.

"Whosoever saves the life of one person, it would be as if he saved the life of all mankind."

Dad was quoting the *Quran* like he'd been doing ever since we heard the news. His voice started strongly, then crumbled as his face distorted. His mouth stretched in a silent scream and his eyes were screwed shut. His thin shoulders shook as wordless sobs wracked his aging body.

Parents aren't supposed to bury their children. It's wrong. It's wrong.

Rage drove my tears away.

I was so angry with Karam. He had no business travelling to Syria during his summer break. He wasn't even a qualified doctor—he still had years of medical school left. But he said he could help the people there. He said he could do good.

Instead he was dead. Dead. And I hated him. I hated what he'd done to our family. We were torn apart from the inside out, hopeless and helpless.

The *hijab* covering my hair and neck was stifling and confining under the August sun, and I felt sweat trickle down the back of my neck, blooming into damp patches under my arms, in the small of my back and at my crotch.

Zada gripped my hand, crushing my fingers together painfully. I welcomed the pain, I embraced the pain. It was something to hold onto, something tangible.

The words from the *Quran* echoed in my mind, but I wasn't sure I believed anymore. If I ever had.

In my mind, I saw my father rising to his feet, trembling and broken as he said goodbye to his only son.

In his hand he held a symbolic fistful of soil to spread across his grave, and the *Imam* would quote another line from the *Quran*:

"We created you from it, and return you into it, and from it we will raise you a second time."

I could see it all in my mind as grief and anger ripped into my broken heart, my shrivelled soul.

"Damn you, Karam," I whispered. "I love you so much, but right now I hate you. I hate you!"

The mourners would pray, asking for forgiveness for Karam, to remind him of his profession of faith. I knew that my father would find it comforting, the way they still talked to Karam through prayer.

My sister picked up the *Quran* and began to read, her voice gaining volume as if she gained strength through the words.

I didn't listen.

And I didn't believe.

May Allah strike me down.

For three days, we mourned. Neighbours and friends brought food and condolences, but none of it could touch our grief, or my deep anger.

I stared out of the window, watching another group of my mother's friends leaving the house.

"You haven't cried yet."

Lost in my bleak thoughts, it was several seconds before my sister's words sank in.

"What?"

I turned abruptly at Zada's accusing tone, and watched, irritated, as her dark eyes filled with tears and she wiped her nose again with a damp tissue. I focussed on the broken capillaries that reddened the whites of her eyes, the eyelids swollen, the snot that she constantly wiped from her nose. Odd how grief makes us ugly.

"You haven't cried for Karam. Not once. Don't you care?"

Her mumbled words wrenched my attention back to her.

"How can you ask me that?"

She shrugged and looked away.

"You act like all this is just an inconvenience, like you'd rather be at work."

She was right. And as she searched for truth, I'd give it to her, rough and raw.

"Honestly, Zee, I would. I don't see the point in this enforced grief —like after three days we're supposed to be okay and go about our lives normally. It's so false."

She stared at me, sniffing softly.

"It's to help us mourn. But ... you seem so ... so angry."

I rubbed my forehead, my fingers catching on the material of the *hijab*. It was just a headscarf to cover my hair during prayers—today my parents wanted modesty, so I had been modest in the way that they needed.

"Aren't you angry, Zee? He was killed while he was working in a hospital. American drones dropped bombs on a hospital! Doesn't that make you angry? That he died for no reason?"

Her eyes drooped to the tissue in her hands as she started to shred it.

"He didn't die for no reason—he saved a lot of lives while he was there. He said so in his emails, *mashallah*."

I held in a groan. *Mashallah—as Allah has willed it*. It sounded like a feeble excuse to me. But my younger sister had always been devout. I was the one who questioned everything, who constantly asked why, who was sent for extra religious instruction when I was nine, because my father didn't know how to answer my myriad questions anymore.

We came to America when I was six years old and Karam was three. Only the haziest memories of the old country remained for me, our previous existence a blur of colours and faces, a few phrases.

In his old life, our father had been a university professor, someone important. But when he was accused of membership of an unauthorized political group, the accusation would have been enough to result in imprisonment and torture. My father's friends warned him that his name was on a government list, so we fled with only the clothes on our back.

For two years we were stateless refugees, asylum seekers, immigrants, use whatever name you like. And then we were granted permission to stay in the Land of the Free.

We settled in Southern California, and my father found a job cleaning the bathrooms in offices. He came home smelling of bleach and stale urine. He said it was honest work and that Pride was sinful, so he prayed every night, thankful to have this chance.

Once I learned English and lost my accent, I was just another dark haired, dark-eyed penniless migrant. People assumed I was Mexican, and I was happy with that.

I only wore the *hijab* on religious holidays.

But Zada had been born here, an American citizen from birth. She willingly studied the *Quran* and always dressed more modestly than me. When she was 15, she started wearing her *hijab* full time. We were as different as day and night. I loved her, but I didn't understand her, and I was always closer to Karam.

Karam. My fun-loving, happy-go-lucky brother. The hipster, the surfer, always smiling, always generous. Never met a stranger in his life.

Dead.

For nothing.

When I finally went back to my tiny, cluttered apartment near Scrips Mercy Hospital, Chula Vista, where I worked as an ER nurse, I wallowed in hatred and anger.

I needed to do something.

Karam's death had to have meaning.

It had to.

CHAPTER THREE

JAMES

I'd been expecting some sort of military transport vehicle to pick me up, but instead a black Range Rover pulled up outside HQ. It didn't have military number-plates either, but the guy driving it was American Air Force.

"Staff Sergeant James Spears?"

"Yep, that's me."

He was probably wondering why I wasn't wearing dog tags. In the British Army, we only wore dog tags on operational duty and even then inside our shirts. Besides, I had another reason not to wear them; I'd changed how I mounted mine because when I was wearing the bomb suit, they hung behind my armoured chest plate and stabbed into me. An Aussie AT I met used to wear his dog tags on his boots because he knew that if he got blown up, the boots would survive.

"Senior Airman John Behrends. Good to meet you."

We shook hands and I chucked my rucksack onto the back seat, followed by my kit bag, closed the door and climbed in the front passenger door.

We drove past the guard hut, and the duty soldier saluted as he raised the barrier and waved us on.

Soon, we were driving through the rolling chalk downs of

Wiltshire, the thin grass turning brown under the scorching sun, then heading up the A34 through Oxfordshire to our destination. It was a ninety minute drive, and we chatted about countries we'd both been deployed to and his opinion on the British weather. After that, we fell silent and I was fine with that—the strangeness of the situation was playing on my mind but I was also enjoying the peace and quiet. You have to find that silence inside yourself when you're living on a base with thousands of military and civilian personnel. I found it easy to be alone with my thoughts in the middle of a crowd.

When we reached RAF Croughton, an unassuming entrance on the edge of a small Cotswold village, my driver dropped me in front of a faceless grey building, pulled my bags out from the backseat, waved and then disappeared behind an empty hangar.

Across the flat airstrip about half a mile away, I could see a Gulfstream C-20 sitting on the runway. And somewhere in the distance, I could hear the familiar *chuck-chuck* sound of a helo.

As I walked inside the building, I handed my orders to a young Airman on duty.

He was the stereotype of a corn-fed, blond haired, blue-eyed American, and snapped a sharp salute.

"Yes, sir. We've been waiting on your arrival, sir. Would you like some coffee?"

"Thanks. Do you have tea?"

He looked at me uncertainly.

"Sure, I think so. Yes, sir."

He left me sitting on a hard seat while he bustled around in a room at the back. Then he proudly handed me a plastic cup filled with tepid water, and dropped a teabag into it.

"I've never made tea for a Brit before," he said happily.

I stared dubiously at the teabag slowly deflating in the lukewarm water. *Nope, wouldn't be drinking that.*

"Thanks."

"You're welcome, sir."

He went back to his computer, happy with a job well done. I carefully placed the cup aside and checked messages on my phone. Nope. No one gave a shit, and even Noddy hadn't replied to my email about where I'd left my bike and keys. *Great.* My Ducati had better be in one piece when I got back, or there would be arses kicked from here to Glasgow.

After a few minutes, the young Airman's desk phone rang and he listened intently, *yessir-ing* a lot. Then he leaped up and grabbed my kitbag which I took as my cue to follow him.

He led me along a twisting corridor that housed a labyrinth of tiny, hutch-like offices, each with sweating USAF personnel sitting behind a bank of computers. A few looked up as I passed, their eyes following my progress until I was out of sight.

Finally, the Airman stopped at a larger office, knocked twice, then opened the door.

A gush of chilled air flowed out, cooling the sweat on my skin.

Behind a slab of oak desk, I saw an older officer. His air of authority had me standing to attention and snapping a smart salute. I side-eyed the star on his shoulder, recognising a Major General of the U.S. Air Force when I saw one.

"At ease, Spears. Take a seat."

"Yes, sir. Thank you, sir."

He leaned back in his chair, his eyes travelling across me dispassionately, and then he spoke.

"You're probably wondering what the hell you're doing here."

"It had crossed my mind, sir."

He raised his eyebrows.

"Well, Staff Sergeant Spears, I have my orders, too. And they're to put you on that C-20 that's being refuelled right now."

I waited for more.

"And that's all I can tell you, son. Good luck."

He stood up and held out his hand. I was so surprised, it took a second for my brain to catch up as I stumbled to my feet and shook his hand.

"Thank you, sir," I said automatically.

The office door opened again, and a different Airman entered, threw a snappy salute, then picked up my kitbag and rucksack.

Back under the brilliant blue sky, he tossed my bags into a Jeep and drove across the airfield at breakneck speed, bouncing over the grass and racing along the tarmac to the waiting jet.

As soon as I'd pulled my bags out, he sped off.

What was with everyone today?

A man wearing jeans and aviator sunglasses stood at the top of the plane's steps.

"Climb aboard, Staff Sergeant. Got a lot of miles to cover today."

I squinted up at him, wishing I'd taken my own sunglasses out of my bag.

"And where are these miles going to take me, exactly?"

His smile was cool and condescending.

"Need to know. I'll tell you once we're in the air."

I glanced behind me, but the Jeep I'd arrived on was already a blur in the distance.

Resigned to the weirdness, I climbed up and squinted into the darker interior, my eyes adjusting slowly from the bright sunlight outside.

The aircraft was much plusher than any military transport I'd been on before, with leather executive seats arranged around a small table, and it was totally empty.

As soon as I was on board, the dude closed the doors, and gestured at me to take a seat.

"Strap yourself in," he grinned. "You're in for a bumpy ride."

Somehow I didn't think he was talking about air turbulence.

The cockpit door shut behind him, and then I heard the engines roar into life. Minutes later, we were taxiing down the runway then lurching into the sky. I peered out of the window, the English countryside shrinking to toy-sized houses and patches of brown and yellow fields, until thin clouds hid the world from view.

I leaned back in my seat wondering what the hell I was being dropped into.

The dude with the sunglasses reappeared after twenty minutes, and tossed me a bottle of water and a bag of peanuts.

"I hope you've got someone flying this kite," I said, sounding like a grumpy bastard.

He laughed lightly.

"Yup, full crew—you, me and the pilot." He grinned as he slid into the seat opposite me. "The name's Smith."

"Uh-huh, and I'm Jones."

He opened his own water and took a long drink.

"Yeah, you're not the first person to say that, but it happens to be true: Nathaniel John Smith. My parents only got imaginative once. Call me Nate or Smith," and he shrugged. "You're wondering what's going on. Well, I'm here to tell you."

"You're not military," I surmised, taking in the long hair curling at the nape of his neck and the scruffy beard.

"I was: 101st Airborne, one of the Screaming Angels."

"And now?"

He shrugged.

"My talents lay outside normal military duty."

"So ... that makes you, what? FBI? CIA? NSA?"

He smiled.

"Something like that."

We stared across the table, weighing each other up.

He was older than me by maybe ten years, a few flecks of grey in his hair, but he was in good shape and obviously worked out. He had a scar over one eyebrow, and the tip of his left index finger was permanently bent.

"I'll never play the piano again," he grinned, his eyes dark and unreadable.

"Are you going to tell me why I'm here?"

He smiled broadly.

"An impatient EOD operator? Isn't that a contradiction in terms? Well, this is your lucky day, buddy, because I'm here to brief you."

He learned forwards, his gaze becoming serious.

"Since ISIS began to lose ground in the Middle East, large numbers of their fighters have been dispersed but not captured, not neutered. Some have re-established themselves into the civilian population, but others have left the country. We suspect that a number have made their way to the U.S., radicalising where they can—disillusioned youth, that kind of thing. The people I work for are pretty unhappy about that."

His words didn't surprise me. Everything he'd said was common knowledge and something discussed frequently in the EOD community. Most British people sleepwalked in the belief that 9/11 couldn't happen there. Until it did. On 7th July 2005, 52 people were killed by a series of bomb attacks across London; 700 were injured.

There were others, of course, then most recently, the bombing at the Ariana Grande concert in 2017 reminded us that the threat hadn't gone away. In the city of Manchester, on a warm May evening, 23 people lost their lives to a suicide bomber, and 139 were wounded. The victims were teenagers. Children.

As a country, we were vulnerable, and people like me were the ones sent to neutralize devices—but only if they were found in time.

Smith's eyes glittered with the fervour of a zealot.

"No one wants to admit it, but we're losing ground to extremism," he said. "We have to fight fire with fire."

"Meaning?"

He grimaced.

"We're aware of a terror cell in rural Pennsylvania, deep in the woods at the foot of the Appalachians," he gave a wry smile. "We're calling this Operation Hansel and Gretel."

"Really?"

He shrugged.

"I didn't choose the name. Anyway, they've been recruiting quietly for the last three months, and it was just by sheer luck that we picked up wind of it. They're more organised than most, training like soldiers. The leaders fought in Syria, Iraq and Afghanistan."

"Why don't you go in and pick them up?"

He stroked his beard thoughtfully.

"That would be a short-term solution, but we want to know who or what they're targeting, and we want to know where they're getting their intel, because it's damn good. Who's supplying the bastards? Who's arming them?"

My lip curled in wry amusement.

"In other words, they've outsmarted you and you can't catch them."

Smith didn't smile back.

"But I don't get it—you've got EOD teams of your own. I've trained with some of them—good blokes."

"We think we have a mole."

I blinked twice and my smile vanished.

"Bloody hell!"

The pieces of the jigsaw started to fall into place—a few were still missing, but I was beginning to see the whole picture.

"Yep. That's why we want you," said Smith, leaning back.

He continued to stare at me, and finally I understood.

"You can't trust your own teams—and because I'm British Army, I have no possible connections to anyone or anything."

He gave the ghost of a smile.

"Got it in one. I was told you were smart."

He pulled a thick file out of his bag and placed it on the table in front of him.

"We're putting together a team to infiltrate the cell. We need the terrorist leader to want their skills so badly, that he'll skip some of their own security protocols to get them."

Smith watched my face then pushed the file across the table.

"And we need you to train them to make improvised explosive devices—bombs."

CHAPTER FOUR

AMIRA

The first person I saw when they removed the blindfold was a tall guy with skin the colour of teak and a friendly smile. But he was wearing the uniform of a soldier and that stole any reason for me to return the smile.

"Hey! You must be Amira. I'm Clay. Welcome to ... well, who the heck knows?"

He laughed but I just stared at him until uncertainty bloomed on his handsome face.

"Uh, you speak English, right?"

He couldn't see the sarcastic curl of my lips as I replied.

"Like a native."

If his skin hadn't been so dark, he would have blushed. Instead, he seemed slightly flustered, then smiled again and held out his hand.

I left him hanging there, surprised he didn't know that a woman wearing a *niqab* would be unlikely to shake the hand of a man she didn't know.

I smiled to myself as I laid my right hand across my heart and bowed.

He jerked his hand back, apologising quickly.

"Damn! I knew that one. No shaking hands. Got it. Sorry, I've been travelling a lot of hours—my brain isn't working on full power. But I promise I'll remember for next time."

It was hard to dislike Clay and his ready smile, but I'd spent the last six months being trained not to take anyone at face value. So I simply stared at him until his tongue stilled and he stood awkwardly, the stretched silence making him sweat.

The man who'd brought me here stepped from the truck and jerked his thumb at one of the cabins: "That's yours."

It looked old, maybe over a hundred years, with a sagging roof and tattered sackcloth for curtains. But the locks on the door were shiny and new, and someone had added a generator at the side, the soft whirr providing electricity. I was hopeful that there was running water, as well.

I picked up my battered suitcase and tugged it behind me, frustrated as the wheels were checked by small rocks that littered the path. I kicked a pinecone out of the way, cursing inwardly as sandy soil slowed my progress. With a final wrench, I jerked it over the threshold and surveyed the place that would be my home for the next few months.

Inside, the cabin was hot and stuffy, the air wood-scented and drowsy.

A table and two wooden chairs stood in the middle of the room under a bare bulb, and twin doors opened into tiny bedrooms with single beds on either side of the cabin. There was a third door that was shut—please let that be an indoor bathroom.

I picked the bedroom that smelled the least musty and hauled my suitcase onto the bed, sitting down beside it heavily.

The frame was old, but the bare mattress looked new, and a small pile of sheets and a pillow were folded neatly at the bottom.

I'd been on the road a long time and I knew that I wasn't in California anymore. Hell, I wasn't even sure I was still in the U.S., but if I had to guess, I'd say we'd ended up on the eastern side, somewhere in the mountains. But equally, I could be in Canada. I'd have to wait for someone to end a sentence with 'eh' to be sure.

I lifted my veil to scratch my cheek, still unused to the press of the *niqab's* material covering all but my eyes.

I jerked the thin curtains together with an angry flick and removed my veil, breathing freely for the first time in too long.

Karam, tell me I'm doing the right thing. Give me a sign!

But only the gathering silence answered me as a narrow ray of sunlight breeched the curtains, illuminating the swirls of dust in the stale air.

There was no going back, no footsteps led to yesterday: the only way was forwards.

Outside, I heard the rumble of a car engine, something large—a truck, perhaps. Two doors slammed followed by a muted conversation. I replaced my *niqab*, lifting one side and pressing my ear against the door, straining to hear, but the words eluded me.

Then the cabin door opened and I heard the heavy tread of a man's footsteps: no, two men.

"Your students have already arrived," said a man's voice. "You'll meet Clay in a moment, the other is in the room over there."

"Just two?"

There was a pause as I pressed my ear more firmly against the door's rough wood.

"Recruitment issues."

The second man grunted a reply.

"Chow time in ten."

One set of footsteps left the cabin, and the floor creaked as the second set headed away from me toward the other bedroom.

I wasn't happy that I'd be sharing with a man. Didn't these idiots know how wrong that was?

But if I was a student, then this new man must be my teacher. I felt a thrill of excitement as well as fear at the thought of what he could teach me, what I'd be able to do after I'd been trained. My breathing quickened as I sat on the edge of the bed.

Karam, I prayed silently. *Am I doing the right thing?*

There was no answer. There was never any answer.

Pressure on my bladder reminded me that I needed to use the bathroom. Door number three? I tugged the *niqab* into place and cautiously left the room. I didn't know why I tiptoed, but I did, moving soundlessly across the old, hand-hewn planks.

But then the door to the opposite bedroom was thrown open and a man stared at me in surprise, for a second his expression open and astonished. His eyes were the palest blue, wide, and fringed with long, black lashes. They were too pretty for a man, especially a soldier, and his uniform told me that's exactly what he was.

He was as tall as Clay but broader in the shoulders, a hint of concealed strength. His cheekbones were high and his lips softly curving as if he was meant to smile. He wasn't smiling now, instead his expression turned cold and detached, deliberately blank as he studied me, and I wanted to squirm at his slow, intent appraisal. His eyes were tired but alert, and I reminded myself that he couldn't see anything but a dark, shapeless mass as I stood concealed by my *niqab*.

Then his eyes fixed on mine.

CHAPTER FIVE

JAMES

A woman. Jesus.

Smith had omitted that tiny detail when he'd recruited me to train his undercover agents. It shouldn't have bothered me, but it did. It bothered the hell out of me that he was going to send a woman to infiltrate a terror cell run by some of the most dangerous and ruthless people on the planet.

The woman matched my gaze, her fathomless black eyes giving nothing away. She was dressed head to toe in black, with her face, neck, shoulders and chest covered, so it was hard to tell anything about her, but I would have guessed that she was about 5'7", between 25 and 40, slender.

She shifted slightly and the robe revealed her shoes—red and white Converse. They seemed a contradiction, but what did I know?

Fuck all, as it turned out.

She edged past me, heading for the bathroom and hurriedly locking the door behind her.

I strode from the cabin, my anger building as I tracked Smith across the compound.

"Hey! HEY!"

He was talking to another guy dressed in civvies, a man with overdeveloped muscles and a *fuck you* expression. I ignored him, my attention on the tosser who'd brought me on this mission without sharing the full story.

"Smith, are you kidding me? A woman?"

He raised one eyebrow and folded his arms calmly.

"That's Amira. She's perfect." But then he let out a sigh that sounded like weariness and a long-standing argument. "She's smart, real smart. She's committed."

"You can't seriously send her against ISIS? Do you know what they'll do to her if they even suspect that she's U.S. military or..."

"She's not."

"What?"

"She's not military. She's a civilian. A nurse, in fact. Works the ER."

I shook my head in disbelief.

"She's a nurse? Are you insane? She won't last a day with those bastards! She's not trained for this!"

He stared at me calmly as I ranted on.

"She'll never make it! I've worked with spies and they need to be streetwise, they need to know how to work with the criminals who'll get them the supplies needed. There's no way she's prepared for anything like that!"

Smith stared me down.

"Take your ego out of the equation, soldier, and listen good. We need someone with above average intelligence so lessons can be quickly assimilated, and with excellent recollection skills both for training and recalling the conversations of the terror cell. Amira is strong in all these areas. We've been working with her for a couple of months now."

"A couple of months? That's it? It's nowhere near enough," I objected.

"And that's what we're here for. As well as your special duties, you and your other student, Clay, will teach her the basics: how to clean and fire a weapon, how to use a knife, hand-to-hand combat. Clay has a black belt in jujitsu. He'll watch her six."

I shook my head in disgust.

"Do you know what they'll do to her *when* they realize she's a plant? Every man in the cell will rape her, then they'll rape her again until every orifice is bleeding and torn. They'll flog her, slit her nose and mouth while she's begging for them to kill her, and then, only then, they'll behead her. And all the time they're violating her in every possible way, they'll be filming it so her family can watch it on YouTube!"

Smith gazed at me, his face closed.

"I know," he said. "She knows, too."

"What?"

"Amira knows the risk she's taking, and she's willing to do it." He stared at me long and hard. "You think we take this lightly? You think we just picked a woman off the street? She has passed every psych evaluation that we could throw at her with flying colours. She wants this—and you'll train her for it."

I started to speak, but Smith and the goon were staring at something or someone behind me. I turned to see the woman standing at the cabin's entrance, her arms crossed in front of her.

"Thanks for your concern, soldier," she said, "but I don't need it and I don't want it. Just do your job ... and I'll do mine."

Her voice was slightly muffled, but pure American, and I hadn't expected that either. My mind was whirring, exploding with new thoughts and ideas, stereotypes folding like a deck of cards.

I wanted to say something, to persuade her to change her mind, or maybe to see her fear and indecision, but she gave me nothing, so there was nothing to say. Those black, black eyes stared out from the shapeless material, remorseless, unchanging.

"So, you're the teacher. Do you have any other specialist skills?"

Her voice was mocking, challenging me.

"Yeah, I'm really good at making things explode."

The tense standoff was interrupted by the arrival of another soldier.

He walked towards me, smiling broadly and holding out his hand.

"The name's Alan Clayton No-name, Master Sergeant, United States Army. I also answer to Clay, dude, bossman, sir—or even bitch if you buy me dinner first."

He gripped my hand tightly, the torrent of words and his friendliness surprising, given the circumstances.

As a Master Sergeant, he outranked me, but that didn't matter when I was in charge of training him. Besides, I was in the British Army, so his rank meant nothing to me.

I studied the new guy and scratched my chin.

"What do your friends call you?"

"Clay, Clayton, I answer to anything if it's time for dinner."

The woman stood silently during this exchange. I had no idea what she was thinking—not being able to see her face threw me off.

Smith clapped his hands together.

"Touching as this is, food's ready."

"Mmm mmm mmm, MREs!" grinned Clay. "Three lies for the price of one: it's not a Meal, it's not Ready, and you can't Eat it!"

He laughed loudly at his own joke.

The woman's eyes widened slightly, but she didn't speak. Instead she shrugged and turned away.

"I have to pray," she said, over her shoulder.

I followed the path of those red and white shoes, small puffs of dirt kicking up behind her. It wasn't right having her here, it just wasn't right. But as she retreated inside the cabin, some of the tightness in my chest loosened.

Smith shot me a look.

"This going to be a problem for you, Spears?"

Yes, it was a huge problem.

"She's Muslim?" I asked.

"Does it matter? My parents were Episcopalians—your point?"

I wasn't sure what bothered me most: this whole situation was weird.

He gave me a small smile.

"Let me worry about what happens when she infiltrates the terror cell: your job is to get her and Clay in there."

I frowned at his non-answer. And it made me realize how isolated I was. With no clear chain of command, with no accountability, I was out here on my own. And right now, I didn't know who I could trust.

I still had the email address at the MOD that I'd memorized, but that was all. I didn't even know whose email it was or if they'd arrange extraction if things got hairy. Smith had taken my phone so I was stranded. Maybe that's why they'd chosen me: ultimately, all EOD operators worked alone.

The woman reappeared ten minutes later, selected a vegetarian MRE pack and returned to her room to eat it alone.

"Is she allowed to eat with men?" I asked, my knowledge of Muslim culture limited.

Clay glanced towards the cabin.

"Looks like she's choosing not to eat with us. But I guess it all depends."

"On what?"

He frowned, deep in thought.

"Family traditions, cultural values. Some Muslims don't have a problem with it; others are stricter about segregating the sexes." He rubbed his eyebrow thoughtfully. "I'm talking about just one aspect here. Many Muslim women socialise widely—but there's huge variety."

His answer left me none the wiser, but the woman didn't return.

"Seriously, James. Just be respectful, and let her guide us on how to behave. She'll soon let us know if we've over-stepped the line. She's one of us now, part of the team."

"You'll be the one going undercover with her," I pointed out. "Are you okay with this?"

"I've worked alongside female soldiers before, but not in combat." He scratched the thin beard on his chin. "'Three things cannot be long hidden: the sun, the moon, and the truth', that's a saying by Buddha, man."

"What's that got to do with anything?" I asked, utterly confused.

Smith laughed out loud.

"Clay's a Buddhist..."

Clay raised a finger.

"A scholar of Buddha, but close enough."

I stared at the two of them.

"I studied philosophy and religion in school," Clay said evenly.

"And you think you can pass yourself off as Muslim?"

He shrugged, seeming unconcerned.

"I'm a brother, still learning. They'll accept that I've recently converted." He stared up at the darkening sky. "There's a lot to be said for Islam—it's a religion based on a concept of peace. In fact, the Arabic word 'salaam' which is a common greeting, means 'secured, pacified, submitted'. It's from the same word stem as

'Islam'—so individual personal peace is attained by submitting to Allah."

Smith gave a wry grin as my mouth dropped open.

"He can't help it," Smith grinned, "but keep listening, you might learn something."

I closed my mouth with a snap: it was hard to believe in a peaceful religion when ISIS—the so-called Islamic State in Syria—had killed tens of thousands of men, women and children with chilling brutality. It was hard to believe in much at all.

I ate my meal out of a plastic box, and sat outside with Clay and Smith, watching the sun sink behind the mountains, the brilliant colours fading to grey. The goon in civvies had disappeared, although Smith said he'd be our go-between to bring supplies once a week.

"You can trust Larson," he said casually.

I didn't trust anyone, and I had serious doubts about this mission. But the only way I was getting out of here was on foot. Technically, I'd be going AWOL which wouldn't do a lot for my career.

Smith tapped my boot with his foot.

"Have you thought about how you're going to start training them?"

Clay looked up, his eyes shadowed in the twilight.

It was clear that we were training hard routine here—rather than just living in a rental and eating normal food, this op was aimed to toughen up the trainees. But I was supposed to be teaching them bomb-making, too, so there were some supplies that would help with my job.

"I need a laptop."

Smith frowned.

"For the purpose of?"

"Are you going to ask that every time I say I need something to do my job?"

He gave a thin smile.

"Yes."

"Fine. I need a laptop because if I'm teaching them what it takes to make an IED, then the first lesson is to show them an explosion in a bomb-making factory that killed four terrorists."

Smith glanced towards the cabin.

"And how will that help teach them the skills they'll need?"

Clay gave a hollow laugh.

"Is that what you call motivation, James?"

I met his eyes.

"I call it encouraging focus."

Smith looked at Clay and they shared an unspoken exchange.

"I'll get the laptop," he said. "But it will be encrypted and you'll have no access to it or to Wi-Fi without my say-so. What else is on your shopping list?"

"A projector: first, because explosions look better on a big screen; and second, I'm not going to teach while I'm squinting at a laptop."

"Anything else?"

"Wouldn't it be better to teach them to make IEDs from universal sources?"

He frowned.

"What do you mean?"

"Commonly available resources: specific chemicals, steel ball bearings, push button switches, battery connectors and cables, ignition systems. Hell, you can buy Thermite on ten different online stores— that's a pyrotechnic composition of metal powder. Or buy enough fireworks and you've got a source of black powder. It's not even that hard to get TATP: triacetone triperoxide, which is a high explosive. One of the ingredients of TATP is hydrogen peroxide—easy to get hold of over the counter at most pharmacists."

"I didn't think TATP was very stable."

"It's not, but it's easy to source." I shrugged. "ISIS and co. use it as their go-to explosive, so they obviously know by now how to make and use it with a degree of safety. The Paris IEDs in 2015 were TATP, and the Brussels airport IED team in 2016 left 200lb of TATP in their flat."

He grimaced and nodded.

"Bomb-makers don't usually care whether or not the people delivering the IEDs will live through detonation. That's why most of them are suicide bombers, whether they're planning to be or not. Or you could get ammonium nitrate, a chemical compound most commonly found in fertilizer—slightly more stable."

"Okay, so you'll teach them to source what they need. But supposing this cell is a little more sophisticated," Smith persisted.

"What sort of supplies would you expect them to have? What resources should they be prepared for?"

"Detonators—what you call caps; det cord; high explosives; munitions; fertilizer; nails or scrap pieces of metal; a dozen burner mobile phones. In eight weeks, I can teach making a basic pipe bomb and pressure plate devices to target military traffic, maybe time devices against infrastructure and RC—remote-controlled—bombs." I stopped to think. "Wire coat hangers, alarm clocks with hands that move around, silver paper, lots of batteries of different sizes, caps from a pop gun. That enough?"

"A pop gun?"

"In the hope that they won't kill themselves the first time they try to make a bomb."

He nodded, then looked over my shoulder. I glanced up to find Amira watching us.

"So you're going to teach me to make things go bang, soldier?" she asked, her tone deliberately taunting.

"Yeah, and it might be you. Better take notes."

Back in the 1980s, the British SAS took the Mujahid to Scotland and trained them to fight the Russians occupying Afghanistan. They let that genie out of the bottle and we ended up fighting their descendants in the Taliban thirty years later.

I saw the flash of hatred in her eyes and regretted my harsh words. Once again I couldn't help thinking that this was a really bad idea.

CHAPTER SIX

AMIRA

My hands were still shaking. I sat hunched on the bed, my knees drawn up to my chin, my arms wrapped around my shins. And still they shook, the tremors running through my entire body. My heart cannoned against my ribcage and I squeezed my eyes shut, my breath coming in short bursts as the panic ricocheted through me.

My body shook the ancient bed so it shuddered in sympathy, the creaks and cracks sounding as if they were coming from inside me.

I gulped and gasped, trying to unhear the words he'd said, but they tunnelled through my brain, echoing louder and louder, warring with my thundering heart.

I was a trained nurse and I knew exactly what was happening to me, but still I couldn't control the terrifying panic that gripped me. I couldn't catch my breath and dark spots danced in front of my closed eyes, disorientating; faintness chased me as sweat broke out in a sheen across my skin. I felt like I was being smothered, and I tore the *niqab* from my face, desperate to breathe.

I pictured it with terrifying clarity—my body flying apart in a haze of red, atomized by the force of an explosion. It could happen to me just like that, it really could.

Minutes ticked past as my rigid body held me in an iron band of terror, then slowly, achingly slowly, the fear leaked away, leaving me weak, trembling like a puppy on the fourth of July as fireworks spun in starbursts around me.

I wiped my hand across my forehead, and it came back slick with my sweat, the stench of my fear filling the small room.

He didn't trust me, that English soldier. And I didn't trust him. Why had they chosen him? Why bring in someone from the British Army? His strange accent, those pale eyes, his stillness, the dislike I saw on his face. And he was attractive, too, with the lean body of a greyhound, and the strikingly handsome features that could have stared out of high-end fashion magazines.

I'd been so certain that this was the right thing to do, even though Karam had stayed silent, but now, hearing the reality of what lay ahead, my nerves failed me.

I was going to die.

I tried to imagine what Zada and my parents would say when they found out. Would they understand? Or would they curse me the way I'd cursed Karam?

I'd had almost no contact with my family for the last six months. They missed me, wondering why I hadn't responded to their calls and messages, bewildered by my silence, becoming desperate. As far as the hospital knew, I'd taken a leave of absence brought on by the stress of my brother's death. But I'd been too cowardly to tell my family to their faces that I was going away, so I'd mailed them vague letters that explained nothing but told them not to worry. I knew they would.

I told them that I needed to find myself. The words were contemptible: I knew exactly who I was and what I had to do.

But I didn't want to die. I wasn't ready to die. I wanted to live and see my sister marry and have children, and maybe she'd have a son named Karam, in honour of our brother.

I wanted to feel free of this burden, this debt that he'd left behind, a debt I was trying to pay in my own way. I wanted to feel free again.

Free of grief. Free of pain.

But when I closed my eyes, I saw the British soldier's eyes and I heard again the dozen ways that I might be tortured before I died.

I feared that more than I feared death.

As the horror of my panic attack ebbed, I unclenched my hands and picked up the MRE pack, still warm but cooling fast.

Even though my stomach lurched and saliva pooled in my mouth, I knew that I needed to eat.

There were several different types of food pouches, but I stuck to the vegetarian ones because I didn't trust the meat was *halal*. Even the ones designed for Muslims serving in the military. It felt strange to think that I was one of them now.

Everything was so new and strange: the training, the effort to be more like my sister, to fit in, and now wearing the *niqab*.

I pulled it off and breathed freely. My hair was a damp, sweaty tangle and my ponytail was a fistful of rats' tails. My jeans hung loosely from my hips—I must have lost ten pounds over the previous months of training. It wasn't just Army rations, it was the workouts that they'd put my body through. Mentally tough and physically tough—that's what they said. I didn't agree—I thought they were training me to be emotionless, to be a good little soldier and do as I was told. They didn't know that I had my own agenda.

I was still getting used to my *niqab*: there were many challenges in addition to feeling hot and stuffy. Just taking a drink of water was a major challenge of *Twister* proportions. But I also felt cut off and isolated from the world around me, and every sound was muted, slightly muffled. At least my eyes weren't covered in the thin veil of the *burqa* that some Muslim women wore, their whole world a dim haze. How could you ever recognize a friend in the street? The first day I'd worn the *niqab*, I felt like a blinkered horse, able only to look straight ahead. But you know what? It was different not to be leered at or looked at, to be too fat or too thin, with too big a bust or too generous an ass, or for wearing last year's fashions. I could wear pyjamas to the mall if I wanted. I was invisible, separate.

Although I got a few nasty comments from the ignorant—men, women and kids—it wasn't *me* but what I represented when I wore the *niqab*. That was a strange and powerful feeling, that a piece of clothing could cause such strong responses. But I understood it, too—the *niqab* was isolating and the woman wearing it in public stood apart. It was a powerful symbol, but a divisive one.

In Austria, the *burqa* had been banned completely, and other countries debated whether women in teaching positions should be allowed to wear them. But in some largely Muslim countries, they were required.

When I heard a knock on my door, I snatched up the *niqab*, tugging it over my head hurriedly, but no one came inside.

"Amira, we train at 0600. Get a good night's sleep."

Clay's voice. I could recognize it already. Wearing the *niqab* heightened my other senses, and I could hear the kindness.

I hated him for that, his kindness. He had no reason to be kind to me.

"Fine," I called out, and bit back the automatic 'thank you' that was on the tip of my tongue.

I pinched the back of my hand.

"Remember who you are," I whispered.

I lay on the hard cot, the air thick and stuffy, and listened to the sounds of the cabin settling into sleep, familiarising myself with the creak of the old wood, the restless rustling of the leaves in the tall trees beyond my window. I listened carefully, but the chirp of crickets mocked me, the sudden screech of an owl making me jump, then laugh at myself.

My thoughts turned to the men I'd be working with. Larson was a brute and I didn't like him; Smith had been efficient and professional; and Clay warm and friendly. But then there was the man in the room on the other side of the cabin. He unnerved me in a new way. I'd met many hardened men over the weeks of training, but he wasn't like them. They'd seen me as an asset to be used; he thought I was in the wrong place. I'd prove him wrong—or maybe I'd prove him right, just not in the way he expected. My heart sped up as I thought of what he was going to teach me: to make bombs.

He was younger than the other men—my age, perhaps. Although I knew that didn't mean anything. Some of Daesh's best bomb-makers were teenagers.

I thought about that a lot, in the quiet of the night when my unquiet mind tormented me. Children forced to fight—you'd never recover from that. The child-soldiers recruited by both sides in a war they didn't understand.

I'd never believed that this war was about religion—wars never are.

They're always about politics, always about power—who has it and who wants it, who is prepared to kill for it. In Syria, there were followers of Daesh or followers of Assad, the Syrian President: one killed with guns and bombs; the other with gas attacks—and both killed civilians.

James.

The British soldier said his name was James. Like one of Jesus' apostles. How very Biblical.

Or Quranic, depending on your point of view. In Islam, Jesus was a prophet and messenger of God, born without sin in a virgin birth. Does that sound familiar? It's no surprise as the three largest religions on earth all stem from the Abrahamic faith: Judaism, Christianity and Islam. All so close. All with similar beliefs. All blindly believing that *their faith* is the one and only.

It would make me weep, if all my tears hadn't died with Karam.

My brother, give me a sign. Am I doing the right thing?

The owl screeched again, and I shivered in the stifling warmth of the tiny room.

I was already on edge, so when a sudden scream pierced the night, this time I really did leap out of bed, searching for a weapon.

I grabbed the heavy brass lamp next to my bed and stumbled to the door, terrified.

Shouting was coming from the British soldier's room, but I couldn't tell how many people were in there.

I gripped the lamp more tightly and strained my ears to pick out words, but the only certain sound was "no!" said loudly and forcefully. I waited, my heart racing, my breathing accelerated, deafening.

The sounds died away suddenly like a radio being turned off, and I held my breath. I heard his bedroom door open and he walked to the bathroom, very slowly, his footsteps heavy. The door clicked shut and I could hear the rush of running water.

My heart rate began to slow as I analyzed what I'd heard—the man had been having a nightmare, a bad one.

Retreating, I jammed the chair against my door and went back to bed.

I still didn't like him, but it made him seem more human.

. . .

Morning came slowly but too soon, and I woke with red-rimmed eyes, drugged with tiredness. I'd sweated through the rest of the night and the scent of my own body odour was strong.

I stumbled from the bed, swatting at the thin sheet that caught itself in knots around my ankles, cursing as my shin banged painfully against the footboard.

Still limping, I pulled the door open and lurched to a halt.

The British soldier was standing by the cabin's open door, his shoulder propped against the wooden frame, silhouetted. He wore only sleep shorts, and the rising sun made his skin glow, casting a halo around his smooth head. He held a cup of coffee in one hand, his head bowed as he took slow, grateful sips. I saw the shadow of a tattoo across his shoulders but I couldn't see the markings clearly. It looked like a clock, maybe.

Infidel.

The word came to me more easily now.

Some Muslim scholars said tattooing was a sin, because it changed the natural creation of God. They caused pain, were impure and therefore prohibited by the Prophet Muhammad (peace be upon him).

The British soldier turned to stare at me, not startled, not surprised, but with wariness in his eyes. He held the coffee cup in front of him like a weapon, and my eyes were drawn to his strong arms, the hard muscles of his chest, dog tags glinting in the light, his flat stomach rising and falling above the trail of light brown hair that led downward.

In my old life, I would have said he was hot, but these days I was training myself to think only pure thoughts. And I had to focus on my job.

His insolent eyes drifted up my legs and across my breasts, lingering on my face.

I was uncovered!

My hands flew to my hair and I stumbled backwards, my cheeks heating with humiliation and shame as I scrambled to find my *niqab*.

I swore silently, then prayed for forgiveness for both sins. I had to do better.

My life depended on it.

CHAPTER SEVEN

JAMES

I'd known that she was standing behind me, watching me. I'd heard the creak of her cot as she climbed off the bed, heard the soft rustle of sheets, and listened carefully as she'd opened the door.

I waited for the soft footfalls that meant she was walking towards me or towards the bathroom, but when I didn't hear anything, I turned around.

She was a mess.

Her left cheek was creased from sleeping face down on her pillow, and her hair was a knotted tangle, stuck to her head on one side, greasy and uncombed. Her t-shirt was thin and her tits pressed against the worn material so I could see the darker tint of her nipples underneath. Her legs were long and smooth, with skin the colour of caramel. And those eyes—the eyes that had seemed older glaring at me through her *niqab* were soft and liquid with surprise, then narrowed in anger, and finally drooping with shame.

She stumbled backwards away from me, slamming the door and muttering to herself.

I didn't know if I was amused, insulted, or just as surprised as her. My dick twitched with appreciation of her curvy figure and a nice pair of legs.

I hadn't expected the woman to be so young, maybe mid-twenties, maybe late-twenties—my age. I *definitely* hadn't expected her to be attractive. I'd imagined some sour, bitter bitch, her sharp tongue cutting chunks off men who got in her way.

But this woman was beautiful. It was probably just as well she covered herself from head to toe in that black sheet. Being attracted to a CIA asset was a terrible idea—and we both had a job to do.

Clay appeared from the other cabin.

"It's a beautiful morning, brother," he smiled.

My brain took a second to reboot then I shook my head in amusement. This guy was congenitally happy—it wasn't normal. My smile faded when I took in how he was dressed: sandals on his feet, and a loose white robe, similar to those I'd seen Iraqi men wear.

"What's with all that?" I asked, nodding at his robe while I sipped my coffee.

"Have some respect, brother," he said, pointing a finger at me, and nearly dropping a handful of sweets in the process. "Damn! You almost made me drop my Gummi Worms. Damn, you made me cuss and I've only just said morning prayers." He sighed. "You're a bad influence, James. And put some damn clothes on."

"What are those sweets you're eating?"

Clay looked shocked.

"You've never had Gummi Worms?"

"Don't think so. They look too much like, well, worms. What are they made of? Gelatin?"

He closed his eyes for a second then squinted up at the rising sun.

"Damn," he said softly. "Gelatin—that's definitely not *halal*. You want them?"

I pulled a face and he dropped the colourful sweets in the dirt, shaking his head sadly.

"This shit is hard."

"But you're not really a Muslim, are you?"

He grimaced, still staring at the dust-covered sweets by his feet.

"I'm a seeker," he said finally. "There are a lot of fine words in the *Qur'an*, but I don't subscribe to any religion in particular." Then he looked at me seriously. "But I'd better damn well convince the ISIS cell that I'm a convert."

"That's why you're dressing like one of them?"

He nodded and stroked the straggly beard that he was growing.

"The robe is a *Didashah*: white for the summer, and darker, heavier fabrics in the winter." He grinned at me. "It's surprisingly comfortable in this heat. Free-balling is mighty fine."

I groaned.

"Mate, I don't want to think about your meat-and-two-veg—that's just nasty."

He laughed and fished in his pocket for some different sweets.

"This hard candy should be okay, don't you think?"

"No idea. Probably not."

"Harsh, brother," he sighed, putting the sweets away again. Then he nodded his head at my cabin. "Better get dressed, James. It will be disrespectful for Amira to see you like that."

I didn't tell him she already had. Instead, I took another swallow of coffee and tossed the rest onto the dusty ground.

"We need to come up with a training programme," I said over my shoulder. "Brain work in the morning, physical training in the afternoon. Okay with you?"

"It's hotter in the afternoon," he pointed out.

"Yeah, but I need you awake and alert for what I'm going to teach you. Working with explosives isn't good if you're half asleep after lunchtime."

"Whatever you say," he grinned. "You're the man!"

As I walked inside to the cabin, the heat was already growing, the dark interior stuffy and airless. I pulled on my desert camo trousers and olive green EOD t-shirt with the badge that said I was 321 EOD & Search Squadron. I was proud of that badge; I'd earned that badge, with blood and sweat.

I began running through what I needed to teach Clay and Amira in the next eight weeks: what was essential to stop them blowing themselves up, and what was ancillary to that. It had taken me seven years to become a high threat operator—how the hell was I supposed to teach them that in eight weeks? It was an impossible task. I'd just have to keep it simple and hope to hell that we all survived.

My old trainer used to say that neutralizing bombs made by the IRA was easier than devices made in Iraq or Afghanistan because they had a better build quality. That sounds messed up, but the truth was, the ISIS leaders didn't care if their bomb-makers had short careers—although it was the suicide bombers carrying out the attacks who were completely disposable: they didn't care about them at all.

Smith was waiting for me outside. I'd heard his truck leave in the night soon after I'd kicked dirt over our small campfire, and Clay had blown out the candles in the old hurricane lamps. But now he stood in front of me, his face lined with tiredness. He looked as though he'd been driving all night.

Pulling an all-nighter on deployment was never fun. Either you were on edge, aware of every noise, squeak, bump or bark; or your eyes were weighted with lead, and forcing your body or brain into action was the only way to stay alert.

Smith jerked his head at the back of the truck.

"Got your supplies. Everything except the projector screen—you'll have to do without that. Help yourself. Laptop's on the passenger seat. I'm going to get some coffee."

He didn't wait for me to reply but headed for the cabin he shared with Clay.

I wondered about that. Wouldn't it have made more sense for the two trainees to share together? If Clay was with Amira, he could have learned more about how a Muslim man was supposed to behave, and I assumed she'd rather share with him than me? Shouldn't they be bonding as a team? But what did I know.

Larson hadn't reappeared and Smith hadn't said where he'd gone. I didn't ask.

The truck was parked in the shade of a towering beech tree. My grandfather had taught me to recognize trees, and I'd loved going traipsing through the woods with him. Nothing like an old poacher for teaching you forest craft.

Although it had been years since the old man passed, the sense of loss was still fresh as I squatted under the tree and let the dry soil run through my fingers. I'd been laid up in Selly Oak at the time, a hospital where they sent all the military's injured personnel, so I hadn't gone to his funeral. I'd visited his grave a month later, my arm in a sling, a patch over one eye, and missing six teeth. Grass and weeds were already growing over the mound but he wouldn't have minded that.

"Nature in the raw, lad. That's the only way it should be."

His voice rang through my memories, his laugh turning into a hacking cough, the sweet scent of pipe tobacco clinging to our clothes.

I pushed back the echoes where they belonged and jumped into the back of the truck, rummaging through bags and boxes. Smith had done well. It was enough to start with.

He'd also taken the time to visit a supermarket, and I grabbed an apple and a banana, shoving them in my pockets for later.

MREs couldn't compete with fresh food.

I poked through the rest of the swag, mentally detailing the resources I had to play with, then Clay wandered out and helped me unload everything into an old lean-to that seemed watertight.

Amira appeared a few minutes later, the black *niqab* in place, but I couldn't forget the image of her standing in the doorway, sleepy and sexy, wearing just a t-shirt. I turned away and gestured to my 'classroom' which was a shady patch under one of the trees, and sent Clay to find Smith.

Amira sat gracefully, arranging her *niqab* around her in the dirt while I stood waiting for my other two students. She kept her eyes down, her restless hands shredding the dry leaves that covered the ground.

I couldn't help wondering about her. Why had she volunteered for this? What drove her to put her life on the line? I was about to teach her skills that would make her a very valuable terrorist asset. Clay was military and had seen action overseas, so I understood why he might have volunteered for this.

Smith arrived and sat on the ground with a grunt, rubbing his eyes as he sipped his coffee. Clay was his usual friendly self, and from the expression on his face you'd think I was giving a cooking lesson, not talking about efficient ways to kill people.

Obviously, I couldn't train them the way I'd been trained. Normally, I'd impart knowledge in the safest way possible, describing the explosive train, the parts of an IED and so on. But that risked using terminology or certain phrases that would be signature to military training. I needed to work differently.

I gathered my thoughts then dived in.

"Today I'm going to show you how to make a basic pipe bomb.

Pipe bombs are anti-personnel fragmentation devices that wound, maim and kill. They're simple, cheap, portable and easily made from components available at any hardware shop. I wouldn't say they're unstable, but they're easy to get wrong; for example, you end up with the black powder functioning if it's caught in the screw threads and just as likely to injure the bomb-maker as the intended target. So do what I say and only when I tell you."

I definitely had their attention.

I squatted down in front of them with the laptop, but the small size of the screen was frustrating and hard for everyone to see at the same time, so I swept leaves from the ground in front of us to make a clear, flat space, and sketched diagrams in the dirt. Then I pointed at the supplies in front of me as I described them.

"The bomb is made from a pipe. Any pipe, like this plastic one a plumber would use—you can get it from a hardware store. Yes, you can use metal pipes, too."

Clay raised his hand.

"I'm guessing you need more explosive power with a metal pipe?"

"Nope, the opposite: you'd use low order explosives like black power, and the compression still gives a decent effect. Plastic pipe can work just as effectively. In 1999, a bastard named Copeland targeted several gay bars in London using plastic pipe bombs. It needed more violence and additional frag—firework-mix and nails. He picked weekends, when there were more people around. Each bomb was hidden in a hold-all and contained up to 1,500 four-inch nails. He killed three people, including a pregnant woman, and injured 140 others. Four of those people lost limbs. Don't underestimate the homemade pipe bomb."

Clay was listening intently but I saw Amira shudder.

"What happened to him?" she asked.

"Who? The bomber?"

She nodded.

"Who cares?"

She dropped her gaze to the floor.

"I was just asking..."

My gaze narrowed on her, but she didn't look up again.

"He was convicted of murder and is serving six life sentences."

Smith had told me she was an ER nurse—maybe she knew exactly the kind of injuries I was talking about. I continued with the lesson.

"The pipe has threaded ends into which two caps are screwed. You drill a hole into one cap and place a fuze inside. Your first choice for that is military grade or civilian burning fuze; second choice is firework fuze. School kids are always using string and constantly have accidents."

"School kids?"

I glanced up, irritated by another of Amira's interruptions. Was she really that shocked?

"Yeah, kids. Happens all the time." I turned back to my explanation. "And det cord isn't used. Low order explosive is then poured into the pipe—I'll show you how to make that from fertilizer and sugar—and then packed tightly with a wad of tissue paper. This prevents the explosive being caught in the thread of the pipe exposing it to friction—that would be bad as it could cause accidental initiation."

Amira raised her hand again.

"Yes," I asked testily.

I was being an arse. Don't ask why.

"Could a ... a pipe bomb this size cause much injury? You said the London one had 1,500 nails packed into it, so..."

"Of course it can cause injury."

"It looks so small."

I gave her a hard look.

"One of the first incidents I was called to was where paramedics were treating a 39 year old man for blast injuries: they intubated him at the roadside because he had a scorched oesophagus from inhaling superheated air; he was bleeding from his ears so they suspected ruptured tympanic membranes—plus various shrapnel injuries."

She didn't look away as I described the scene, heard again the shouted chaos, felt the man's fear and panic as his body thrashed while medics fought to sedate him.

"He'd been a passenger in the back of an open pick-up truck when an unstable pipe bomb exploded in the driver's compartment—they'd gone over a speed bump at 25 mph." I paused. "The driver's head was found by police 30 metres away. Does that answer your question?"

Her eyes widened but that was the only reaction I could see.

"That's what you're being trained to do, Amira."

She shook her head.

"No, I need to *look* like I can construct a bomb and..."

"Are you that naïve?" I asked softly. "Do you really think that they'll trust you with the intel you're being sent to collect without having to prove yourself? And how do you think you might do that?" I let the question hang in the air.

"Come on, man," said Clay, his eyes darting to Amira.

"She has to know. There are always casualties of war."

My voice was bitter.

It was Amira who spoke first.

"I can do it."

My lips curled in a sneer.

"You think you can take another human's life?"

Her head jerked, but her voice was confident when she answered.

"Yes."

I leaned toward her.

"You think you can look a living, breathing human being in the face, and pull the trigger or set the timer and watch as their body is blown apart?"

It looked as though she'd taken a deep breath, but I couldn't be sure, and her eyes were hidden by the deep shade of the tree's branches.

"Yes," she said. "I can do that. The same as you."

Smith's gaze bounced between us.

"Right, James," he said calmly. "Moving on."

My eyes were still fixed on Amira, and she didn't look away.

For the rest of the morning, I taught them the basics: what length to cut burning fuze for different timings, and described where to place these IEDs for the best results that would cause the most casualties. Often terrorists prefer high numbers of casualties to the death of a single target: casualties tie up more resources for a longer period of time—maximum impact.

Amira fumbled, her hands clumsy under the *niqab*. Her peripheral vision was limited, too, and she stopped me several times because she couldn't always hear what I was saying. I tried to speaker slower, more clearly, but sometimes even my accent confused both her and Clay.

It was frustrating for all of us.

But part of me had descended into that ice-cold place where reason and rationality existed without emotion. I was a robot teaching another robot how to kill humans as efficiently as possible.

I'd been trained to think like a terrorist: that was the slow poison of my job.

I could never un-see what I'd seen, the bodies ripped apart, the lives mangled and destroyed. But that wasn't all. One aspect of my job was to collect samples from devices that had functioned so that DNA could be analyzed with the aim of ultimately finding the bomb-makers. And neutralizing them. There could be DNA samples on the Velcro straps used by a suicide bomber, but we collected all samples to be examined—and by samples, I mean body parts. Ears are particularly resilient since they're just gristle. Heads always pop off because necks are the weak spot. So part of my job was to collect body parts of suicide bombers. It was sickening work. And it marked a man.

Clay worked slowly and methodically, absorbing everything I said. His jaw worked constantly, sucking on sweets or chewing gum, a slight frown on his face.

The day grew warmer and sweat trickled down my back. I could see beads of perspiration on Clay's face, and Amira's head covering grew damp and she kept wiping her eyes.

I could tell that Smith had done this before—where and when, I didn't ask. I wondered if he'd worked with EOD in another life. If he had, he wasn't saying.

Finally, each of my students had a viable pipe bomb. The last lesson of the day was to see how well they exploded.

Smith led us through the woods to a small depression in the ground about a mile from our camp. I could see why he'd chosen the place—it was more enclosed, more sheltered, so the blast radius would be contained. I'd have to take his word for it that there was no one near enough to hear us.

I handed out ear protectors before I tested Clay's plastic pipe bomb first. It did a reasonable job, blowing apart and sending out an arc of plastic shrapnel that shred the canopy of leaves above the explosion. Amira jumped when the bomb functioned but tried very hard to look calm.

Smith's metal pipe bomb was good, as I knew it would be, scaring the crap out of Clay and Amira, and sending a shower of shrapnel thudding into the trees, severing branches and twigs, studding the heavy trunks like a medieval castle door.

Amira's plastic pipe bomb fizzed and died without detonating.

She stood with her hands on her hips.

"Ah, come on! I did everything you said!"

"Get down!"

"What?"

"Get on the fucking ground now!"

With wide eyes and a jerk of her head, she did as I ordered, dropping flat, belly down.

"Listen carefully and don't ever make that mistake again," I said, my voice grim. "Burning fuze is unreliable compared to an electric detonation, so there is always, *always* a mandatory waiting period—in the Army it's 30 minutes from when the last smoke was seen." I softened my voice. "That fuze can still function, so give it at least a few minutes before you go check what went wrong. Understand?"

She nodded her head sullenly, and my irritation level was up to 11 again.

"Let me hear you say it!"

"Yes, sir," snapped Smith and Clay.

Amira followed a second later.

"Yes. I understand."

I took a deep breath and softened my voice.

"The hole you drilled was too large so the fuze was loose. It came out when you placed the bomb. You should have checked."

"You didn't tell me to check that!" she snapped back.

I gave her a hard look.

"It was in my original instructions—that's why I showed you how to pack it with tissues. This isn't nursery school. I'm not here to hold your hand and wipe your arse." I took a breath. "You can learn more by a failure than you do by following instructions. Use your common sense: if the fuze doesn't reach the explosive, nothing will happen."

Her eyes narrowed and she glared at me.

Smith nodded.

"Here endeth the lesson."

"Amen," said Clay.

CHAPTER EIGHT

AMIRA

He was obnoxious. I wanted to take that pipe bomb and shove it up his ... no, that was the old me. I shook my head, clearing myself of impure thoughts.

We lay on the ground under the trees for the full half hour before James found my pathetic pipe bomb and made it safe. Since it hadn't exploded, I already thought it was safe, but apparently that wasn't enough.

We made our way back toward the cabins, the heat and humidity oppressive. As I glanced away from the group and peered upwards through the canopy of green, I realized that the sun was high in the sky and close to midday—time for me to pray.

I moved as gracefully as I could, hampered by the folds of material, and headed to my room to unroll my prayer mat for *salat-al-zuhr*.

Prayer was the second pillar of Islam, and the devout prayed five times a day. I'd come to look on it as meditation, the only peaceful moments in a crazy life.

I knelt down.

"Karam, I made my first pipe bomb today. It wasn't very good and it didn't explode. I'll try and do better but ... give me a sign, please! Am I doing the right thing?"

As usual, there was no answer and after I waited, my knees aching, I sighed, climbed to my feet and rolled up my prayer mat.

I peered out of the window and found that the men were all sitting in the shade eating, and the one named Larson was back. He scared me: so silent, so angry, the overt aggression a thick miasma around him.

If I had to guess, I'd say that he'd enjoyed blindfolding me, enjoyed pushing me into his truck and leaving me there; enjoyed telling me what to do on the long journey to this training ground. The man was a bully with a badge and a gun. I hated him.

But then again, I hated a lot of things these days.

James.

He'd deliberately set me up to fail. I found it hard to accept that there was any truth in what he'd said. I'd followed his instructions religiously, but it was more complicated than he made it seem, and the diagrams that he'd scratched in the dirt were hard to understand. There was so much information to take in. Clay had managed though, and that made me feel pathetic and useless.

I learned best by being able to study textbooks in peace; but here there were no books, nothing was written down, and I had to memorize everything. It was hard. Everything about this was hard.

My stomach growled, reminding me that I needed to eat, and I decided to venture out of the stuffy cabin to find some food.

I opened the door to leave my room, only to find James coming toward me carrying a grocery bag.

"Your lunch," he muttered, pushing the bag into my hands.

I was so surprised, I didn't say a word, and just watched as he strode outside again.

I retreated to my room and inspected what he'd brought me.

I was amazed to find two vegetarian MREs and a small pile of fresh fruit. I guessed Smith must have brought the peaches, bananas and apples back with him, but I was touched that James had brought them in here for me because he knew I didn't eat with the men.

I would have liked to eat outside, but in the world I was entering, a Muslim woman didn't eat in public because part of her face would necessarily be exposed.

I sat on my bed and gorged myself on ripe peaches, the juice dripping down my chin as I luxuriated in their sweetness. Then I ate a couple of bananas for energy and finished off with a piece of pita bread.

I remembered too late that it was our first P.T. session this afternoon, and I'd eaten more than I should. I hoped I wasn't going to throw it up later.

Running in a *niqab* was definitely a challenge, but I'd bought myself some CoolMax clothes to wear underneath—fabrics that wicked the moisture away from my body.

And suddenly an image popped into my head—a shopping trip with my mother and sister. My mother didn't like to break a sweat but Zada used to tell her that exercise was part of Islam since the Prophet Muhammad (*pbuh*) had once run a race with his wife Aisha.

Mama said that she still had no intention of breaking a sweat on purpose.

We'd laughed so hard. I remembered...

By afternoon, the temperature was in the high nineties, the mercury approaching 100°F. Any sane person would be indoors with air conditioning or taking a nap. Instead, I was about to follow Clay and Smith around a five mile-circuit and then do press ups, sit ups and throw some rocks around to build strength. I was dreading it. At least Larson had disappeared again.

Smith told us to look out for snakes, but not to worry about black bears since they ran away from humans. Then he gave us a quick lesson in identifying poison ivy, poison sumac and poison oak. That was a lot of poison. He also lectured us on all the bugs that could get us: mosquitoes, black flies, and the deer ticks that could spread Lyme disease. I sprayed myself liberally with DEET and set out to join the men.

Clay was his usual happy self, still wearing his *Didashah* and sandals. But I was surprised to see that James was joining us, too, still in his camo pants, t-shirt and desert boots. He also had a heavy-looking pack on his back, but seemed unfazed by the sweltering heat.

Smith also wore camo pants but had an assault rifle slung across his shoulders—a shiver ran through me.

I hated guns. I'd dealt with enough gunshot injuries in ER to loathe them, but now ... something else I had to get used to. The mission was everything.

Smith set a fast pace through the forest, following some narrow animal track. Branches plucked at my *niqab*, and roots tried to trip me. Soon, I was sweating hard—so much for CoolMax. It didn't have a chance to work with the *niqab* covering so much. I'd thought that I was pretty fit, but that was the sin of Pride, because my breath was coming in heaving gasps and I felt like I was drowning under the confining cotton. I concentrated on putting one foot in front of the other, eyes on Clay's robes, bright white even in the forest's shade. Smith insisted that I ran in the middle of the pack with James at the rear. He said you didn't put the weakest person at the back because you'd always be looking over your shoulder to see if they were still with you.

He was right: I was weak, but I was trying to be strong.

Karam...

Sweat ran into my eyes, making them sting. I blinked hard and tried to follow the sound of Clay's sandals slapping against the dry earth.

My breathing grew more laboured and swirls of light danced in front of my eyes. I didn't know if it was the dappled shade under the trees or...

"Amira's down!"

From far away, I heard the voice say my name. My eyes rolled in my head and my brain felt as though it was being slow-cooked in a hot oven.

Someone tore the *niqab* from my body, then water was flowing over my face and into my hair, and I gasped at the precious liquid, my hands flailing.

"Is she okay?" asked Clay, sounding concerned.

"Take it slow," said James, his voice so close to me. "Just a few drops at a time ... ah shit!"

I threw up, the whole of my lunch making a return trip. All over James.

I was too ill to be embarrassed, my ears ringing and my stomach cramping.

"Damn it, Smith! She's got heatstroke! She can't train in that outfit."

"I'll take her back to the cabin," offered Clay.

"I got her," James muttered.

My limbs felt floppy and uncooperative, but then I was rising through the air, the scent of vomit sharp and acrid in my nose.

My eyes fluttered open. James was carrying me—one arm around my shoulders and the other under my legs. This was so wrong! I squirmed feebly but he just tightened his grip.

"Stop it. You're not fit to walk."

I didn't have the energy to fight either, flopping against him. I was tired, so tired, and I let my eyes drift shut. I was aware of the movement of his body as he strode through the woods, his chest damp against my side, the rhythm of his steps strong and steady.

I drifted away, vaguely aware that heatstroke could be serious. Yes, I needed to ... what did I need to do? My brain wouldn't function.

When I felt the light on my eyelids change, I squinted at the dim interior of the cabin, then gasped as James dumped me on the bathroom floor and turned on the shower, cold water drenching both of us. The blissful cool water poured down, and I closed my eyes as he propped me against the tiled wall, his hands wiping the water from my eyes.

"Drink this," he said, forcing a bottle of water into my hands. "Drink slowly."

I was so thirsty, so horribly, desperately thirsty. I started to guzzle the water but he ripped the bottle away from me.

"Slowly!"

He slid down next to me, letting me take small sips from the bottle, the drink cooling me from the inside and the shower from the outside, until gradually, my body temperature started to return to normal, and awareness came back in fits and starts.

My brain rebooted slowly and I stared up at James, his pale eyes cool as he watched my face.

"Better?"

I nodded automatically, but my head wobbled on my neck as if it was too heavy to be supported. I tried to thank him but my throat seemed bone dry and the words turned to dust.

He grunted something then picked me up again, making me gasp.

My sodden *niqab* twined around his arms as he dumped me on my bed, his hands gentle as he touched my forehead briefly.

"Get changed," he said. "I'll be back to check on you."

I waited until the door closed behind him, prepared for the wash of shame that he'd seen me uncovered for a second time, but it didn't come.

True, it had been a medical emergency, but, but...

I was exhausted. It took forever for me to shed my wet clothes and crawl into a clean t-shirt and a pair of shorts. My hair was still damp and a bird's nest on top of my head, but I couldn't care less. I certainly wasn't suffering from vanity lately.

After a few more minutes of feeling sick and very sorry for myself, I heard a light tap on the door.

"It's Clay. How are you?"

Was I disappointed that it wasn't James who'd come to check on me like he said he would? I reminded myself that I wasn't supposed to trust him—I wasn't supposed to trust any of them.

I wrapped a simple cotton scarf around my head and called out with a hoarse voice.

Clay opened the door, peering inside but not crossing the threshold. He gave me a small, compassionate smile.

"How are you doing?"

I shrugged.

"Better now. Embarrassed mostly."

He grinned.

"It was pretty spectacular the way you hurled over James. I've never seen projectile vomiting like it."

I gave a shaky laugh despite myself.

"You know," he said kindly, "The *Quran* 24:31 obliges men to observe modesty: *Say to the believing men that they restrain their eyes and guard their private parts. That is purer for them. Surely, Allah is well aware of what they do.*"

"I know that," I said acidly. "What's your point?"

"That's it's up to the men to look away, not for you to cover yourself up and make yourself sick. You have to trust us, Amira. Everyone here wants this mission to succeed. Passing out during training is not helping. Wear a *hijab* if you feel you must, but don't knowingly make yourself ill again—that is also *haram*. We need you."

He gave me a long, knowing look, then he closed the door behind him as he left.

Was he right? Was this one of those occasions where Allah would forgive me? I had no one to ask, no one other than Clay who'd called himself a searcher.

The rising tide of Islamophobia made wearing the *niqab* a political as well as a religious statement. Our rights were being eroded across Europe: *niqabs* and *burqas* had been banned in Denmark, Austria, France, Belgium, Bulgaria and Latvia. And it wasn't just Europe: the ban also applied in Tajikstan on the frontier with Asia, as well as several countries in Africa, and also China. My human rights to dress as I chose were being swept away. So much fear. So much hatred.

I lay back on my narrow cot, but before sleep stole me, my thoughts whirled like leaves in the Fall, as I tried to catch them.

I thought about what I felt and what had happened. It was impossible for me to spend so many hours with James and not see little clues about him, even clues he was trying to hide about the man inside the soldier. James was kind, I could see that now. He tried so hard to be an asshole around me, but his humanity bled through, he couldn't help it.

And Clay, he was a total sweetheart and much more willing to let it show.

James.

I couldn't be attracted to him.

No, no, no.

CHAPTER NINE

JAMES

I woke up sweating and choked with fear.

I'd been dreaming about Afghanistan again. I hadn't done that in a while—such a mindfuck that it had happened both nights since I'd been here.

My room was stifling, even with the window as wide as it would go and my bedroom door propped open. The slight breeze had fallen away at sunset and the forest around us seemed to hold its breath—silent, watching and waiting.

Sweat coated my body and I decided that a low tech solution for heat reduction was needed. If you don't have air conditioning, wear wet socks in bed or lie on damp towels. It helps.

I sat up reluctantly, wiping my forehead. The air was thick and muggy, tugging at limbs that felt heavy and awkward. I took a long drink of tepid water from the chipped mug I'd left on the wooden crate that served as a bedside table and swiped my arm across my face again.

There was no moon tonight and the cabins were sheltered by the broad branches of the oldest trees.

Moving silently, I made for the bathroom. The water in the taps wasn't cold, but anything was better than this hellish humidity. I stuck my head under the flow of water and splashed my neck, back and chest. Relief.

Sleeping outdoors would be only slightly cooler than the oppressive cabin, but I'd take that tiny increment of comfort—although I'd need a mosquito net or I'd be bug food by morning.

Behind me, the floor creaked. I froze, alert to every sound. If Amira was trying to be silent, she was failing miserably. I heard her bare feet shuffle across the wooden floor, the warm timbers groaning quietly. She sighed heavily, and I heard the brush of material against skin. I decided to give her fair warning.

"I'm in the bathroom, Amira."

She squealed and stumbled backwards.

"Oh, dear Allah!"

"Yeah, I guessed you didn't know I was here. Sorry."

There was a pause as she took a breath.

"No, I'm fine. It's so freaking dark. How come Smith insists we can't use the generator at night now?"

"He wants you to get used to hard routine training."

"Excuse me?"

"Making you do without—toughening you up."

She made a snorting sound then sighed again.

"It makes a twisted sort of sense. So ... are you finished in there? I need some water—it's so hot!"

"Yeah. I'm going to sleep outside anyway."

I brushed past her as I exited the bathroom, and I was close enough to smell the sweat clinging to her skin. It wasn't unpleasant—slightly sweet, slightly spicy.

"James?"

Her voice was hesitant.

"Yeah?"

"Thank you. For today. You were kind. And you had no reason to be."

An uncomfortable sensation woke something inside me—an alert, a warning.

"I was just helping a member of my team. I'd have done the same for anyone."

"Oh, sure. Well, thank you anyway."

"No worries. Night."

"Goodnight, James."

I took my pillow, blanket and mosquito net from my bed and headed outside, but my thoughts stayed with Amira.

Was I beginning to understand her? She tried so hard to act tough, but that's all it was—an act. There had been moments today when she'd joined in with us, laughed at one of the dumb jokes that Clay was always cracking, but then she stopped herself and retreated again.

Something was driving her to do this, and I wanted to know what that was. Smith said she'd passed all the vetting procedures, but Smith had his own motives for bringing Amira here—and he wasn't sharing those.

I wasn't supposed to know any background, but it bothered me. I'd worked with undercover agents when I was out in Afghanistan. They were men motivated by money or manipulated into working for the allied forces. Only one I'd met had done it for idealism, and his eagerness got him killed.

Ahmad had been a nice kid, eager to learn. I never learned who recruited him—hell, he probably approached us. He had an older sister that he looked up to, and he'd hated the way she was treated, hated that the Taliban had closed her school. During training, we all told him to act tougher, be harder, hide who he was—but ultimately, he couldn't do it—idealism marked him. And that's what he became—a marked man. Dead at seventeen.

I'd known from the first day I met Ahmad why he was so driven.

Amira was an ER nurse. Hadn't she seen enough violence? Enough shootings, stabbings, car-jackings, sudden and violent death? But here she was, learning how to maim and kill. It didn't make sense to me.

In my experience, people spied for different reasons: greed, resentment, blackmail, ego, ideology, or a combination of all of those things. Did that mean for Amira it was about ideology: she was angry with how ISIS twisted her religion, so infiltrating them was a way to even the score? I wished I understood.

I was still thinking about her as the forest closed around me, cocooning me in its darkness, its strangeness, encouraging the thoughts and memories of my 29 years, rolling and pitching inside me. And when I dreamed, it was of her eyes.

I slept fitfully and woke just before dawn as a soft footfall penetrated the thin curtain of my consciousness. I rolled to one side automatically to avoid a blow, but became tangled in the mosquito net that I'd hung from a low branch.

Larson laughed as he stood over me, watching as I flailed around, caught in the netting.

"Sleeping beauty, you ain't," he grinned, holding a cup of coffee in front of him.

"If you're Prince Charming, we're both fucked," I grumbled, fighting my way free of the netting.

He muttered something under his breath and strode away.

The man walked softly, and he'd returned on foot. His Jeep was nowhere to be seen, and I'd definitely have heard that. Engine sounds travel a long way in the night. He'd probably stashed it a couple of miles away and walked in on foot. All the same, I'd keep an eye on him.

"Today I'm going to teach you how to make homemade explosives: method one is fertilizer and sugar or ANS; and method two involves hydrogen peroxide.ANS was the mainstay of the IRA because it's pretty much idiot proof—you grind the prills in a coffee grinder then mix it with sugar in a cement mixer. The hydrogen peroxide stuff is completely different: it's chemistry and takes longer. We're going to make both."

"Um, what's a prill, man?" asked Clay.

Damn, I was using EOD jargon again.

"Prills are the pellets of any substance formed by the congealing of a liquid during an industrial process."

"Got it."

I'd already gone over the key points of pipe bombs again, but saying there was a lot of material to get through was like saying Mount Everest was quite a large hill. And I was getting the impression that I had to pare it down even more.

"In 2010, a crude car bomb was discovered in Times Square. The device was made from petrol—gasoline—propane and fertilizer. But the bomber wasn't too bright and used a type of fertilizer that isn't explosive."

I gazed around at my class.

"It can be tricky to make explosives from fertilizer because of the chemistry involved. I'll tell you what type you *can* make use of. Look for one with ammonium nitrate, but you'll need to mix it in the correct quantities with fuel, and you'll need a detonator to generate enough energy and..."

Amira raised her hand.

"It seems to me that getting the raw materials is relatively straightforward, but where can you get detonators?"

I glanced up briefly.

"Radio Shack."

"I'm serious!" she snapped.

"So am I. Wasting time now won't help when you're on your own."

Having her in my class brought out the bastard in me. I knew why —I was attracted to a woman I had no chance with. After this time was over, I'd never see her again.

I turned away, ignoring Clay's raised eyebrows, and continued the lesson without interruption. Amira sat silently, still wearing her *niqab*, despite the heat and her collapse yesterday.

After lunch, Smith took over. I wasn't essential to this section of Clay and Amira's training, but I sat in anyway.

"On this assignment, you will be under stress," he intoned, his face hard. "Failure will cost you your lives and the lives of others. You will be isolated. The chances of you being left alone together are low—they won't trust either of you. You will have no one to talk to, no one to confide in. You will have to rely on yourselves."

Despite the day's heat, I saw a shiver run through Amira.

Smith lowered his voice and continued.

"Some agents enjoy the freedom that undercover work offers and decide to do things their own way. Don't. It will get you killed. Neither of you have the experience to pull that off. Following the plan is your best way of coming out of this."

Alive.

He didn't say it, but that's what he meant: *the best way of coming out of this alive.*

Clay stared at Smith, his dark eyes unblinking and serious. He wasn't cracking jokes today. Amira was silent and unmoving. I wanted her to get up and walk away. I wanted her to say that she couldn't do this. But she didn't. She sat there, listening, absorbing his words, taking it all in.

"You may begin to feel sympathy for the terrorists as you get to know them. Maybe you'll feel sorry for them and be motivated to help them. Don't. They're excellent liars—they wouldn't have gotten this far without that ability. *Do not trust them*. It will get you killed." He paused. "You die, I have to take a pay cut."

Clay snorted and grinned; Amira didn't react.

As the afternoon grew hotter, Smith led us out to a small clearing in the forest where Larson had been busy chopping down some of the smaller saplings to create a shooting range.

Amira was given some basic gun handling training, but her hands were slick with sweat and she found it hard to grip the pistol butt. I was tempted to show her how to hold the pistol steady with two hands, but that was a stance used by both the police and the military—it would be a dead giveaway. Instead, she struggled on, hot and frustrated, her aim getting worse instead of better.

Clay had it easier since his story was that he'd found his faith while in the military, and had seen how his 'brothers and sisters' were treated in Iraq. The closer the undercover role to your real personality, the easier it would be to succeed.

"What story are you going with, Amira?" Clay asked during a short break.

She glanced up then away, still hesitating.

"I thought we weren't supposed to talk about that."

Clay shrugged and smiled.

"Ain't nobody here but us chickens."

"What?"

He laughed.

"You don't know that song? Jump blues? Louis Jordan, 1946? Am I the only one here who knows the good stuff?"

Amira turned away from Clay.

"Only music that is devotional is *halal*."

Clay smiled sadly.

"Any instrument is lawful when used for permissible music such as accompaniment to devotional songs."

She didn't look at him again.

"I doubt that your chicken song is devotional or permissible."

Clay sighed.

I wasn't a praying man—I hadn't talked to God much when I was younger and not at all since Afghanistan—but I'd always believed that music soothed the soul and there was a time to dance. I couldn't remember where I'd heard that.

I was surprised when it was Smith who seemed to read my mind.

"*'To everything there is a season, and a time to every purpose under the heaven: a time to be born, a time to die; a time to plant, and a time to pluck up that which is planted; a time to kill, and a time to heal; a time to break down, and a time to build up; a time to weep, and a time to laugh; a time to mourn, and a time to dance.'* Ecclesiastes."

Smith had surprised himself, blinking in the afternoon heat.

"Shit! I don't know where that came from! Guess those Bible study sessions with sweet Sabrina Olsen taught me some things after all."

A time to kill.

That's why we were all here.

CHAPTER TEN

AMIRA

A storm was coming. I could feel the electricity by the way the hairs on my arms stood up, a sizzle that filled the air with static.

It began with just a few drops plopping onto the dirt at my feet, and I watched with fascination as the yellow-brown soil darkened steadily. I closed my eyes, turning my face upwards, feeling the first cooling drops across my eyelids and the bridge of my nose—the only part of my face that was exposed.

Soon the drops began to gather speed, slipping and sliding off the broad beech leaves and tumbling to the forest floor. The thick canopy was no longer protection against the growing torrent.

"Better get out of the damn rain," muttered Smith, jogging towards the cabins with Clay.

But I didn't want to. I wanted to feel the cool drops on my face, feel my *niqab* grow damp and heavy, feel the splash of rain on my upturned palms.

The sky cracked open and a bolt of lightning speared through the sky. It was wonderful! The most awesome light show on earth, free and fearsome.

The rumbling threat of thunder was followed by a loud crash that made me jump and then burst out laughing.

I felt so alive, so free.

A dash of movement beside caught my eye. It was James, like me, standing in the rain, a huge smile on his handsome face as he allowed the rain to soak him, his arms outstretched, the wet material of his thin t-shirt clinging to his shoulders and the muscles of his chest.

He opened his eyes and grinned at me, his voice rising above the crashes and rumbles.

"Isn't it amazing!" he yelled, wonder and happiness spilling out of him.

"It's incredible!" I yelled back, but of course he couldn't see my huge smile.

Perhaps he knew it was there.

He closed his eyes again, pure joy on his face.

The walls around my heart cracked dangerously and my arms fell to my sides.

Slipping in the mud, I hurried back to the cabin, glancing once over my shoulder.

James was watching me, his expression disappointed.

In my room, with a chair against the door handle, I stripped off my wet clothes, towel drying my damp hair.

It had been a moment of joy, a moment of madness, and now my emotions were dangerously untamed.

I sent up a prayer asking for guidance, pleading for strength.

Karam, I need you! Please, tell me—what do I do?

His silence felt like censure and I was close to tears.

Suddenly, the cabin's lights failed, and the familiar whir of the generator stilled.

There were voices outside and a moment later, James knocked on my door.

"Smith turned off the power because of the storm. Dunno what difference it makes, but that's what he said. Sleep well, Amira."

His voice faded and I started to breathe again.

As the hours of evening slipped into night, the storm grew wilder, howling around the tiny cabin and shaking its frame. The trees creaked and groaned, the smaller limbs snapping and spinning against our cabin.

I'd never known a storm so loud, never heard the wind tearing at the shingles on the roof before. The power of nature threatened to overwhelm our little shelter. I couldn't sleep with the wind shrieking so accusingly.

Slipping on my *niqab*, I headed into the darkened living area, edging around the kitchen table.

I squealed when I touched something warm, something alive.

"Don't freak out," came James' voice. "I couldn't sleep either."

"I'm going to put a bell around your neck," I groused, trying to calm my leaping pulse. "You scared the living daylights out of me."

I heard his quiet laugh and a flash of lightning illuminated his face briefly.

"I should go back to my room."

My voice was hesitant.

"Whatever," he said abruptly. "I don't know how to talk to you anyway, when I can't see your face."

His frustration halted my return to the bedroom.

"Because of the *niqab?* It's night! You couldn't see my face regardless!" He didn't reply and his silence defeated me. "I'm still a person, James. The same person."

He mumbled something I couldn't hear, and the low rumble of his voice made me long for human connection that I'd denied myself for too long, the weeks bleeding into months. I wanted to talk. I wanted to hear more than my own voice, or the echoes in my head.

Maybe if Karam had answered me I would have gone back to my room. Maybe not.

I pulled out one of the wooden chairs and sat down, a rustle of material as I pulled my *niqab* over my head and tossed it onto the chair beside me.

"There. I've taken off the *niqab*. Now we're just two people, two voices in the dark."

And we were, but it was the sudden flashes of light that were thrilling as I caught glimpses of James watching me.

"I've always loved lightning storms," I said. "My sister was scared of them and used to hide in the closet, but I'd go sit in the window and watch them with my brother. Did you know that there's no thunder if the lightning is over the ocean?"

James laughed softly.

"Yeah, I knew that."

"Of course you did."

There was a pause.

"You've got a brother and a sister?"

Oh no. Why did he have to ask that?

I didn't reply because I didn't know what to say and I was afraid that I might say too much.

"It must be nice," he said, his voice reflective, "to have family."

The resignation I heard touched me.

"You don't have any family?"

I thought he wasn't going to answer because the silence was strung out between us for so long, a thin thread that could snap and be lost forever.

"I probably do," he said at last, his voice truthful in the darkness. "I don't know who my dad was. I vaguely remember my mum, but I was taken into care when I was six. I haven't seen her since. I might have half-brothers or sisters by now, but I don't know." He paused. "I was close to my grandfather even though I only saw him once or twice a year. He died three years ago."

My heart softened as I imagined James as a small boy, how lost he must have felt, lonely and abandoned with nothing constant in his life, not even a parent.

"You've never wanted to find your mother?" I asked cautiously.

"No. She didn't come back for me, so why should I?" He paused. "She might not even be alive for all I know."

"I'm sorry."

"No reason why you should be sorry," he said gruffly. "You didn't abandon your kid."

"No, but I'm sorry anyway."

There was silence between us before he spoke again.

"I know I've been tough on you, tougher than I have on Clay, but it's because you're the least trained. What you're doing is dangerous. Are you sure you want to do this?

"Yes," I said.

It was half truth, half lie.

"Okay," he sighed. "I'll do my best to train you before I go home."

"Where do you call home?"

He gave a harsh bark of laugher.

"Wherever the Army sends me. I bought a flat in Reading, just outside London, so I'd have somewhere one day. I rent it out, but that's all. I didn't want to live in Aldershit."

"Really? There's a place in England named *Aldershit?*"

He laughed.

"Nah, not really. It's called 'Aldershot' and it's a big squaddie town. But it's a dump, so everyone calls it 'Aldershit'."

It sounded sad to me, but his voice had cheered up again.

"When did you join the Army?"

"When I was eighteen."

"That sounds so young."

"Best time to be trained—the body can take it," he chuckled. "Once you get past 30, everything gets harder. Carrying all that pack weight around in your Bergan—your rucksack—it's hard. Or try wearing 80 pounds of bomb suit made of Kevlar and armour plating: stand, kneel, stand, kneel, lie down, kneel. It kills your knees and back. I'll be an old man if I make it to forty."

If.

I hated that he said that, but he was right. There are no guarantees in life. I knew that better than anyone.

But I was fascinated and I wanted to keep him talking. Now that we'd started.

"Obviously you don't usually spend your life playing Hansel and Gretel in the woods and teaching people to make bombs, so what do you do, James?"

He laughed quietly, the sound lost under a loud crash of thunder that made me jump.

"Most of my work is the complete opposite: neutralizing devices wherever they're found. The team gets call-outs several times a week."

I was shocked.

"So often?"

"Yes, but a lot of those calls are about devices from the Second World War, believe it or not. Every time there's building work in Liverpool or Manchester or any of the port cities, someone digs up a rusting bomb, and we get called in. The Germans bombed the hell out of London during the Blitz from September 1940 to May 1941.

Millions of tons of explosives were dropped, especially on the docks where shipping brought food and supplies right up the Thames to the city. About a third never functioned and just got buried over time. Those devices are more than 70 years old now, so they can be pretty unstable from lying in the ground all these years. But the oldest device I ever neutralized was a mine from the First World War. It was found lying half buried in mud outside a major naval base on the South Coast, and the tide was rising. That was a tough one."

I tried to picture it in my mind—James in his bomb suit, sinking and slipping in mud as the tide kept coming, rising higher and higher, time running out, but not being able to rush, the clock ticking.

"That sounds ... really dangerous."

If he heard the quaver in my voice, he didn't comment on it.

"I don't think about it."

"How can you not?"

He paused, and I wondered if I'd pushed too far, but eventually he spoke.

"I have to switch off my emotions when I work. I have to concentrate on the job. If I stopped to think that I might lose my hands this time, or see it explode in my face, I'd lose focus. I have to analyze the task ahead. I have to see it in my mind, each step that will lead to me stopping the device from functioning." He paused. "I'm told it's like being a surgeon—that if you start to think about the person you're operating on, that they've got a wife or husband or parent or child waiting for them, that you wouldn't be able to concentrate on slicing into their flesh with a scalpel and working your way into a body cavity. I concentrate on getting the outcome I want, and that's what I think about when I'm doing my job."

I shook my head, ideas and fears spilling out of me.

"I guess I thought that you spent all your time dealing with terror attacks."

"There's that. But you'd be surprised how many times I get called to schools or homes because little Johnny has been playing with the chemistry set and something has gone bang."

I laughed, half surprised that he could so playful. Or maybe he was deflecting. I didn't know him well enough to tell the difference. But I didn't call him on it, I was enjoying talking to him too much. Much too much.

"I kind of imagine you were like that as a kid—seeing how big a bang you could make."

Again, I heard his quiet laugh, half lost as the wind howled outside.

"I may have had my share of emptying the powder from fireworks to see what else I could make."

"I definitely believe that," I said, glad he couldn't see me rolling my eyes.

We sat in silence as the storm shook the cabin with an angry fist, the rain rattling against the windows like bullets.

"Tell me about your tattoos," I said abruptly. "Sorry, I was just wondering. I know tattoos can be personal." He didn't reply. "It's none of my business."

"No, I'm just surprised ... I forgot you'd seen them."

I was so glad he couldn't see me blushing in the dark as I remembered the way my eyes had travelled over his back in the half-light of dawn, trying to understand the shadows I could see.

"I have two, they're separate and were done at different times, but they're linked, as well."

His chair creaked and I wondered if he was leaning back or leaning forwards.

"The one across my shoulders was my first. It says, 'The game starts after you score.' I used to play basketball when I was at school and it was something my coach used to say. It stuck with me."

Now I understood.

"He was someone important to you."

"Yeah, you could say that. He was the first person who believed in me. He taught me that when the other team scores, you have to set up the offence then score, then have a defensive strategy so they can't score again. It's like when life knocks you down, that's when you have to stand up and fight. I got the tattoo at a time in my life that was hard and I felt ... I guess 'lost' is the word that fits."

He gave a small huff of embarrassed laughter.

"A metaphor, yes, I can see that. And the other one?"

"It's a compass with the word 'pathfinder'. I had it done just before I joined the Army."

"So the Army was you finding your path."

He paused.

"Yeah, I guess you could say that."

"Working in bomb disposal?"

"I didn't plan that, it was just one of the trades—one of the specialities—on offer. It sounded interesting."

I shook my head in amazement.

"You risk your life to do this because it sounded *interesting?*"

"Why does anyone do what they do? Everything is a risk. Why are you here, Amira?"

"Because I have to!"

I blurted out the words without thinking.

"You *have* to?"

"I can't talk about it."

He sighed and his chair creaked again.

"No, I guess you can't."

Once again, the raging storm filled the emptiness between us.

"I heard you screaming," I said quietly. "Twice now. I wondered if..."

"I can't talk about that either," he said, his tone turning from surprise to something darker.

"Okay. Sorry."

He gave a dry laugh.

"Is there any topic out there that we *can* talk about?"

We sat in silence, listening to the wind moan, and the cabin creak and groan.

"You don't have to answer," I said at last. "There's no reason why you should ... but why do you shave your head? I know it's not because you're bald—so, I just wondered..."

My words limped to an end. It was another personal question, but no more so than him telling me about his parents or his tattoos. Even though the conversation was one-sided, I didn't want it to end.

"Have you ever had lice—body lice, hair lice?" he asked.

"What? No! Is that why?"

"When you're deployed in some shitty stone-age village where there's no access to running water and you've got two hundred blokes all crammed in together, it happens. They get in your hair, in your clothes, in your armpits ... and elsewhere—it's miserable. There's no way to wash your kit because water is flown in and rationed, so you hang your uniform over a fire and smoke the little bastards. Then heat up your bayonet or your knife and press it against the seams like an iron to get rid of their eggs. But for your hair, best thing is to shave it off."

"Wow! I never thought about that!" I reached up to scratch my head.

Now he'd talked about it, I imagined that my scalp was itching.

"That's just horrible!" I said, recoiling slightly.

"Yeah, not nice." He hesitated and I could hear him drumming his fingers on the table. "But it's not the real reason I shave my head. Although I would have. A lot of the lads shaved their heads on that deployment—a battalion of baldies!"

"So if it wasn't that, why did you?"

He gave an embarrassed laugh.

"I did it when I was 17." He hesitated. "You really want to hear this stuff?"

I nodded even though he couldn't see me.

"Oh definitely! I can tell there's a story here!"

"Okay, fine," he sighed. "Everyone at school called me a pretty boy, so I shaved off my hair so I'd look hard. Then it grew back a little bit but I didn't like it afterwards, so I just kept shaving it off."

I burst out laughing.

"A pretty boy? Well, sorry to burst your bubble, James, but you're still pretty!"

"Oh, cheers for that," he said, his tone ironic. He laughed lightly. "I've never told anyone that before."

His voice sounded contemplative.

"Yes," I acknowledged quietly. "It's easier to tell the truth in the dark."

I realized that we were heading for dangerous territory again—I couldn't afford to tell him the truth about myself.

"What reaction did you get when you first did it?" I asked quickly.

"Well," he said slyly, "girls liked me even better but the boys couldn't say anything after that. I suppose they were still pissed off— maybe even more so."

"Hmm, I bet they were. Is it typical, in the Army, I mean? If a guy's naturally bald..."

"I just about got away with it. The grooming standard is about being smart and uniform. I don't think a commander would object," he paused again, "unless it was tied to something like the National Front."

"Oh, is that a political party?"

He snorted.

"Just a right wing fascist organization. I don't want to be associated with those arseholes."

"But it can be slightly intimidating," I said. "It's aggressive."

"No, I don't see it like that. Buddhist monks shave their heads."

"Buddhism doesn't equal pacifism," I pointed out. "Buddhist teaching doesn't stop their believers from fighting in defence of their way of life."

There was another of the silences as I waited for his reaction.

"You sound like you know a lot about it."

"I had a friend who was a Buddhist ... not now, of course."

"You can't have Buddhist friends?"

"We were roommates at college but lost touch after graduation."

"But can you? You seem pretty hardcore about your religion—can you have non-faith friends?"

I sighed, not really wanting to get into this.

"It's always easier to be friends with people who are like you, from your tribe, you know?"

"My tribe?"

"Well, your tribe is the Army, isn't it?"

"Oh, right, I guess. What's yours?"

I can't tell you. I hesitated, uncertain what to say.

"The *Quran* says: 'Do not take the Jews and the Christians for your allies', and that part gets quoted a lot by those who are intolerant of the faith. But you have to read the whole book to understand, because later on it says, 'God does not forbid you to show them kindness and to behave towards them with full equity: for, verily, God loves those who act equitably'."

"You didn't answer the question, Amira." James' voice had become sharp. "I asked if you could have non-Muslim friends. What you've quoted to me says that you can be kind towards them but it doesn't mention friendship."

I slipped my *niqab* back on and stood up. The conversation had run its course.

"I can't be friends with you," I said.

I ran back to my room, my hurried footsteps lost in the fury of the storm.

CHAPTER ELEVEN

JAMES

She was driving me crazy. Warm, friendly and funny one minute; cool, distant and hostile the next.

It also pissed me off that she was more relaxed with Smith and Clay than she was with me. I knew that was my fault, but there was a push and pull between us that I couldn't ignore.

In the darkness, with the storm battering the cabin, I'd found myself talking to her in ways I never usually did with a woman, not for a long time. I'd told her personal stuff, things that were private that I never told anyone, and for all I knew she could use the information against me. I'd let her get inside my head, and that wasn't good—it was very, very bad.

I sat at the wobbly kitchen table with my head in my hands, frustrated that I'd given so much away.

Jesus, I'd even told her about the World War One mine that I'd been called out to, although I hadn't told her the details. I hadn't told her that I'd spent nearly 11 hours up to my thighs in mud that kept trying to suck me down, trying to force open a rusted mine that was covered in barnacles and not get blown to kingdom come. And I hadn't told her that I'd earned the Queen's Gallantry Medal for that job.

I hadn't told her about the nights I woke up gasping for breath because I dreamed that my hands had been blown off or turned to blackened stumps in front of me, curled and burned into claws, the nightmares that plagued me.

I hadn't told her about the high risk training with IEDs, the roadside bombs I'd worked to stop detonating in Afghanistan, or the ones we didn't get to in time, the ammo demolition that went so badly wrong.

And I hadn't explained that it's not about individual glory or even individual achievement: every bit of knowledge was saved and stored and taught to the next generation of ATs. All the knowledge accumulated from UXB teams during the two World Wars, the years of living with the threat of IRA bombs in Northern Ireland and on the mainland, it all added up. We'd learned to adapt as the terrorists had adapted. We even had a museum of devices so new recruits could learn from the ground up. Because although terrorists were becoming more sophisticated, you could equally be called to a primary school or a building site, and you had to be ready for what you'd find. Although conventional tasks of making ordnance safe added to our explosives knowledge, so granddad's grenades had little bearing on our counter terrorism expertise.

Even so, I'd told her more than enough.

I thought about the very tiny pieces of information that she'd given away: that she had a brother and sister; that she'd gone to college and roomed with a Buddhist, so presumably she hadn't always been so ... was 'devout' the word? Maybe that's why she seemed to schizo—at times joining in with us naturally, at other times stand-offish and awkward.

It had been good talking to her tonight. She said that the truth was easier to say in the dark.

And then I remembered something else ... when I asked her why she was here, she said, *because I have to.*

What did that mean? That something was driving her to go through with this, or that some outside force was compelling her. She'd certainly shut up quickly enough afterwards, and I guessed that she was even regretting telling me she had a brother and sister.

The CIA or NSA or whoever Smith worked for—they would have trained her not to give away personal information because it can be used against you. She'd been a hell of a lot better at keeping quiet than I had.

But it had seemed like something else at the time, that there was another reason she wouldn't talk about her family. I wondered if they knew what she was doing.

And then it struck me: had I been chosen for this op because I didn't have any family? After all, who would notice if I never came home? Noddy would hold onto my bike and maybe ask around, but what if the 'paperwork' just got lost? I moved around so much, would anyone from my regiment realize before half a year had gone by? And by then, the trail would be cold.

I was being paranoid. The British military was so small, we were down to 80,000 personnel. Just enough to fill Wembley Stadium, although the Navy would have to park their battleships outside. But there were even fewer ATs, maybe 350 to 400, and only 30 operators on teams in the UK. Surely someone would notice? Eventually.

A prickle of unease swept over me: *what the hell am I doing here?*

I was tired, and maybe that was the reason I was seeing conspiracy theories everywhere. With the storm still raging around us, I knew that sleep would be far away, so I put my restless brain to work on planning tomorrow's ... today's lesson.

By morning, the storm had blown itself out. The day felt fresher and I could see things more clearly.

The first job was to get rid of the branches, twigs, leaves and other debris from around the cabins, then restarting the generator that coughed and gurgled painfully.

We all knew how to make a fire and boil water in a mess kettle, but the Army has a saying: any fool can be uncomfortable. I was very happy turning on the generator to make use of the coffee machine.

I made two cups and left one outside Amira's door.

She ate alone, as usual, and I felt a pinch of anger mixed with sadness. It was hard to bond with the team when you isolated yourself for long periods of rec time. But maybe that would work in her favour when she was moved on.

Clay clapped me on the shoulder.

"Deep thoughts, brother?"

"Nope, I'm paddling through the shallow end right now."

He laughed.

"I somehow doubt that. So, Teach, what pearls of wisdom will you be casting before us today?"

Amira poked her head out of the door, once again dressed in her black *niqab*. I was beginning to hate the sight of it. There was no sign of last night's shared secrets.

"Timers," I said. "How to make them and how to use them."

Once we'd cleared a space outside, we made ourselves comfortable on the ground and I began.

"Okay, first lesson in making a device with a timer. You need a non-digital alarm clock and some silver paper. Take one of the hands and wrap it with silver paper. Push a nail or tack into the clock face. Take a battery, nail file, dental floss, glue, pliers, a pop gun and a mousetrap."

I laid out the components in from of me—all easily available.

"Strip the wire, silver paper over the top, bend the wire back and glue to the clock. Take the caps from a pop gun and glue to the mousetrap. Attach the battery and clock, then wire together. Glue the unit to the mousetrap. Thread the dental floss through the mousetrap —or cotton if you don't have floss—and glue to the battery. Lift up the mousetrap and you've armed the device. When the hand hits the nail, it'll trigger the caps of the pop gun ... which you'll have attached to a bloody great explosive device." I paused. "Easy. Kids make them all the time."

I saw Amira's eye twitch. I'd learned to read a lot from those dark, expressive eyes, probably because that was all I could see of her. And I could tell that this made her uncomfortable.

Smith didn't join us today. He'd seemed distracted during breakfast and had disappeared into the forest. He didn't say where he was going.

It occurred to me that if he didn't come back, we'd be stranded here or have to make our way out on foot. And none of us knew where we were. Oh well, survival training 101—follow the river downstream.

But Smith returned in the afternoon, just as Clay and I finished a workout. Amira said she'd train in her room. I didn't know if she was avoiding me. It gave me a headache trying to second guess her all the time. It would be a hell of a lot easier if I could just ignore her.

But I couldn't. Those eyes. Those damned eyes. I felt her watching me, and even when she wasn't there, I found myself looking for her.

Smith jerked his head at me, indicating that I should follow him.

He walked a couple of hundred metres into the forest then sat down on a log.

"How's the training going?"

"I've really only just scratched the surface of what they need to know. Clay might remember a few things, but Amira … I'm not so sure. She makes mistakes that will get her killed. Even Clay is nowhere near competent. Why? We've got seven more weeks yet."

He sighed and shook his head.

"We really don't. Can you get them ready in ten days?"

I thought he was joking but the smile froze on my face.

"Is that a serious request?"

He grimaced.

"An order from above. There's been a significant increase in radio chatter from the terror cell—my bosses think something is brewing, and they want the assets in place now—yesterday would be better."

I shook my head.

"No, not possible. It's too soon. They're not ready."

He looked away.

"Ten days. It's all you've got."

"If you send them in now, posing as bomb-makers, they won't last a day—it'll be a suicide mission, and you know it!"

He stood and glared at me.

"You think I don't know that? We have *no choice*. Whatever they're planning, it's big. We haven't intercepted anyone travelling through the U.S. so we suspect, hell we're fairly certain at this point, but we think they've got a bomb-making factory on U.S. soil."

"Bloody hell!"

"Exactly. You know what that means. So getting the assets in as quickly as possible is our only chance of finding out when, where, who and how." He ground his teeth. "I can risk two assets—I can't risk letting this terror cell slip away again."

He turned and left, calling over his shoulder.

"Ten days, James."

The assets had names—and I had ten days to prepare them to enter Hell.

. . .

That evening, we were sitting around the campfire, making it smoke as much as possible by piling on green leaves. It helped to keep the bugs and mosquitoes away, even though it meant that we all smelled like barbeque flavour. I'd sprayed myself with insect repellent as usual, but the little sods kept finding a patch of skin to munch on.

Smith was staring into the fire, his expression fixed, a frown on his face. Then he looked up at me and I knew it was time.

"Team meeting," he said. "Clay, go get Amira—she needs to hear this, too."

"Yes, boss."

As soon as Clay and Amira were seated by the bonfire, Smith stood up.

"The deadline has changed," he began. "We have intel that leads us to believe that the terror cell is planning something big, and soon. We need to get you in there as quickly as possible." He paused, looking at both of them in turn, but neither spoke. "I'm aware that your bomb-making training is sketchy at best, but it just means we'll have to spin your cover story slightly differently. It might even work to our advantage that you're only partly trained since no one expects military precision from most ISIS bomb-makers."

"How much time do we have?" asked Clay, his face solemn.

"Ten days."

Smith turned to me, nodded, and I began speaking.

"I'm going to abbreviate the programme, so there's a lot you won't get to see, but I'll teach you what I can with the emphasis on keeping you safe—and make sure that it sinks in. Tomorrow, at daybreak, I'm going to show you how to search for IEDs: what to look for, what kind of devices you might come across—and how to deal with them."

I was staring into the darkness, but my mind was thousands of miles away, remembering.

"What I've taught you so far is small fry stuff: a few pipe bombs, basic timers. You'll be useful but not indispensable to the terrorists. I can't teach you expertise in ten days. But you can still make a difference. We'll use the time to cover as much ground as possible."

I looked up. Clay was watching me silently and Amira's dark eyes glittered in the firelight. I had no idea what she was thinking, no clue what she was feeling.

"Smith's team believe that the cell are connected to a bomb-making factory on U.S. soil. We're talking large scale here, not just a few pipe bombs. We could be talking about a new 9/11. So I'm going to tell you what a bomb-making factory looks like, so at least you'll know it when you see it, and the kinds of jobs you might be asked to do."

I reached into my rucksack and showed them a smooth metal tube with wires coming out, no thicker than a pencil and half as long.

"This is a typical detonator. These are sensitive and where most accidents happen. Don't hold it in your hand for long, because body heat can be enough to make it function—you'd lose your hand."

I let them hold the inert detonator, feeling its weight, studying the wires that hung from it.

"Next: if they've got C4 from Iran, it often comes wrapped in green plastic, but inside it's white like putty and sticky to the touch. Most terrorists prefer military explosives, but if they want to make a large bomb, they'll make their own. They'll have a room that looks like a workshop, tools and equipment on the tables and with someone connecting wires to saw blades—these are used for switches. As each switch is finished, it will be attached to a battery and a lightbulb."

I took a length of wire with a bulb attached, a battery pack wrapped in rubber made from bicycle tyres and ran the wire along a patch of soil a short distance from the fire.

"Once the wire is laid out, they'll connect one wire to a lead from the battery and then touch the other wires together."

The bulb gave a bright flash and Clay jumped.

"That's how you blow up a convoy. The exact moment of explosion is less important with several vehicles to aim for, because if you miss the first vehicle, you'll hit the second: either way, if there is a big explosive charge, the road will be damaged and you'll be able to immobilize the convoy for your attack with small arms fire.

"If you're targeting a single vehicle, a professional terrorist group would tell you to practice 'trigger time' where you get used to the delay between touching the wires together and the bulb coming on."

Amira was looking between me and Smith.

"I ... I won't be able to remember all this! I can't, I..."

"No one is expecting you to—I'm just trying to make you aware of the possibilities. If the cell is as organized as Smith's bosses think, they'll only use people with electronic skills to build the circuitry. In all likelihood, you'll be doing the mundane leg work like making HME ... homemade explosives—shovelling fertilizer into modified coffee grinders."

Amira's hands were shaking, but there was no time to stop. I had so much to tell her, so many things that she needed to know to keep her as safe as possible—every second was precious.

I ran my hands over my head as I felt her frustration.

"If you see a uniform grey-coloured powder ... that will be the aluminium. They mix it with fertilizer. It looks like this."

Smith had done his job when I'd asked for my supplies, and I showed them a packet of the powder.

"Most HMEs will be packed into pressure cookers or homemade metal cases made from gas pipes, cut into sections and welded closed. Some are put into large plastic drinks containers. You'll see the det-cord hanging out from pre-drilled holes."

I carried on.

"Things to notice: anyone working with peroxide, it often bleaches the skin white. It's more obvious on darker skinned individuals, and obviously any transit through airports would risk being swabbed and lighting up the explosive trace machines. That's one of the reasons why Smith thinks the devices are being made on the U.S. mainland.

"Now I need to tell you about booby trap devices, pressure plates being hugely common, and of course devices attached to a suicide bomber where..."

Amira fainted.

Grumbling softly to himself, Clay picked her up and carried her to her room.

I stared at Smith, my gaze hard and accusing.

"If you send her into that terror cell in ten days, you'll be sending her to die."

CHAPTER TWELVE

AMIRA

Clay hovered by my bed, trying to make me sip some water. He was kind, but I didn't want his company. The horror of James's words hung in my head: *suicide bomber*. Because suddenly I knew—that's what I'd been recruited for. Fewer people suspected women, fewer believed that we were capable of atrocities. But we were.

And yet faced with that stark reality, it had been too much. I was disgusted by my weakness.

The fact that I hadn't eaten much all day was definitely a contributing factor to my embarrassing dive into the dirt, but more than that, it was those words.

"Amira," Clay said softly. "There's still time to walk away. You don't have to do this."

He didn't understand. How could he? I'd never told anyone why I had the compulsion to do this, why I *had* to continue.

"I'm fine," I mumbled.

"You're not fine," he sighed. "At least eat something. You'll make yourself sick by not eating. I've left you two vegetarian MRE packs— just about edible cold. Eat something."

I didn't want to tell him that I still had the two that James had left for me.

I heard the door close behind him but I stayed curled up on the bed. I was tired, so tired. If I could just stay here forever…

When I dreamed that night, it was of my family. Zada and my parents were standing together, looking into the distance, the wind whipping their clothes. I called to them, but they didn't hear me. I kept calling, but my voice was swallowed by the roar of the approaching storm. I screamed their names but they never turned to look at me, didn't see me, couldn't hear me. And all through this, Karam was nowhere to be seen.

The next morning, I was determined to show them that I wasn't weak, that I could do this.

I ate two of the MRE packs that had been left for me and attended James' lessons with a new drive and focus.

I think I surprised everyone, not least myself.

Today, we'd learn how to locate hidden devices.

At dawn, James had been awake before us all, and set up a number of training devices so we could practise searching for them.

"At a roadside, you're looking for a mound of soil, something that's been moved, unusual bumps in the road; sometimes slight indentations where the soil has sunk. Look for anything unusual, especially wires sticking out anywhere. And where you find one device, expect two. You find two devices, search for a third. A large device may have booby-trap switches to catch out someone interfering with them or trying to defuse it—and it could have more than one, sometimes two or three."

Then he showed us how to do a fingertip search of the area around the cabin, working from a starting point and making our way forwards. It was slow and tedious and sweat was pouring down my face, making it hard to see. I used my *niqab* to wipe my eyes because my hands were so filthy from filtering dirt.

"Man, this is backbreaking," sighed Clay.

James didn't crack a smile.

"Yeah? Well, imagine you're doing this with a limited amount of time because insurgents will be arriving any second to shoot your arse off. Remember, the longer you're searching, the more vulnerable is the team watching your back."

We searched for the rest of the morning, our frustration growing.

"I'm beginning to think you didn't hide any devices out here," Clay groused, his usual good temper wearing thin.

Then his expression changed.

"Wait! I think I just stepped on something."

James nodded and sighed.

"Yep, pressure plate device. You're dead, mate."

Clay gave a half smile as he removed his foot from something buried beneath him.

"Does that earn me a ten-minute break and some iced tea?"

"You can have five minutes and some water if you tell me what signs you missed."

Clay stared at the dirt under his feet, his forehead wrinkling.

"The dirt is a different colour there," I said suddenly. "It's been disturbed recently."

James's gaze swung to me as admiration shone in Clay's eyes.

"Good call. But is it safe for you to continue?"

I crouched down, studying the dirt in front of me, eyeing the bushes at either side warily. Minutes passed and my thighs began to cramp. Was there anything? Was I seeing things were there were nothing?

In the end, I huffed out a breath and rubbed my aching muscles. As I started to stand up, I bumped my head on something hard. Expecting to see a tree branch, I was surprised when James shook his head.

"You're dead, too. Look up."

We all looked up at the tree branch above my head. There, hidden in the foliage, was another device. I'd walked right into it.

"Don't forget to look up, don't forget to look down: always check out nearby drains and sewers. Look everywhere. Suspect everyone."

Between James and Smith, and occasional fleeting visits from Larson, Clay and I were worked around the clock.

We were woken in the middle of the night, had our sleep disrupted, and every psychological trick in the book was used to break us. But the harder they tried, the more determined I became. I was starting to understand what James meant when he said he locked his emotions away to do his job. As a nurse, I'd certainly had to learn to function without being overly emotional, and at the end of a shift, it had taken a few hours to feel like myself again after an especially bad day; but this was at a new level of intensity and it didn't end. There was no 'off' button anymore, no end to my shift. I wondered if I'd ever reconnect with my feelings again—they seemed so far away, so unimportant.

The physical workouts intensified, too, and I was exhausted all the time. Larson, in particular, took great pleasure in noticing when I was close to falling asleep, and once he pushed his boot into my ribs to wake me up.

"Get used to it," he sneered. "It's going to get worse."

I didn't know if he meant here at the camp, or when I became an asset, when I was sent to the terror cell. Maybe both.

But he was excellent at teaching me how to use weapons and the basics of loading, firing, cleaning, disassembling and reassembling a Smith & Wesson handgun and an AK-47.

During those lessons, he was surprisingly patient, but hand-to-hand fighting brought out the beast in him.

"Jesus, Larson," snapped James. "You'll break her bloody arm!"

"She's weak!" he snarled. "Being weak will get her killed."

"Well, she'll be no use to anyone if you break her first!"

I wasn't a person anymore. I'd become a toy, a weapon. I was becoming an asset.

I didn't care.

But I wasn't weak. I'd show them how strong I could be.

Karam, give me strength. Show me how to be strong.

A breeze rustled through the leaves above me, and it felt like an answer at last.

This time when Larson attacked me, I fought back with everything I had. He used his greater height and weight to pin me down, but I bit him on his cheek; even through the *niqab*, I left a mark.

"Damn!" he said, rolling off me and rubbing his face.

His eyes narrowed and I wondered if he'd hit me, but then his hand shot out and he hauled me to my feet.

"Better," he said. "Now do it again."

I glanced across to James and Clay, but they were engaged in their own battle, each using wrestling tricks to out-manoeuvre the other.

Sweat glistened on their faces and on James' arms, now streaked with dirt. Suddenly, he bent low and Clay seemed to fly over James' back, thudding onto the forest floor, winded.

"Sneaky, brother!" he gasped as James stared at him, then shrugged.

Oh, I knew all about being sneaky. I'd learned that over the past year: hiding who I was from Zada, from my parents—I'd learned plenty of sneaky tricks before I'd ended up here.

Larson's fist in my chest threw me to the ground.

"Concentrate!" he barked as I tried to catch my breath from his attack. "No distractions! Allow yourself to be distracted and you'll be dead!"

His eyes darkened with anger or maybe dislike, I couldn't tell, but something inside changed in that moment. A deep well of hatred had grown inside me: Larson had just lit the fuse.

As I prepared to fight again, I saw that James was watching me again, his face a mask of blankness.

That evening, he was sitting at our tiny kitchen table when I walked past him to my room.

"You're doing well," he said, without looking up.

I was surprised that he'd spoken to me; for the last few days, we hadn't had any conversations other than during training.

"Does that mean I get a certificate?"

He laughed, and it was such an unexpected sound after the seriousness of the day.

"Yeah, I'll make you a certificate with a gold star," he smiled.

"I must have a good teacher."

He grinned, his eyes crinkling at the corners.

"I'd have to agree."

Curious, I stepped closer.

"How long have you been doing this, working in bomb disposal?"

"It took me seven years of training to be a high threat operator. Lots of studying," he sighed, yawning as he stretched.

"I'm sure your grandfather was very proud of you."

I didn't know why I'd said that, but I felt it must be true.

He hesitated before he answered.

"I hope so. Yeah, I think so. But I wasn't there when he needed me either. When you join the Army and you promise to serve your country, family commitments come second."

He was right, and the pain in my heart when I thought about my family grew daily.

"Thank you for your service," I said quietly.

"I should be saying that to you."

I nodded and continued to my room.

CHAPTER THIRTEEN

JAMES

Clay had mad skills at Ju Jitsu but I'd been a streetfighter since I was six. Being sent to an orphanage at an early age had toughened me up—you had to fight to survive. At six years old, I'd been a skinny little runt of a kid, so I'd had to learn to fight dirty. And right now that was serving me well. I was winning because Clay couldn't break a rule if he drove over it with a tank.

I'd put him on his back again and was laughing my arse off at his surprised expression. But then Amira walked past, muttering about taking a nap. The moment I took my eyes off Clay, he swept my legs out from underneath me.

I was winded by a stabbing pain in my side.

"You're always telling me to focus," laughed Clay, but then he saw I wasn't getting up. "Damn, brother! Are you okay?"

I groaned as I sat up, clamping my hand against the side of my back that I'd landed on, surprised when my hand came away wet with blood.

"I think I landed on a rock or a pinecone or something. Hurts like a mother!"

Clay helped me up, then looked at the wound.

"It's small but looks deep. You'd better get it cleaned up. Better still, get Amira to take a look."

"Nah, I won't bother her."

"Don't be a jerk. That looks nasty, and she's a nurse."

"Blimey, since when did you become my mother?" I grumbled as I walked back to the cabin.

But I still went to do as he suggested, and knocked on Amira's door.

"Yes?" she called, her voice sounding tired.

"I could use a bit of First Aid," I sighed.

I heard her moving around in her room, then the door opened.

"What happened?" she asked.

I turned around to show her my back.

"Ouch! What did you do?"

I told her about wrestling with Clay as she led me to the bathroom.

"This is going to sting when I clean it. I can't risk leaving any dirt in there."

She washed her hands, then gently cleaned the wound, her hands sliding over my skin. As she applied peroxide, prodding around until it felt like my back was on fire, I gritted my teeth as she finished cleaning it.

"That's better," she said at last. "But I think it needs a stitch, maybe two. Go lie down on your bed and I'll be there in a minute."

Feeling stupid and sore, I lay face down on my bed and waited for her. It wasn't long before I heard her soft footfalls and reassuring voice.

"You'll feel a sharp prick when I inject some anaesthetic, okay?"

I already felt like a prick, but I didn't say that.

Once the needle went in, a cool, numbing sensation spread across the side of my back. Followed by that weird tugging that meant I was getting a new collection of stitches as she sewed me back together.

"You have a lot of scars," she commented as she worked.

"Yeah, well, I've been in the Army for 11 years—I have more scars than medals."

"Hmm," she said. "I don't think that's a fair swap. You should complain."

I grinned at her words.

"I'll tell my C.O. that."

"You should!" She was silent for a couple of minutes before she spoke again. "How did you get these scars?" and she ran her fingers down toward my hip, making me shiver.

I didn't want to talk about that.

"Seen a lot of wars—too many."

"I see," she said quietly. "Well, you're all stitched up now, James. I'll put a dressing over it, but I'll need to change it every time you shower for the next three or four days, then I'll see about taking the stitches out. Normally, I'd use dissolving stitches, but these ones I'll have to take out by hand. Right, you're good to go. Oh, and James?"

"Yeah?"

"Try not to do anything crazy and tear the stitches."

I laughed.

"Yeah, right. I'll try not to. Thanks, Amira."

She left my room and I lay there for a while longer before I sat up reluctantly. It occurred to me that it had been our first real conversation in daylight, even though she'd been sewing me up at the time.

I liked it, I liked talking to her. And I liked her hands on me.

I kept telling myself that it was stupid to be attracted to someone that I would never see again once the training was completed, but I couldn't help it.

The following day was another long one: EOD tasks in the morning, arms and combat in the afternoon, and a lecture from Smith in the evening about the psychological impact of going undercover—the pressure of maintaining their identities, the strain on family relationships, the isolation, the loneliness.

I wished she'd change her mind, but she seemed more focussed than ever.

That evening, I took a quick shower before bed, and Amira dressed my wound again.

"What did you think about Smith's lecture?" I asked.

She took several seconds to answer.

"I'm trying to prepare myself," she said, "but it's hard, it's such an unknown."

"Are you sure you want to..."

"James, please," she said softly. "Don't question me on this. It's hard enough already."

I lowered my voice.

"Sorry."

"It's kind of you to worry, but it's not your concern." I felt her press another dressing over my wound. "All done," she said.

She stood up to leave the room.

"Amira?"

"Yes?"

"It is my concern—you and Clay."

Her eyes slid away from me.

"Thank you."

I wouldn't say things were easy between us, not with that pulse of attraction that I felt—and I was beginning to wonder if it was as one-sided as I'd been thinking—but it was definitely easier.

She dressed my wound every day, and I looked forward to those brief chats. On the seventh day, she removed the stitches.

"That looks healthy," she said. "It's healed well."

"I have a great doctor."

Her hands stilled on my skin. My casual words had meant something to her, but I wasn't sure why.

"Just a nurse," she said at last.

"You never thought about training to be a doctor?"

"No. Not me."

She cleared her throat and her hands left my body.

"Did you ever think about doing something other than joining the Army?"

"Nah, not bright enough to do anything else."

She paused, surprised.

"You have to be pretty smart to do what you do. Why would you say that?"

I felt an unaccustomed heat in my cheeks.

"Never much good in school," I muttered. "Not very clever."

There was an uncomfortable silence for several seconds.

"I think you're clever."

And then she walked away.

. . .

Ten days had slipped away like sand through my fingers and we were shipping out in the morning.

Clay and Amira would be joining the terror cell, Larson would be their handler, and I was going home. I didn't know about Smith—he didn't say and I didn't ask.

It didn't seem possible that only two weeks had passed since I'd left the UK—it felt a hell of a lot longer. I'd changed. I'd never had a problem saying goodbye, but now it wasn't easy indifference I was feeling.

Two long weeks, but not long enough. What I'd taught them, I hoped it would help, hoped it would protect them, hoped it would keep them safe, but the weight of their probable mistakes was bloody heavy.

Clay had become as close as a brother to me. We'd shared time, shared meals, swapped stories about deployments, talked while we worked; and I'd learned a lot from him, too, about his philosophy of life, his belief that it was his duty to make a difference. He'd also laughed when he said that, because apparently it was prideful to think he was important. He was also very calm about where they were sending him and what he was about to do. You could even say that he'd made his peace with whatever would happen.

He admired Amira, I could see that, as well. He promised that he'd look after her, as much as he could, but we both knew that the cell leaders were likely to keep them apart. It could be months before they were trusted. Somehow, they had to prove themselves invaluable and trustworthy in a much shorter timeframe if they were going to get the intel that was needed.

After eating the last of our MRE packs, eking out the final hours of his freedom, I sat with Clay around the campfire for longer than usual, knowing it was our last night together as a team, as friends maybe. I was disappointed when Amira disappeared to her room as usual, and I followed her with my eyes.

She was a mystery that I still hadn't solved.

"She's a hell of a woman," said Clay, watching her leave.

"Yep."

"You care, brother," said Clay.

My gaze snapped to his.

"I don't know anything about her."

He gave me a knowing smile.

"And yet, you care."

"And you're saying you don't?"

He looked down.

"I wouldn't stand in your way. You know, if you and her..."

"You're talking bollocks, Clay. There's nothing between us."

He looked thoughtful, but I shrugged because there was nothing I could say. I knew that I'd never see her again, but I had to admit the thought stung. It shouldn't have, but it did.

Clay promised to stay in touch after—and neither of us voiced the reasons why that might not happen—saying casually that Smith knew how to find me. It wasn't safe to swap email addresses or any other details, even our surnames, so Smith was the go-between who knew everything.

I wondered what he knew about Amira, what secrets he was keeping.

As the fire died slowly, the flames shrinking to glowing embers, we talked late into the night.

"Lollipop?" Clay offered, holding out a brightly coloured sugary thing on a stick.

"Nah, you're alright, mate. I want to keep a full set of teeth. The amount of sugar you eat is unreal."

"Every man's gotta have a hobby. Besides, I'm stocking up. 'Cause I tell you, brother, going without my sugar rush is going to be the hardest part of this op."

I laughed.

"Yeah, definitely the hardest part, you nutter!"

We both knew that he was full of shit, but we laughed and pretended to agree it was true. Tomorrow, he'd focus on the job and try to believe he'd get home again one day.

When the night was half gone and getting a few hours sleep seemed like a good idea, we shook hands. Then Clay hugged the hell out of me. For a second, I was surprised, but managed an awkward pat on his back.

"Look after yourself, James."

"Yeah. You too, Clay."

He grinned at me in the darkness.

"You're not bad for a Brit. Shoulder to shoulder, brother."

I laughed as we bumped fists.

Weariness that was part mental, part physical pulled at me as I plodded toward the cabin. Clay was still chuckling to himself while he walked away and I turned to look, but he'd already vanished into the night.

My bedroom was hot and stuffy as usual, and as we were shipping out at dawn, I decided to shower now.

I stripped off my uniform and picked up the threadbare towel and my sleep shorts to shuffle to the bathroom. The tepid water of the shower was cooling and I stood with my eyes closed under the weak jets of water.

Yawning, ready for sleep, I pulled on my shorts over my still damp body and opened the door.

And stepped back in surprise when I saw Amira standing in front of me.

She was wearing a thin t-shirt that reached mid-thigh, just like the first morning I'd seen her, and just like that day, my eyes followed the length of her legs and the swell of her tits.

"I can't sleep," she said, her voice trembling, her eyes brimming with unshed tears. "I'm scared."

As soon as she said the words, her shoulders began to shake and tremors ran through her. She held herself rigid as she tried to stop herself from crying, and her hands were knotted into tight fists while her teeth chattered. She seemed so defenceless without her veil, so vulnerable. Her eyes squeezed shut and her panting breaths came more rapidly. I recognized the onset of a panic attack half a second before she collapsed against my chest, her knees buckling. My clothes and towel dropped to the floor as I caught her, my arms automatically surrounding her, supporting her.

I lowered her down, tucking her against me as the panic held her hostage. Her long hair swept over my skin, her chest heaving as she tried to catch her breath.

I held her, trying to protect her from nameless fears. Every soldier has them—it's the mental battle we all fight alone. This was all I could do to help her, so I held her, reassuring her with my arms.

It took a long time before her shaking subsided, but she'd kept her tears tightly under control.

As her body loosened, I tucked her head under my chin, wishing that I could help her: do more, be more.

I knew what she had to face and I knew she wasn't ready.

"Shh," I said, rocking her gently. "It's okay to be scared."

Slowly, her hands crept around my neck, brushing over my bare shoulders, her touch warm and soft.

She took a shuddering breath.

"I'm s-s-s-sorry."

"Nothing to be sorry for. It's okay."

Her lips were so close to my skin and I could feel the soft puffs of breath as she spoke.

"I don't want to be alone, James. Can I stay with you? I mean, just stay?"

I knew what it was like to crave human touch, that connection with another person. The last night before deployment left you open and exposed, a weakness that disappeared at dawn because it had to.

I kissed her hair lightly.

"Course you can."

Her head hung down as she slowly released me and climbed unsteadily to her feet. Then I took her hand in mine, leading her to my bedroom.

"Which side do you want?" I joked, as we stared down at the narrow single cot.

She shrugged and rubbed her eyes.

"I don't care."

"Okay, well, you take the wall side, then if I roll over, I'll just fall out instead of flattening you."

Her laugh was shaky, but she nodded and clambered wearily under the thin sheet.

I squeezed in behind her, lying on my side, wondering what to do with my arm. In the end, I draped it over her waist.

She hesitated for a moment then snuggled against me.

It felt new and familiar at the same time. I wanted to find the words that would reassure her, but my body had woken up to the fact that a beautiful woman was pushing her backside into my crotch.

I inched away from her. My brain knew that she needed comfort not sex, but my dick hadn't got the message. Typical.

She grumbled softly, then wriggled around until she was facing me, our knees knocking against each other. With my curtains open, I could see the outline of her body as the moonlight washed over us, giving me glimpses of smooth skin, dark hair and darker eyes.

"Don't tell Smith," she said.

"Tell him what? That you're nervous? Amira, you wouldn't be human if you weren't feeling pretty freaked about now."

She chewed on her lip.

"Then how come Clay isn't in here, begging you not to leave him alone?"

"Because he's too damn big for this bed," I grouched.

She snorted and pushed a finger into my chest, then sighed.

"But it's true. He's not freaking out."

I stared into liquid brown eyes that I'd been dreaming about since I met her.

"He'll be having a few quiet moments of his own—we all do before an op. And you're forgetting that he was a soldier for years before he signed up for this. Smith told me you're an ER nurse. That's a pretty full-on profession, but it doesn't prepare you for going undercover. I'm not sure anything can."

She leaned her head on my arm and I couldn't see her clearly, but I knew that she was staring up at me.

"I'm so scared, James. I keep thinking about what's going to happen, thinking that I'm going to die, and it's like looking into the future and seeing nothing—not day or night, just nothing; an endless nothing, and it's terrifying."

I squeezed my eyes tightly shut, because I knew, I knew *exactly* what she meant. And I was afraid she was right.

But I couldn't tell her that.

"Amira, you're a strong woman and..."

"No, I'm not strong," she interrupted forcefully. "I've tried so hard to be strong, but I'm weak. I should be on my knees praying to God to give me strength, but instead I'm in a stranger's bed clinging to some stupid hope that if no one can see me in the dark, then I'm invisible and I'm safe." She took a shuddering breath. "Or maybe I don't exist, because if I don't exist then dying won't hurt, will it?"

My personal belief was that dying could hurt like hell, but living was more painful. Being dead was simply the end: no more pain, no more disappointments, no more fighting.

"Do you think about dying?" she whispered. "When you're working to neutralize a bomb. Do you think what will happen if you get it wrong?"

I shook my head.

"There's too much else to think about. It's a technical challenge—part chess game, part mechanical. In the early days, I'd be trying to remember what the instructor had said, but also trying not to panic, trying not to let my brain go into freefall. What do I do? Pull the wire? Shoot the batteries? Blow it up? And in a hostile environment where there are insurgents hoping that you'll fail, there are also a dozen of your own men counting on you. So I have to focus—nothing else matters. And I rely on the men guarding me to take care of any unfriendlies who might be about—I can't think about them."

She shook her head, and silky hair swept across my skin.

"You're so brave."

"Don't mistake bravery for training. I do what I'm trained to do." *And I relive it over and over again in my nightmares.* "You, Amira, you're brave."

She gave a hollow laugh.

"Yeah? That's why I've spent the last few hours shaking so badly that I couldn't pick up a glass of water? I kept going over the worst case scenarios, over and over; and when I couldn't stop the images, I tried to go through your training, but I couldn't remember anything. Not a single thing. I started to panic, and it was like nothing I'd felt before, I couldn't control it. When I heard you come in," her voice shook, "my legs were trembling so badly I could hardly stand, but I *had* to see another human being before I went crazy."

Her head shifted slightly and I saw the glint of her eyes as she stared up at me.

I was so tempted to lean down and kiss her, tasting her lips, but I didn't—because I didn't want to be one of those men who takes advantage of a woman when she was vulnerable. But she wasn't making it easy.

Instead, I turned my head to stare at the ceiling.

"Every soldier feels that—the fear of the unknown—but our training teaches us to control it or to use it be a better soldier."

"What do you mean?"

I tried to explain.

"In any regiment, there'll be one or two headcases. They'll take stupid risks because they think they're in a game of *Call of Duty* or something. They're the ones who'll charge the enemy uphill with only one clip of ammo. And when it works, they're heroes."

"And when it doesn't?"

"They're the poor sods who got killed because they didn't follow their training or listen to orders. Or the arsehole who got his buddies shot, too."

"So it's just the outcome that makes them a hero or a fool?"

"Pretty much."

She hesitated.

"Which one am I?"

"I think you're incredible," I said honestly. "I've never met anyone like you."

My arms tightened around her compulsively, and when she slid her legs down the bed and over mine, it felt as though we'd been doing this the whole of our adult lives.

Restraint snapped and I kissed her hard, the shock of her lips on mine sending sparks shooting up my spine.

When she moaned and clawed at my shoulders, my dick went from hard to rigid and pulsing with need. It became a raging necessity that this didn't stop.

"Oh God, I shouldn't but I need this!" she cried out in the darkness.

I kissed the smooth, soft skin of her neck, her chin, her cheeks until she sat up and pulled off her t-shirt. Immediately, I was touching and tasting her full, heavy breasts, feeling their weight in my groping hands as her knees clamped on either side of my hips.

I pressed one hand between us until I reached the apex of her legs, surprised and excited to find that she wasn't wearing underwear; she wasn't waxed either, and my pulse accelerated. Instead, I felt wiry hair coated with moisture and my fingers sank in easily, in and out, then circling her clit. Her back arched as she sat upright.

"Yesss," she hissed, "like that, don't stop!"

She sighed and writhed, moaned and scratched her short nails down my chest aggressively, her fingers tangling in my dog tags. When she gripped my leaking cock, I nearly levitated off the bed. She was trying to angle my dick towards her, ready to sink onto me.

"Can't!" I said with gritted teeth. "No condoms!"

"Don't care," she breathed against my chest. "If this is my last night on earth, I don't care."

It went against everything inside me: as a kid who'd been abandoned by his parents, and as a man who took his responsibilities seriously. But she was asking me, saying it could be her last night, and I wanted her badly. Right now, this second, this moment, I needed her as much as she needed me.

And my brain disconnected as I pushed inside her eagerly, thrusting against her bucking body, grunting as her nails scored tracks across my shoulders, then flipping us over and grinding her into the bed with my weight.

Her feet hooked behind my arse, urging me on as she muttered words that melted my thoughts: *harder, faster, more.*

Electric sparks sizzled across my skin and the base of my spine while my hips pumped furiously. My balls tightened and with a curse, I pulled out of her, cumming over her stomach as orgasms ripped through us both.

Her body shuddered with pleasure as I panted above her, my arms trembling and sweat dripping from my face.

Unexpected emotion was close to overwhelming, but her next words made me laugh.

"A tactical withdrawal?" she asked breathlessly.

"Something like that," I grunted, falling onto my side and feeling her nestle against me.

We were silent for several seconds.

"That was intense," she said softly.

My eyes were already closing as I smiled to myself. But then she pressed her lips against the heart that beat steadily inside my chest.

"I shouldn't have done that."

My eyes snapped open as awareness of the time and place flooded back.

"Don't, Amira. Don't beat yourself up."

"I really shouldn't have done that. I'm ashamed ... but I don't regret it either. How can I feel both those things together?"

I had no clue.

"I should have spent the night on my knees, praying, preparing myself."

I was wide awake now.

"You don't have to do this, Amira. You don't have to go tomorrow."

"I do! Smith said..."

"He's not the one putting his life on the line."

She laid her finger across my lips, silencing me.

"I've made my choice, James. If I was stronger, I wouldn't be so scared, but it doesn't mean I've changed my mind."

The resignation in her voice was painful to hear.

"I don't understand. Nursing is a profession where you save lives— it's important, it matters, and you can help so many people that way. I don't get why you're doing *this*."

"I don't expect you to understand," she said stiffly.

"Great, because I don't!"

"We fuck once and then you think you can say what you like? Because you're kind of being an asshole right now."

I took a breath, trying to peg back my frustration.

"I didn't think good Muslim girls were allowed to say that, or got into bed with strange men they don't know."

She sighed and shook her head.

"I'm a work in progress—always have been," she added more quietly. "Is that what you think?"

"I'm sorry. I was just teasing. I was trying to make this..."

"Easier?"

"Yeah, something like that."

"You're right," she said softly. "I shouldn't be here—sex outside marriage is definitely *haram*. But you're wrong, as well: you're not a stranger and I do know you. I may not know your last name, but I know what's inside here," and she laid her warm palm over my heart. "And it's good, James. You're good, a good man."

I tugged her hand into mine and kissed it lightly.

"Say the word, and I'll get you out of here. Now. Tonight. Just say it, Amira, and we can leave together. We can go far, far away from here —forget this place ever existed."

I felt her warm breath fanning over my chest.

"That's a tempting offer, but I can't. And neither can you. No one made me sign up for this..."

"They didn't?"

"No."

"Because I'd wondered about that."

She moved restlessly in the bed.

"You thought someone was forcing me to do this?"

"It was one of the possibilities."

"No. No one's forcing me."

"Okay. Then ... will you tell me why? Here, in the dark, with no one else to see or hear. Can you tell me the truth?"

"Here, in the dark?"

"Yeah, because someone once told me that it's easier to tell the truth in the dark."

She laughed quietly, the gentle movement rocking the old bed so it squeaked sympathetically.

"I'm doing this for Karam. And that's the truth."

A flare of jealousy burned through me. *Boyfriend? Husband?*

She continued quietly, her words anonymous in the dark.

"He was my little brother."

Was.

"He was killed in Syria. He should never have been there. He was such a fun person, you know? He loved to surf and hang out with all his beach buddies. Even when he'd gotten into medical school, he was always at the beach, always catching one more wave. And then one morning he woke up and said he was going to Syria to put his medical training to use. He wasn't even a doctor—he'd done one year of med school! We all tried to talk him out of it, but he was so ... so certain. He said he was needed, that he could do good. He promised he'd be there for one summer and come home to finish med school."

Her voice trailed off.

"But he never came home," I added, and it wasn't a question.

It was a long while before she replied.

"He came home in a coffin," she said bitterly. "My parents were devastated—their only son."

I was putting the pieces of the jigsaw together.

"He was killed by Daesh?"

"Daesh?" She gave a long, low laugh that chilled me. "Did you know that ISIS have threatened to cut out the tongues of anyone who calls them 'Daesh'? It's an acronym for the Arabic phrase al-Dawla al-Islamiya al-Iraq al-Sham, which means the Islamic State of Iraq and the Levant, but it's very similar to the word 'daes' which means 'one who crushes, or tramples something underfoot'. No, ISIS didn't kill my brother—it was American drones that bombed the hospital where he was working."

I froze. I literally froze. My blood ran cold at her words and my skin crawled as she cuddled against me.

I'd just spent the last two weeks training her to make bombs, passing on my knowledge and skills, when her little brother had been killed in a U.S. air strike.

Was I sleeping with the enemy? I was wrong, I must be wrong.

"I hate them," she said, her voice shaking with fury and loathing. "I really hate them."

CHAPTER FOURTEEN

AMIRA

Sunlight on my eyelids woke me, but when I sat up, I was alone in James' bed.

Every memory from the night before rushed back, and my cheeks heated with shame at the thought of how whorishly I'd behaved, what I'd said, what I'd done, how I'd begged him.

I'd been trying so desperately to be good, to be worthy, trying so very hard. But my fears had overwhelmed me and the need to feel something other than crushing terror had led me to his bed. It was so many types of wrong, even though he'd been amazing. A different heat flooded through me, and I felt the stretch and pull where he'd taken my body, where'd he'd filled me with his own.

But as my gaze drifted lazily around his room, I realized that it wasn't just the bed that was empty, every part of James was gone—his clothes, his backpack, the book he'd been reading, everything.

I sat up and squinted at the light filtering through the dirty windowpane. The sun was climbing in the sky and we were long past dawn.

In a panic, I shot out of bed and found my t-shirt, neatly folded on a chair. I yanked it over my head and scurried back to my room, falling to my knees as the bedroom door slammed behind me.

Karam, forgive me! I'm trying so hard to be strong—it was one moment of weakness. I'll do better, I promise. But please, something, a sign—am I doing the right thing?

When the silence became too painful, I climbed to my feet and wiped a solitary tear from my eyes, disgusted at my weakness, loathing my pathetic neediness.

I didn't have time to be weak. I had to be a warrior.

I dressed quickly, but this time I exchanged my *niqab* for a *burqa*—even more concealing. My vision was immediately limited as I viewed the world through a one-piece veil that covered my face and body, leaving just a mesh screen to see through. It felt like putting on armour. I felt like I could face everyone—even James.

I packed my small bag and left the stuffy room that had been my home for the last two weeks and headed outside.

The *burqa* took some getting used to. My peripheral vision was nonexistent and even staring straight forward, what I could see was limited, hazy and indistinct.

Clay and Larson were staring at me, but I felt protected, invisible even as their eyes followed me.

I nodded at them both, and Clay gave a gentle smile, taking my bag from me and stowing it in the bed of the truck.

I couldn't see Smith or James and glanced around.

"They've gone," said Clay, his voice oddly flat as he spoke. "They said ... to say good luck."

Disappointment that felt like pain filled me. *He didn't even say goodbye.* After the secrets we'd shared, the hungriness of his kisses, after the way we'd shared our bodies, not even a word. But maybe it was better like this—I didn't need the distraction. And I certainly regretted my ridiculous attraction to James. But still, saying goodbye wouldn't have killed him, would it?

Larson didn't say a word, his cold eyes watching me closely. I wished it was Smith who'd be my handler—I felt a lot more comfortable with him. But I didn't have a choice, and Larson was the man I'd have to rely on. I was so glad that Clay was going to be there. Even if I wouldn't be allowed to talk to him, just knowing he was near would be enough.

I sat in the back of the truck, my mind whirring dully, watching the road stretch endlessly, wondering where it would take me. And wondering if I'd ever return.

I should banish all my memories of James, the memories of his hands on me; forget how it felt when he pushed inside me; ignore the moment of connection that had sparked between us. I shouldn't have used him like that. When he'd offered to take me away, even if it meant going AWOL, he would have done it. I could hear it in his voice—he'd have given up everything for me. I had a guilty conscience about James. I must have hurt him—the fact that he hadn't even stayed to say goodbye showed that. But since I'd never see him again, I had to forget it all. As if last night had never happened.

In some ways, I felt as though I'd already passed on from this life. Whatever happened next, it would be like nothing that had gone before in the first 29 years of my life.

I felt unconnected, adrift, alone.

We drove for four hours straight and by then my bladder was bursting for relief. Larson wouldn't let me leave the truck at any of the rest stops we passed even when he filled up with gas, saying that my 'bedsheet' would cause too much comment. I knew he was right, but I still thought he was a sadistic bastard, Allah forgive me.

I couldn't even perform *salah* properly, but I knew that Clay was praying at the same time when I saw him bow his head and mouth the words of prayer.

Finally, Larson stopped at a more secluded, heavily wooded part of the road, and we were allowed to leave the truck. I walked as far into the forest as I dared, then squatted over a dry patch of dirt to relieve myself.

When I returned, Larson tossed a boxed salad at me that he'd bought earlier. I lifted my veil and ate as discreetly as I could, ignoring the glances that Larson threw me in the rearview mirror.

I had too much time to think, but every moment my thoughts drifted to what I was about to do, panic threatened to take over, and that was going to get me killed.

I took a savage bite of my salad, yelping as I chomped down on my own tongue. Tears pricked my eyes, but I wouldn't give in. I'd never give in. Not while there was breath in my body.

Although maybe that wouldn't be for much longer.

From the position of the sun, I could tell that we were travelling north, but I still wasn't sure where we were, the names of the small towns and villages meaning nothing to me, and Larson had chosen to avoid any of the main roads.

I don't know how he found his way along all the small, dusty tracks without GPS, but he drove unerringly, so either he had an amazing memory or he'd been here before. Maybe both.

His phone rang once on the journey, and he pulled over, parking on a patch of gravel. As he climbed out of the truck without speaking to either of us, he grabbed the keys out of the ignition, then strode away to take the call.

Clay turned and smiled at me.

"He's pretty intense—I think I need to get him a stress ball."

I laughed because he was ridiculous, smiling to myself as Clay winked at me.

"How are you doing?"

"Fine."

"Really?"

"Well, as fine as I can be. You?"

He hesitated.

"Look, if it gets too much, just say the word and I'll get you out of there, okay?"

"Clay..."

"Promise me."

His dark eyes burned with intensity.

"Okay," I said softly. "I'll tell you."

Something like relief passed over his face and he nodded.

But when Larson returned to the truck, he was frowning. Whatever had been said, it didn't make him happy. Although I'd never seen him smile. Ever.

"Change of plan," he growled at us. "You two are going in as a married couple."

Clay looked worried.

"Why?"

"Change of plan," Larson repeated, his face becoming expressionless.

"But we hardly know each other. It's going to look weird if we…"

"An arranged marriage—Amira, your parents found Clay on the internet."

"Damn, man!" said Clay. "This isn't what we planned! We don't even have wedding rings."

"We don't necessarily need them," I said quietly. "Although it might look a bit weird that you didn't even get me an engagement ring," I said, trying to smile. "They'll probably just think you're cheap."

Clay gave me the ghost of a smile.

"Better learn fast," scowled Larson, always short of patience. "Get in the back with her and get to know her."

Raising his eyebrows, Clay slid onto the back seat next to me.

"What else don't I know?" he asked, his smile strained.

"Wedding rings signify a sort of ownership over the other person. But in Islamic belief, there is no ownership of your partner. That's why Muslim women don't necessarily change their last name to their husband's."

Clay sighed.

"We'd better get sharing if we're going to pull this off. Where did we meet? Where did we marry? What internet site did we meet on? Had I already converted? Wait, I must have if your parents found me. Who's my family? Who's your family? There's a lot of ground to cover, Amira."

The change of plan threw me. I had to start thinking of Clay as my husband. I guess that meant we'd have to sleep together. I liked Clay, he was kind, so maybe it wouldn't be too weird…

I swallowed my fear and nodded.

Clay gave me an encouraging smile, but I could see the strain behind his eyes.

CHAPTER FIFTEEN

JAMES

I lashed out with both feet at the car door, kicking as hard as I could.

"Jeez, calm down, James!"

I recognized Smith's voice at once and paused.

"I've got the child locks engaged—you won't get out that way. But if you keep pissing me off, I'll have to put you out again."

Vague memories coated in candy floss floated around my mind. I'd told him something important—what was it?

Gradually, the fuzziness cleared and everything came flooding back. I remembered: the argument, his insistence that Amira could be trusted, and Larson putting me in a choke hold until I'd passed out.

My throat was still raw.

Bastard!

I kicked the driver's seat for good measure.

Smith swerved slightly and I heard another car honking at him. I would have smiled, but the gag in my mouth stopped me from doing anything.

"Christ! You'll get us both killed if you carry on like that. I don't want to hurt you, James. I like you. Just hold it together for a few more hours and I'll take off the handcuffs and gag. Scouts honour."

I muttered something that was unintelligible through the gag, promising myself that I'd show Smith how seriously pissed off I was, as soon as I had the chance.

But for now, I had no choice but to lie back and think of England.

The turn of events had blindsided me.

After Amira's admission in the night, I knew that I needed to tell Smith everything I'd learned. I'd waited until she was asleep, then slipped out of bed and gone to find the CIA handler. He'd listened to me calmly, then told me that he already knew about how her brother had died.

I'd stared at him in amazement.

"Then you must know that the mission is already compromised! You can't send Clay in there with her. What the hell is going on?"

"Clay already has as much data as he needs."

"Then I'll tell him!"

And that's when Larson got me in a choke hold that rendered me unconscious in seconds.

Sick and woozy, I'd woken up in the back of a car, bound, gagged and blindfolded. Metal restraints were fastened around both wrists, securing my hands behind me, and sending sparks of pain shooting into my shoulders every time the car turned a corner. My mouth was dry and I could taste blood. I struggled to sit up, banging my head against the car window in the process.

"Good choice," said Smith dryly.

I tried to spit out a few mumbled swear words, but he just ignored me.

He didn't speak again, but drove for at least two hours, and I didn't know how long I'd been unconscious before that.

Finally, Smith slowed the truck, the wheels thumping over the kerb, and he cut the engine.

I listened hard. I could hear traffic and police sirens, so I must be in an urban area.

Smith opened the door and I tensed, waiting for my chance to escape, but I could hear more than one voice, maybe three people. I doubt I could have fought anyone in my current state, certainly not two people, so I didn't struggle as they hauled me out of the car.

"This him?"

"Yeah, Staff Sergeant James Spears, British Army, EOD high threat operator."

"How long?"

"As long as it takes.

Hands gripped my shoulders and then I heard the car engine start. I could smell the fuel, and the sound told me that I was in a garage, so no one would be able to see me if I struggled. Then I heard the sound of an electric motor and the garage door clanged shut.

Someone released the restraints around my ankles and I was pushed forwards, stumbling slightly, then told to take two steps up. The air was cooler here, so it was probably a building with air conditioning. I was led upstairs.

"Sit," said the voice.

Shuffling forward, I lowered myself awkwardly, finding a soft mattress underneath me.

The blindfold and gag were removed and I blinked madly, my eyes watering in the bright electric light. When I was able to focus again, I squinted up at a hard-looking man who was wearing a gun on his hip.

"Where am I?"

"A safe-house."

What?

"Why am I here?" I asked, my voice scratchy and hoarse.

"You're staying here until Smith says otherwise. There's a bathroom over there," and he nodded to a door on my right. "Clean clothes, shaving gear. I'll send some food in."

A second man entered the room and uncuffed my hands.

"Don't make trouble," he said, "and in a few weeks, you'll walk out of here."

Then they locked the door behind them.

A few weeks!

I yanked back the curtains, but thick bars lined the windows and there was no other way out.

What the hell was going on?

CHAPTER SIXTEEN

AMIRA

I thought they were going to kill us.

We were more than a mile from the terrorists' camp when our car was flagged down by a man with an automatic machine gun.

"Showtime," Clay whispered. "Stay calm. Follow my lead."

I nodded, my heart thundering in my ears, fear clamping a hand around my throat and squeezing shut any words I might have said.

"Get out of the car and toss your keys on the ground. Hands on your head."

The man gestured with his gun.

"We've come to join you in the fight against the Infidel," said Clay, his voice clear and strong as we both stood clear of the car. "We wish to join the Jihad."

The man didn't reply but crept closer, keeping his gun trained on Clay. Then he stopped and looked directly at me.

"Show me your shoes."

With trembling hands, I lifted my *burqa* a few inches, revealing my red and white Chucks.

The man nodded and I dropped the material.

I realized that he'd been checking that I really was female. A *burqa* hid many secrets.

He walked closer, then thrust the barrel of his gun into Clay's stomach, winding him.

Clay dropped to the ground, wheezing and holding his belly. I was frozen to the spot, utterly unable to move, my whole body shaking.

The man spoke into a mouthpiece, staring at me coldly the whole time while Clay lay on the ground, and a minute later a Jeep came bouncing over the dirt track with two more armed men.

They blindfolded us and bound our hands, hauling us into the Jeep, then pushing us out roughly a few minutes later.

I landed on my knees, immediately falling face down. I lay in the dirt, breathing in the clean smell of soil through my *burqa*, panic gripping me, and I wondered if after all this, I'd be dead within the first minute.

But the seconds ticked by and I heard murmured voices discussing us, so I struggled to sit up.

"Well, this is interesting," said a cultured voice with a British accent. "I'm told you wish to join the Jihad."

"Yes," said Clay, keeping his voice subservient.

I was ridiculously relieved to hear him speak.

"American?"

"Yes, sir. My wife and I are both American, but her family is from Syria."

There was a short pause, then the man spoke again.

"I'm more concerned in hearing how you found us."

Clay gave the speech that he'd been rehearsing.

"I served in the U.S. Army until ten months ago," he lied. "I was given a dishonourable discharge for refusing to fight against my brothers in Syria." His voice became bitter. "I served 18 months in a military prison, then they kicked me out after 11 years without a pension." His voice became impassioned. "They're killing children over there. They killed my wife's brother."

Another pause and then the man's voice was closer to me.

"Was your brother Jihadi?"

He was so close to me I could smell the spice on his breath from his last meal. I shook with fear that was definitely not faked.

"No, sir," I whispered. "He was a med student. He volunteered at a hospital in Raqqa. He was killed in a U.S. airstrike."

"Hmm. And what was his name?"

Even though he couldn't see my face, my lips trembled.

"K-K-Karam Kousa."

"And your name?"

"Amira Kousa."

It wasn't my real name. Smith had produced a set of documents for me and a paper trail that would show that Karam Kousa had lived in So Cal since birth and died in Syria.

"And you?"

I heard a thud and a muffled *ouf* from Clay, and guessed that he'd been kicked in the ribs.

"Clay Allen, sir," he gasped. "I've been a convert for three years, sir."

"You still haven't explained how you found us," the man said, his voice dangerously quiet.

"I met a brother who was friends with Ali Muhammad Brown."

I held my breath, knowing that Brown was an extremist convert born in the U.S. and allied with Al-Shabaab, the Jihadist group from East Africa. He'd also murdered four men several years back: three in Seattle and one in New Jersey. His defence had been that the killings were in retaliation for U.S. government involvement in Iraq, Afghanistan and Syria.

There was an even longer pause this time. Then the questions began in earnest: where was I born, where did I go to school, who were my friends, where had I worked, where had I met Clay, how long had we been married, who were his friends, on and on, the same questions over and over as the heat of the day intensified and my brain felt like it was being boiled. I tried to remember every detail that Smith had drilled into me, but sometimes I had to improvise, and that scared me, so I kept as close to the truth as I could.

I told them that I'd been planning to join Karam in Syria but he'd died before I could go. I said that it was Clay who'd taught me basic bomb-making, skills that he'd picked up in the military.

Then the questions began for Clay: who were his family, when was he recruited, who was his Iman when he converted, where had he served, who did he know, where had he met Brown's friend, repeating the questions, trying to trip him up, trying to find inconsistencies in his story, but Clay remained controlled, calm, thoughtful, just as always.

Finally, the questions ended.

"Take them to the hut and secure them. Then we'll see if their stories check out. If not, cut their lying tongues from their throats."

The man's voice was conversational in tone, and that scared me more than if he'd been ranting.

I was hauled upright, my arms twisting painfully, as I half walked, half stumbled, gripped on both sides.

Eventually, we were dumped on the floor, presumably in the hut that had been mentioned, and left there.

I heard shuffling and then felt Clay's body pressing against mine.

"How you doing over there?" he asked quietly.

My mouth was so dry, it took me several attempts to reply.

"Scared."

"You're doing great, *ya amar*."

A surprised cough that could have been a laugh escaped.

"*Ya amar?* You're calling me 'my moon'?"

He laughed softly.

"Works for me."

Clay was doing what he always did—making the horror a little easier.

"What's going to happen to us?" I whispered.

"They'll find that our stories check out, then decide if they'll put us to work or..."

"Get rid of us?"

He hesitated before he answered.

"No, they won't want to do that."

I wasn't so sure, but I prayed that Clay was right.

Karam, I need you more than ever.

But after another few hours of intolerable heat, fear was eclipsed by thirst.

My lips were cracked and my mouth and throat were as dry as dust.

For hours, we'd been left alone, our hands and feet bound. We could hear the sounds of the camp around us, a car engine starting up, people talking with a variety of accents, although I couldn't hear what they were saying.

The air in the hut was stifling and the confining *burqa* made it hard to breathe.

I concentrated on relaxing my muscles one at a time, as much as I could—trying to ignore the baking heat and the lack of water.

Finally, the door opened and the intense heat lessened slightly as cooler air spilled inside.

My blindfold was ripped off by a hard-eyed man with a long scar down one cheek, and my hands released. A bottle of water was dumped by my feet. I worked my stiff fingers, wincing as the blood flow was restored, then awkwardly lifted the bottle under my veil to take long sips of tepid, plastic-tasting water.

Clay was untied, too, but the gunmen clearly regarded him as a much greater threat than me, watching him closely.

"Umar wants to see you," said the scar-faced man, brandishing his gun.

We were led blinking into the sunshine and then told to kneel in the dirt.

And that's when I saw Umar for the first time.

He was tall and slim with a handsome face, dark hair and a tidy black beard. He smiled, revealing even, white teeth.

"Welcome, brother and sister," he said.

It was with a shock of recognition that I listened to his cultured British voice. This was the man who'd threatened to cut out our tongues.

I trembled, shaking like a leaf in the wind as he continued to smile at me and made us welcome.

We were given more water and plates of reheated food, then provided with a set of blankets in the room that had been our prison.

"It's the best accommodation we can offer to a married couple," Umar said regretfully.

Clay thanked him and we carried our blankets to the shed to make ourselves as comfortable as possible.

We were several hours further north here, and the temperature as the sun set was cooler. I eyed the blankets, wondering who'd used them before us and how clean they were.

Clay seemed unconcerned, but I shuddered, remembering what James had said about lice. Ugh, please no! I grimaced as Clay laid the two blankets on the dirt floor, kicked off his sandals and stretched out on the makeshift bed.

"Come and get comfortable, wife," he grinned up at me.

Muttering under my breath, I pulled off my *burqa* and folded it neatly, then laid my Chucks, socks and jeans on top of it.

I felt very exposed, very aware of how I must appear to Clay—it was stupid to be so awkward, but I couldn't help it. Clay was a genuinely nice guy. He was handsome, strong and kind, clever, too. I was so glad that we were in this together, and my heart rested a little easier.

Stupid heart. Didn't know what was good for it. I'd always scoffed at the idea of an arranged marriage, but if you trusted your parents, maybe there was something to be said for it, because I'd made one lousy choice after another.

The last guy I slept with didn't even wait to say goodbye.

Asshole.

The hut was still stuffy and airless, and my hair was a sweaty, matted mess, but there was nothing I could do about it, so I just left it loose and laid down on the blankets next to Clay.

"This feels weird," I whispered.

"Aw, now don't go saying that, *ya amar*. I was enjoying myself."

I poked him in the arm and he pretended to yelp.

"No need to get violent on my ass!"

"I have no intention of going anywhere near your ass or anything else," I hissed at him.

He chuckled in the gathering darkness, as shadows grew from the walls.

"Don't worry, James would kick my ass just for looking at you. I hope to hell he never finds out that I slept with you."

I froze, my fingers clinging to the rough blanket as if it was a life-raft in a turbulent sea.

Clay rolled onto his side.

"Too soon?" he asked gravely.

I swallowed and forced myself to release the blanket.

"You know?"

He grimaced.

"It was kind of obvious when..."

He stopped suddenly but I could guess where that sentence was going.

"I got scared," I shrugged. "It wasn't my finest hour."

"So ... you and James aren't...?"

"Definitely not."

Clay didn't speak again, but squeezed my fingers then let go.

He fell asleep almost immediately, but I lay awake, listening for footsteps in the dark and ruthlessly exorcising any memories of a man with ice-blue eyes.

CHAPTER SEVENTEEN

JAMES

Time dragged and I was bored out of my brain.

I went over and over that final conversation with Amira, back and forth—one moment convincing myself that I'd misunderstood her, then wondering why the hell Smith had brought me here. If she wasn't a threat, why keep me here? If I was a threat, why keep me alive? None of it made sense.

I wished I could speak to her. Hell, I wished I could see her. But now she was deep undercover, that wasn't happening. I drove myself crazy thinking about her, wishing we'd had more time.

Instead, I tortured myself by going over every conversation we'd ever had, and that one surreal night that we'd spent together.

Shit, if they ever let me out of here, I'd turn into her stalker.

They fed me three times a day on a diet of take-out food, and the brands of restaurant chains that they used confirmed my suspicion that I was still somewhere in the U.S. and probably near a city.

They said it was a safe-house, and as they hadn't killed me, it probably meant that they were government spooks like Smith: CIA or FBI or NSA. Probably. They tossed a few books into my room, but never answered any of my questions.

I marked the plasterboard with a fingernail so I could count the passing days.

And I set about trying to escape.

It became clear within the first thirty seconds that my room was a cell. The bars on the windows were cemented into brick walls, and I couldn't shatter the glass by hitting it with anything I found in the room. The floorboards were all nailed down solidly, and I bloodied a few fingers before I gave up on that.

The plasterboard walls came apart easily, but behind them was solid brick.

So I started studying the teams guarding me. They were professional. Always working in pairs, never giving me a chance to jump them and grab a weapon. I was tempted though, and devised intricate plans in my head, maybe faking an illness or an injury, but I didn't think they'd fall for it.

I tried to get them to talk to me but that didn't work either, so I tried to piss them off as much as possible, just being an awkward bastard to see if I could get a reaction.

I complained about the food all the time, about the coffee they gave me, about the water having a weird taste. I tore the sheets off the bed and told them they had bed bugs, but they just left them on the floor. I threw food at the walls, but that just meant I didn't have anything to eat. I tried not washing, but they didn't care if I stank and the only person who had to put up with it was me.

So far I'd been here three weeks and two days.

I wondered what they were waiting for.

I spent a lot of time thinking about Clay, wondering where he was, where Amira was and what was happening, torturing myself with ideas that they were already dead. But then I persuaded myself if that was the case, Smith would let me go—or kill me. Keeping me prisoner didn't add up.

I went over and over the idea that Smith already knew Amira had every reason to hate the U.S. government, and yet they'd blithely brought me in to train her to make bombs. My instinct told me to trust her, but I was a long way from having all the pieces of the puzzle.

We'd been honest with each other, I thought, but if she hated Americans, why had she been recruited? Maybe she just hated the military, but she hadn't been like that with Smith or with Clay. Not even with me that last night. I found myself thinking about her too much, even dreaming about her. She was the only woman that I'd felt a connection with in a long time. And now she was deep undercover, risking her life every day.

Out of sheer boredom and frustration, I spent several hours a day working out as best I could: sit-ups, push-ups, running on the spot, star jumps, anything and everything to keep busy, to keep fit.

I had no idea what was happening in the world outside and lived in a bubble of my captors' creation.

The teams changed shift every eight hours, but I recognized the faces: the short one, Scarface, Mr. Armani, Lady Gaga, Lucifer, Smoky Joe. I didn't know their real names, of course, but that was how I categorized them in my head. *Know your enemy.*

I calculated that there were five teams on shifting rotas. That was a lot of manpower to guard one pissed off AT.

And then, on my twenty-fifth evening in solitary confinement, the protocols changed. It was between shifts and not a mealtime, but I heard voices outside my room.

They'd made sure that there was nothing I could use for a weapon except myself, so I tensed, wondering what was coming next.

But when the door opened, it wasn't any of the teams that I'd grown used to.

It was Smith.

CHAPTER EIGHTEEN

AMIRA

For the first ten days, we were watched, expressionless eyes following our every move. We were given menial chores and only allowed to join the others for prayers or when Umar decided his followers all needed 'some education', as he put it. These were long-winded rants about Western immorality, Infidel governments, and how we were the chosen ones, all part of a great cause, a mighty Jihad, and would be celebrated throughout history.

Other than that, we learned little, but it soon became clear that there was a second camp somewhere nearby in the forest. Sometimes we could hear vehicles in the night, and strange men came and went, most of them were dressed in western clothes, unlike the rest of us.

At times like that, when I felt their cold eyes on me, I felt very grateful for the shapeless *burqa* that concealed me.

My entire existence was a performance, and I found that exhausting. I couldn't understand how people did it for years at a time. *How?* And I also questioned *why?* I was so lost and scared, so sure I'd made a terrible mistake. But I was here and I had to stay.

As I was watched less than Clay, and because I was the only woman, I was allowed a little more freedom to go into the woods as there was no toilet facilities within the compound that I was permitted to use.

This meant that usually it was left to me to check in with Larson, but sometimes Clay was able to slip away, too. He wanted to find out where the second camp was located because it was clear that the bomb-making factory wasn't here, so it must be at the second site. So far, he hadn't been able to find it.

Our camp had eighteen people, although that number fluctuated depending on who was sent to collect supplies. It was usually a guy named Adam from Chicago who was chosen, and he'd change out of his *Didashah* into jeans and a t-shirt, then return with bags of groceries a few hours later.

We never saw Larson, but we saw evidence that he was around, evidence only we knew to look for, and we were able to relay information about the number of people we'd seen, the existence of the second camp, and the fact that every three days, trucks or vans could be heard in the forest at night. Twice, I'd been able to get close enough to see the licence plates. I was going to try again soon.

Larson had set up places in the woods around the camp where we could relay information, expertly hidden in the trees. He'd told us where there were remote mics, pre-planted bugs, (ones that could be switched on and off to defeat bug detectors), ways of capturing all the intel we could collect. I wondered who else was listening.

The terrorists covered their tracks well, and Smith had told us that they'd been discovered in the first place via air search, and planes equipped with infrared and thermal imaging sensors that pinpointed body heat. Whether that was through other intelligence or a lucky strike, neither Smith nor Larson had told us. Not that Larson had been talkative at the best of times, communicating only what he deemed us worthy to know. It was Clay who'd shared his theories with me. Clay trusted me.

We'd become closer since we'd been here, sharing what we'd learned each day. And of course we slept together at night. I felt ridiculously safe in our shed with his warm body close to mine.

During the day, we went about our chores, and at night we spoke in whispers. He told me about his family, not that he was close to them, and I told him about Karam and Zada and my parents.

We also planned our getaway, when the time became apparent, and getting word to Larson. Clay discussed the 'extraction', but that always made me think of dentists. Clay had laughed about that.

I trained myself to remember all the licence plates that I saw—until the day one of the men saw me spying on him.

He pointed his gun at me and I turned and ran, cringing as the sharp *crack* of a bullet rang out in the trees. I ran as fast as I could, the *burqa* hampering my movements. I could hear him shouting, his feet thundering behind me.

If I could just get to the main camp!

It was within sight when he caught me.

He grabbed a fistful of the *burqa* and I was jerked backwards, falling with a shriek.

My veil had been twisted around, so I couldn't see anything either, but I heard voices in the distance and I screamed for Clay and kicked as hard as I could.

A boot thudded into my stomach and all the air whooshed out of my lungs. I scrabbled on the dirt floor, nauseous and gasping for breath

"What's going on, brother?"

It was Umar who'd spoken, but not to me.

"I caught this bitch spying on us! She was watching the trucks—I saw her!"

Someone touched my shoulder and I cringed.

"It's okay, it's okay. Stop fighting, *ya amar*."

Clay's voice was tight with concern as he tried to reassure me.

"Actually," said Umar, "I'd be very interested to hear why your wife wandered so far from camp."

Clay helped me to sit up and I clung to him.

"I ... I just went to the bathroom. And ... I went for a walk. I heard trucks and I wondered what they were. I'm sorry!"

"Hmm," said Umar, stroking his beard thoughtfully, his eyes hiding his true emotions. "Tell your wife that it's not safe for her to go wandering into the woods. Accidents can happen all too easily. She could have been shot today. Next time," and he lowered his voice, "she might not be so lucky."

Clay thanked him and promised to keep better control of me. Then he helped me up and we retreated to our hut.

"Are you okay?" he asked, his voice soft and concerned.

"I think so," I said, trying to stop my voice from shaking.

"What did you see?"

"More trucks," I whispered. "I got the licence plates of two of them, but then that man saw me."

I shuddered, the tremors running through me as adrenaline leaked from my body.

Clay nodded.

"They're moving large quantities of something—my guess is TATP. Sometimes I've smelled chemicals in the air."

I sat up, wiping my eyes.

"Me, too! Only a couple of times and faintly, but I thought it was odd."

"I have to get the intel to Larson tonight. Tell me about the licence plates you saw."

Once he'd memorized the numbers, Clay told me to stay in the hut and not to leave it again today.

Later that night as we lay on our makeshift bed, he held me against the fear and the dark, and feeling that everything was spiralling out of control.

That wasn't the first time that he'd held me in the night, stroking my hair and telling me it would be okay.

I'd drifted asleep when Clay touched my arm.

"I'm going out now. Don't leave the hut, okay?"

I nodded, wishing he wouldn't leave.

"Be safe!"

He gave me a wide grin and slipped out of the hut.

I couldn't sleep after that, jumping at every noise, freezing at every voice, every step as the sentries patrolled.

Clay returned at dawn, saying that he'd managed to get to one of the listening stations, but his face was grim.

"What else?"

"Amira, I don't think you should go into the woods again. Stay near me or in the main camp."

"Why? What's happened?"

I couldn't see his face in the gloom of the hut, but I felt him reach for my hand.

"I heard one of the guards talking. He said that Munassar has been bragging about following you into the woods and ... hurting you."

I stopped breathing.

I'd seen the way some of the men looked at me, studying my body as if the *burqa* didn't hide me. But now, being the only woman in the camp was beginning to be even more dangerous.

"Amira?"

"Yes, okay. I'll be careful," I said, trying to sound tough.

But inside, I was terrified.

So every day, I washed the men's clothes, and at mealtimes, I ate alone in the hut. I was careful when I had to make a bathroom visit, and Clay always came with me. And every night I slept next to Clay. It was strange, but comforting, too.

"He cares about you, you know that, right?"

Clay's voice was thoughtful in the darkness, and I remembered what I'd said so many nights ago to another man, to another voice in the dark, about the truth being easier when the daylight had fled.

"Who?" I asked stiffly.

Clay laughed quietly.

"As if you don't know who I'm talking about!"

I shrugged in the dark.

"It doesn't make any difference now. Besides I told you—it was just convenience, nothing more."

Clay was silent, and James was never mentioned again.

I slipped into a twilight world where I felt expendable by both sides: Umar stared at me but never spoke, and Larson's visits seemed less frequent. Even Clay seemed rattled, and I knew he was wondering how long we'd be here.

Umar still sermonized enthusiastically about Jihad—the great struggle against the oppression of Western governments.

I listened, but I didn't react.

He lectured, and I took it all in.

"What you have to understand," he said, in his hypnotic, educated voice that reminded me of a British royal, "is that the West have no morality, no conscience. The American government is ruled by the Republican Party—the Grand Old Party—but their foreign policy is decided for them by Israel. The Israelites want to attack Iran, but then you had your General Petraeus—the grand old philanderer..." and he laughed at his own joke, "who has stated that the presence of Iran in Iraq is the greater danger. It's a complete mess." His eyes darkened. "And while these so-called world powers squabble amongst themselves, we will rise triumphant."

He talked endlessly as he described the iniquities of the Middle East, the children he'd seen gassed by the Syrian government, bombed by the Russians, killed by the Americans; and his eyes glittered with fury as he detailed the rotting bodies he'd seen in the collapsed hospitals, the devastated communities.

He played on our emotions, and isolated as we were from the rest of the world, from any other perspective, it would have been easy for someone angry and dispossessed to fall under his spell.

Smith had tried to warn me that in the early days the terrorists would show me their most human face. Their sorrow and outrage when I told them about Karam was genuine—and all of them had similar stories to share.

"My father was a detainee in Guantanamo Bay for twelve years," Umar said bitterly. "My childhood ended the day they took him. He'd been a teacher, but they broke his mind with ritual torture and humiliation. He was shackled with heavy irons, blindfolded, made to stand for hours at a time, stripped naked, denied water and deprived of sleep. He was forced to drink seawater until he was sick, then beaten again and again. That," he said, jabbing his finger into the air, "is American justice. Twelve years! Twelve! An innocent man! Broken on the yoke of Western brutality! I say, no more! We will rise up! We will teach them the meaning of fear—and the streets will run with the blood of the Infidel!"

As he spoke, I saw it all in my mind, but I also saw images from CBS and Fox News of the graves in Syria of men, women and children who had been murdered in their thousands by ISIS, the torture, the rape, the beheadings on YouTube.

No one dared question Umar, and we all listened to his lectures as he taught us how to think.

Umar's right hand man was the scary guy that Clay heard wanted to hurt me. Munassar was a Yemeni from Aden, heavily pockmarked and rather short, but he reminded me of Larson with his silence and hard eyes. He was also the only person at the camp, other than me or Umar, who hadn't been born in America.

And when I thought about it later, it was an odd mix of people. Apart from Munassar who unnerved me, they were just people who genuinely believed that the government didn't speak or act for them and therefore they weren't bound by laws of the land.

Adam, the former teacher from the Windy City, explained to me.

"What you have to understand, sister," he said, his brown eyes filled with passion, "is that our mission is the source of pride and dignity for this nation. Now it is time to act, and I'm prepared to die for my country, to make America a better place."

I listened and nodded, but I was itching to ask him why he thought that such sacrifice was a better way than staying and being a teacher and training young minds.

I was stunned to hear that he'd spent the last two years fighting in Syria and now wished to share his 'expertise'.

I didn't dare ask what sort of expertise that might be.

I didn't speak much, but I listened. And that's when I began to see the common thread amongst them: the decision that the only strategic way to make the U.S. government listen, as a way of achieving their political and religious aims, was through terror.

Umar smiled benignly, as if he was sharing a great joke:

"Kill one, terrify ten thousand," he said, laughing loudly. "I didn't even invent that—it's a Chinese saying," and everyone laughed with him.

Clay squatted beside me, perhaps recognizing how disturbed I felt, or maybe just realizing how those words would affect me.

But it was Umar who spoke to me.

"Your husband is very proud of you," he began, nodding at Clay.

I bowed my head and stayed silent, wondering where this was going.

"I knew your brother," Umar said. "In Syria."

My head jerked up as I stared and doubted.

Umar's lips twisted as if he knew what I was thinking.

"He was at the National Hospital, yes?"

I nodded wordlessly.

"Your brother was a great soldier—you should be happy that he is in Paradise now."

I swallowed, afraid to disagree with our great leader.

"My brother wasn't a soldier. He was a volunteer in the hospital. He was at med school, he..."

Umar smiled coldly.

"I'm sure that's what he would tell his *sister*," he said, a slight emphasis on 'sister' that sounded contemptuous. "But I knew his commander. They say he fought with great honour—a true warrior."

Rage roared up inside me. Pure rage that he'd sully my brother's name like this.

"Of course," said Umar. "I didn't know him as Karam Kousa—he was called Karam Soliman then." His smile was glacial, his dark eyes glittering. "But so many people used false names in our great defence of Raqqa."

Panic flashed through me. How did he know Karam's real name? Did he suspect me? Did he suspect Clay? Had Clay told him? And oh, Allah, please no—he must have been lying about my brother! He *must* have.

Umar's eyes grew dull and distant.

"Our days began with air raids piercing the dawn. At first, like a wind, but then comes the crash of bombs dropping. And after, when the world is still, the stench of death hangs in the air and the streets are full of the dead, rotting under rubble in the summer heat." He turned to me.

"Why did you lie about your brother's name?"

Fear trembled in the air and I held my breath, waiting for the words that would end my life.

I waited, spending my last moments on earth praying for a speedy death.

I waited for Umar to condemn me, to tell me to my face that I was a liar, an Infidel, and death would be slow or swift, but soon.

"I'm sorry I lied to you," I stuttered. "I ... I..."

"You should speak your brother's name with pride!" Umar chastised.

Stung, my head snapped up.

"I *am* proud of him!"

Umar smiled and turned away.

"Walk with me, both of you," he said.

We followed him without asking why, my steps stumbling and awkward as Clay reached out his hand for me.

No, we didn't ask where or why, because questioning was not allowed. And I was too shaken by what Umar had said.

Clay squeezed my fingers and he stared at me with a worried frown, but he didn't say anything.

Umar stopped to shout at two of his underlings, striding ahead and leaving us behind.

"Clay!" I hissed. "He *knows!*"

"Hold it together, Amira," he said, his voice firm but gentle.

"But he knows! If he knows Karam's real name, then he knows mine, too. How could he know that? Who could have told him? He can find my family—my parents, my sister! Oh dear Allah, what have I done? What have I done!"

Clay grabbed my shoulders and shook me.

"Stop it! This doesn't mean he's onto you, or onto us. It just means that he knows you gave him a false name. But he also knows that Karam is real, so he knows your story is real. This could be a good thing for us, Amira."

"But he can find my family," I wailed. "They'll never be safe!"

He didn't have a chance to reply because Umar waved us forward.

Clay's face closed down.

"Just hold on, Amira. Hold it together for a little longer. I'll get us out of here, I promise."

I didn't believe him.

All I could do was go on, tortured with images of what a man like Umar could do to my family.

"Clay, my brother, I have a selected you for a special job," Umar said with a smile.

"I'm honoured," said Clay, bowing his head slightly.

"Excellent!"

We followed him silently as he strode into the forest.

I was desperate to ask Clay where he thought we were being taken, but he squeezed my fingers hard and frowned at me.

The narrow track was well trodden, but fringed by large trees, the leaves tinged with copper as the year faded toward Fall.

Finally, the track opened out in another compound, a collection of ramshackle sheds and old cabins.

We'd already learned that the camp was in two sections, but up until now, we'd only been allowed to see one part. Perhaps, today, we'd finally learn more—and actually have something worth reporting back to Larson other than the names of the other people that Umar had recruited—assuming that any of them were using their real names.

In the dead of the night, Clay had whispered encouragement to me. He said we were making progress; he said we had to carry on, that we had no choice.

I wanted to run away, to forget this mad dream to give meaning to Karam's death. But now it seemed like I'd be the one to die—and at a time of Umar's choosing.

I was sinking into Hell, and I didn't know how to climb out.

My mind spun in different directions, so I did what Clay told me, because I was stupid and weak and out of options.

Because I'd come here willingly, and now I'd pay the price.

As we walked into the second camp that afternoon, I noticed several differences between our camp and this one—and between Umar's followers and this group.

There were nine men in their late teens and early twenties who spent most of their time on this site. I'd seen a couple of them before, very briefly, but I'd never spoken to any of them, and they kept to themselves.

Umar regularly took this group into the woods for 'study time' as he put it. He told Clay that they had neglected their studies growing up, and he was helping them. Our guess: he was teaching them to become martyrs. I suspected that we'd found the suicide bombers who would undertake the attacks.

They seemed so young, so driven by disillusionment and hatred. In Umar, they had found the perfect reason for their existence on Earth.

It was terrifying. And so very, very sad.

We'd learned that Umar had trained in Pakistan and Iraq, and had fought in Afghanistan, as well as Syria. And now he was determined to bring the Jihad to America.

"Clay, you will be going with two brothers to bring supplies," and then he turned to the youngest member, a boy who was small and slightly built, no more than seventeen. "Eiliad, find jeans and a shirt for Brother Clay."

The boy waved at Clay to follow him, then turned silently.

I wasn't happy that Umar was splitting us up, but there was nothing I could do about it.

"Sister Amira, you have your own work," he said.

Ushering me ahead of him, we walked toward a series of large sheds arranged around the main courtyard, but when Umar took me inside, my mouth dropped open.

Even though the windows and doors were wide open, the first shed was filled with the smell of chemicals. Umar smiled proudly as showed me where acids, acetone and peroxide were mixed together. I watched silently as two of the men wearing masks and gloves packaged the dried powder into bags the size of a packet of sugar.

"These are boosters for bigger devices," he said conversationally. "As you can see, we're packing these thin tubes and wiring them for use as detonators."

The two workers glanced up briefly then ignored us, concentrating in silence.

Then Umar led me to the second shed.

By contrast, it was noisy with a party atmosphere, and three men were wearing splash suits and masks as they shovelled fertiliser granules from giant one-ton bags into modified coffee grinders. The whirring and grinding drowned out most of the shouted conversations as the granules were turned into a fine powder, dropping into sacks underneath.

Everyone was covered in the dust from the grinders, but as I watched, one of them struggled with the weight of the sack and dropped it, launching a huge cloud of powder into the air. He emerged coughing, so covered in powder that he was as white as a ghost, and everyone laughed.

I was standing in a bomb factory.

CHAPTER NINETEEN

JAMES

I hadn't seen Smith since the day he'd brought me here, but I had spent a lot of time planning to punch him in the face if I ever saw him again.

He smiled warily as he kept his distance.

"I know you feel like kicking the shit out of me right now, but can I come in without risking a beatdown? I need to talk to you."

I watched him cautiously, wondering what new mindfuck was coming my way, then jerked a thumb at him.

"Maybe. I'll decide later."

He nodded.

"Good enough."

He walked into the room and sat on the edge of my bed.

I studied the lines of exhaustion around his mouth, the smudges of black under his eyes that told of long nights and untold stress. *Nope, zero sympathy.*

He looked up, meeting my angry gaze.

"We need your help."

It was so unexpected that I laughed out loud.

"Very funny. You can forget that, you bastard! I've been locked in here for three weeks and..."

"Clay's gone missing."

My furious words shut off immediately.

"What happened? Define missing."

Smith rubbed his forehead.

"The last communication we had with any of them was 72 hours ago. Larson said that Clay had left with two other men from the cell for the regular resupply trip. Usually, that takes between seven and nine hours, depending on which town they use, but this time..."

"Clay didn't come back."

"No, and we haven't heard from him since. The last report from Larson was that Amira had been taken to the second camp that he believes is where the bomb factory is situated. He hadn't been able to get close enough to see inside, but he said the smell of chemicals was strong—and when the trucks were followed by other agents, we knew he was right. It also fit in with intel received from Clay previously. But Larson also thought that his own camp had been found. He'd been sleeping rough within a few miles of the terror cell and hiking in every day. He said he might have to go dark ... and that was the last we heard from him." He scratched the stubble on his face. "Amira hasn't reported in since she was sent to work in the bomb factory..."

"Which means the last time you heard from either of your *assets* was ... what... four days ago?"

He nodded slowly.

"Yep."

"And you're here telling me, so you must want something. You've got a fucking nerve."

He looked up and met my angry gaze.

"I know you and Clay are friends."

I stared at him in disgust.

"Yeah, we are. But you've lost him—he could be anywhere by now or..."

I didn't want to say it, but we both knew that the chances of him being alive were slim.

"Amira?"

Smith shook his head.

I frowned, and Smith's eyes narrowed.

"James, she's on our side."

I stared at him coldly.

"'I hate them,' that's what she said. 'I hate them so much,' and she wasn't talking about Marmite sandwiches."

"James, buddy, just..."

"Prove it. Prove to me that she's not your mole. Prove that Larson isn't your mole."

He grimaced.

"It's not that simple."

"It never is with you spook types."

He gave the twisted shadow of a smile.

"Yeah, that's fair. Look, James, we can't force you to help, but I'll tell you what I know and answer any questions I can, then let you make up your own mind."

I stared at him warily. I didn't trust him any further than I could throw him, and I definitely didn't think he'd tell me everything, but I was prepared to listen to his story.

"We've been monitoring Amira for a long time, over a year, ever since her younger brother, Karam, showed signs of heading out to Syria. Truthfully, we thought that it would be her sister that we'd be recruiting, but that's not the way things worked out."

"Recruiting her for what?"

"Exactly what I told you on the airplane the first day we met: to go undercover with a terror cell that has the potential to set up a bomb factory on U.S. soil—which we now know that they've done. Clay knew her story and was there to try and keep her safe—she's our most valuable asset."

"But ... that makes no sense," I said, confused as hell. "Her brother was killed by U.S. drone bombers—she hates you, she said so. How can you trust her?"

He shook his head.

"No, you're wrong. She hates Daesh and all they stand for. Do you really think we'd recruit someone who could be turned? No. She hates war, period. The thought of an atrocity here in the U.S. was something she was prepared to put her life on the line to prevent. She's the real deal, James—a patriot."

His certainty made me pause, and I went over her words again: *I hate them, I really hate them*. I assumed that she'd been talking about the American military, but now I thought about it, her words could be interpreted differently.

And that changed everything. If Smith was telling the truth.

"You think I'm going to fall for that?" I said dismissively. "You think I don't know your bullshit when I smell it? I don't believe a word you've told me. You're probably not even CIA? I have no idea who you are."

Smith watched me intently.

"I know that you and Amira became ... close."

His words sparked the memory of her body beneath mine, memories that I'd been trying to suppress ever since.

"She wouldn't have told you about her brother otherwise. Frankly," and he frowned, "she should have known better than to share that with you anyway. If she'd kept her mouth shut, we wouldn't have had to detain you." He gave a grim smile. "But as it happens, that's worked in our favour."

He sounded pretty smug, but I ignored that, as well.

"So let me go," I said, folding my arms. "You've got no reason to hold me."

He grimaced.

"I told you, it's not that simple. We really need you, James. If you won't do it for Amira—which frankly surprises me—do it for Clay."

He was chipping away at my resolve. I didn't know what to believe. If anyone had told me thirty minutes ago that I'd even consider helping Smith again, I'd have laughed in their face.

"Give me a timetable of events," I said grudgingly.

He rubbed his hands over his face then flopped down onto the bed again.

"Clay and Amira were successfully inserted into the cell as husband and wife just over three weeks ago and..."

Thick, syrupy jealous clogged my veins.

"What? What do you mean 'as husband and wife'? That wasn't the plan. They weren't even supposed to know each other. Why the change?"

Smith frowned.

"For the same reason that you were recruited in the first place."

"Your mole?"

"Yes, we needed to switch up their stories to throw the mole off the scent for as long as possible."

He sighed.

"At first, reporting was regular, and Larson was getting some good basic intel. The terrorists were definitely collecting the raw materials for mass producing HMEs, but then Clay hinted that something big was going down and he was trying to get more details—a date, a target, something. He went off the grid the next day and we haven't heard from Amira either. Like I said."

"And Larson?"

"Nothing."

I leaned against the wall, my arms folded in front of me.

"How well do you know Larson?"

Smith curled his lip in irritation.

"As well as I know myself. He's not the leak."

I rubbed my chin.

"Then where is he? He could be captured and spilling his guts right now."

Smith shook his head.

"He's alive, but he's gone dark."

"How do you know?"

"Because he's a hard man to catch or kill—and because he said he might have been compromised on his last transmission. Trust me, Larson is still out there."

Un-fucking-believable.

"You want me to trust you? I'm more likely to chew off my foot up to my elbow."

He laughed. He bloody laughed at me.

"I didn't know you held a grudge, James. But we still need you."

I ignored his dig.

"I'm an AT not Special Forces! Call in a SEAL team to extract them —someone trained for this shit!"

"No, for two reasons: we don't want to extract them if they're still viable assets and can get intel out; and second, since it's a bomb-making factory, I want you on site." He frowned. "I can't force you and I know I'm not your favourite person right now, but this is the line in the sand, James, and we need you. Your friend needs you." He pressed his lips together. "Amira needs you."

CHAPTER TWENTY

AMIRA

"What do you think?" asked Umar, his dark eyes gleaming.

"Incredible," I croaked.

"Yes, isn't it? We're able to produce high quality explosives here. I think this work will suit you very well."

And he raised his eyebrows as if waiting for a response.

"Thank you," I said weakly, desperately searching around for Clay.

"Ah, you're looking for your husband. I'm afraid that he's already left," Umar said blandly. "He'll be gone a few days, but you'll see him again soon."

I thought I was going to be sick. For the past weeks, Clay had been my rock—now I was alone with a cold blooded killer, a man whose twisted dreams made him want to kill large numbers of people in the most efficient way possible. I'd never been so scared.

The *burqa* hid my expression, but I stood there, my knees trembling, before Umar decreed what would happen next.

He smiled, and it felt like I was paper thin and he could see right through me.

"Well, now that's agreed," he said, clapping his hands, let's see how well you've been trained."

. . .

From that moment on, I was set to work making improvised explosive devices. I kept waiting for Umar to say something about Clay, but it was as if he'd never existed. When I worked up the courage to ask, I was tersely told that he was collecting supplies. I knew that couldn't be right—he'd been gone too long. I was completely alone.

I was trapped.

After that, no one spoke to me, except to yell orders.

That first night, I ate alone and lay awake most of the night, waiting for them to drag me from my bed, then question, torture and kill me.

I didn't fear dying—I didn't. But I was terrified of the moments leading up to death. I was scared of the pain that seemed certain to be coming my way.

When I thought they were all sleeping, I tried to leave the camp to get a message to Larson, but a cold-eyed guard sent me scurrying back to my lonely corner of the bomb-making factory floor, where I slept each night curled into a tight ball on a mattress in the corner, shaking with cold and fear.

The following morning, I went to relieve myself in the forest, I knew I was being watched, and after that I was never completely alone. Larson had told us not to leave any written messages, nothing that could be incriminating, and I couldn't see any sign of him—but then again, I wouldn't expect to.

On the third day, I scratched a message in the dirt: Clay's name with a broken heart around it. I hoped that Larson would at least realize how worried I was.

But nothing changed, nothing happened, and instead I spent my days working in the bomb factory. I had too much time to think.

Hour after hour, I sank deeper into fear and paranoia. There was no one I could trust, no way out.

Where was Clay? What was happening to him? Had he abandoned me? Was I here on my own? Where was Larson? Was he nearby? Would he come when I needed him?

On good days, I let myself believe that I could trust them, and this would all work out; on bad days, I was sure that they were both dead already and I wouldn't be far behind.

It played on my mind constantly that Karam could have gotten mixed up in more than volunteering at the hospital, as Umar had suggested. In my head, I went over the emails that Karam had sent, searching for any clue, any hint that Umar was telling the truth about him. I couldn't believe it—and yet, Umar knew Karam's name, his real name. It just didn't seem possible that my beautiful, kind brother could be allied with ISIS. Or, more truthfully, I didn't want to believe it. Maybe this was just more of Umar twisting the truth to suit his plans. I wished I could untangle truth from lies. I wished many, many things, without reaching any conclusion.

So I worked.

Because I had small hands, I was the one who packed the thin tubes to make detonators. I quickly became adept at it, using every part of training that I could remember. Umar was very pleased with me.

He gave me my own bench to work at, and agreed that I could wear my *niqab* rather than the *burqa*, so I could see more clearly.

I found that ironic.

We worked 15 hour days, stopping only for food and prayers. My back and hands ached, my eyes burned with the smell of chemicals and I had a constant headache.

The other men ignored me completely. They talked openly in front of me, about the mighty plans that Umar had, about 'the great reckoning' or the 'Day of Judgement' that was coming, and it worried me that they didn't care what they said in front of me. Clearly, I wasn't considered any sort of threat to them—I was insignificant.

I still didn't know what Umar was planning, when, or what his targets would be. It seemed likely that there would be multiple strikes, probably simultaneous.

I prayed that I was wrong.

I knew that I was right.

And then one night, with the smell of chemicals clinging to my hair and clothes, when exhaustion had left me weak, and despair had left me hopeless, Umar came for me.

CHAPTER TWENTY-ONE

JAMES

I knew I was being manipulated—and it was working.

"Did anyone ever tell you that you're an utter bastard?"

Smith shrugged.

"It doesn't matter what you think of me. Do you want to help your friends or not?"

As he sensed me giving in, his eyes gleamed, but he just had to twist the knife a little deeper first.

"The rescue mission is going ahead with or without you, whether you believe in me or not. Our chances are ... fair, but we'll all have a better chance of getting out alive if you come with us."

He'd hit me with a low blow and he knew it. I caved.

"What's the plan?"

He nodded and a small smile played on his face, but I read relief in his expression, too.

One of the men standing by the door as backup in case things had gone tits up, handed him a laptop. Smith propped it on the small table and brought up a map.

"This is their last known location—a remote site in rural Pennsylvania, but still only a 90 minute drive from Pittsburgh or Philadelphia; two hours from here."

"Where is here, since we're being all buddy now?"

Smith gave a grim smile.

"You're in one of our safe houses on the outskirts of New York. Welcome to the Big Apple."

"Fuck off."

He grinned at me then turned back to the laptop.

"It seems likely that the attack will be here, Pittsburgh or Philly— maybe all three cities simultaneously. But that's on the assumption they won't want to transport large quantities of explosive material too far across the country. Also, they've been stockpiling at these locations," and he pointed to several suburbs ringing the cities he'd mentioned. "We have all of these under surveillance, but there very well could be others that we don't know about."

His frustration was obvious and I understood it. I'd been on the receiving end of briefings in London when a new terror cell was found. Some intel was good, some bad, and some so wrong, lives were lost.

"Do we know anything about this group, the sort of hit that they're likely to choose?"

"A little but not enough," he admitted. "We've been able to identify their leader as a Brit named Umar Khalidi—educated at Oxford and post-grad at Harvard. His father was a Guantanamo Bay detainee, and he was already on the MI5/MI6 watch-list. He's got a particular hate on educational institutions, so the target could be a school or college, but just as likely a crowded shopping mall, or something symbolic like the Liberty Bell, the One World Trade Center, even the 9/11 Museum, for all we know."

"That narrows it down. Shit!"

He scowled.

"We've alerted the agencies in these cities. Our job is to find out what's happening at the two camps. I've been giving some thought to how we'll go operational here. It would normally encompass a three-man team—driver, cover, commander—and we go in with a Quick Reaction Force comprising Special Forces to swing into action if it all goes belly up ... we need to stop the cell from splitting and running."

"You forget that the three guys on task would have a very short life expectancy if they get pinned down without a QRF," I pointed out.

"I'm volunteering as team commander," he said quietly. "Clay is your friend and Amira is ... but Larson saved my life." He paused. "You in?"

Everything in me screamed that this was the worst idea in a career of mouthing off to commanding officers and a lot of years of picking the wrong side in an argument.

The last time I'd had a bad feeling like this, I'd ended up in Selly Oak hospital for a month with bone shrapnel that had once belonged to my best friend peppering my arm.

I brushed my fingers over the lumpy white scars on my forearm.

"I'm in. Tell me everything I don't know."

Smith nodded, and asked the other men to bring food and coffee. It was going to be a long night.

"First of all," he said, "I'm not FBI. This operation is outside their jurisdiction."

I raised my eyebrows.

"You mean it's unauthorized?" Smith just stared back. "Bloody hell! Do you have any clearance for this op at all?"

He thought about his answer before he replied.

"The Feds are running scared. They're worried about the legal side."

That was such shit. I was a soldier, and giving rights to would-be terrorists was hard to stomach.

"So, that makes you CIA?"

Smith smiled.

"Something like that. The people I work for prefer to go under the radar..."

"Which means black ops?"

He shrugged.

"If you want to give it a name."

I knew he wouldn't give me anything more about who was running this team.

"Where does Amira fit in?"

"Ah, the beautiful Amira," he grinned, which pissed me off no end.

"The legend we created for her is very close to real life. She really is an ER nurse and her younger brother really did die in Syria. He was a med student at UCSD, and that's where he came to our attention. There was a group within the university who were working to radicalise students. Several of the students who moved in his circle went to Syria to fight with Daesh that summer. Karam was with them, but we think his intention was to work in medicine. That's what he told his family, and it seemed genuine."

Smith sighed.

"When he arrived in Syria, things get a little muddier. He certainly did volunteer at the main hospital in Raqqa, but it's not clear whether he was also recruited by Daesh at that point. We suspect that pressure was put on him and he was coerced to join—it's always a great coup for them when they get foreign fighters, especially from Europe and the U.S. We lost track of him after that, right up until he died. We'd certainly have put a watch on him, had he come back."

"So when he was killed, your attention turned to his family?"

"Got it in one. We thought it would be the younger sister who'd be most susceptible to an approach, but in fact it was Amira who came to us."

I closed my eyes, part of me not wanting to hear this.

"You'd have been surprised what she was like then, James: no *burqa*, no *niqab*, not even a headscarf. She was like many other modern, Muslim woman in the U.S.—respectful of her faith and family, but wanting to have a life and career beyond that. She's a strong woman— and very brave. She upturned everything in her life to help us. She wanted to give meaning to her brother's death. We gave her a forum to do that."

I snorted, unimpressed.

"Yeah, you took someone who was mourning the death of her brother, someone vulnerable, and you manipulated her into helping you."

Smith didn't even bother to deny it.

"Pretty much, yeah."

"You bastard."

He gave me a hard look.

"This terror cell wants to plant multiple bombs on U.S. soil. I say, whatever gets the job done."

Arguing with him about it was getting me nowhere.

"Tell me more about the cell—what else do you know?"

He brought up a map on his laptop.

"Two camps, about three miles apart. The first one is where they sleep, eat and pray; the second is the bomb factory. Clay reported that a truck comes every three days and removes up to a quarter of a ton of HMEs as well as detonators."

Jesus.

"But thanks to that intel, we're able to track each delivery and have eyes on. We know where these explosives are being stored and the people who are involved, but there could well be other places that we've missed—deliveries made before the assets were in place. We'd been waiting for the right moment, when we're certain that we haven't missed anything. What we don't know yet, is the intended targets or when a strike might occur—but we were already thinking it would soon, the way they're stockpiling—and then the flow of intel was interrupted which meant we knew we'd run out of time. The explosives are being stored in a ring of shops and houses grouped around DC, and a second grouping around New York, and a third around Pittsburgh. It seems fairly clear that those are the cities that will be targets."

He showed me three more maps on his laptop, indicating where the HMEs were being kept. It was a relief that the spook squad knew and had the means to get it off the streets soon.

I turned to look at Smith.

"So this is intel that you got from Clay and Amira?"

"Yep. Once we learned of the second camp, we would have followed trucks going in and out anyway, but we only know about the HMEs and detonators because of what they've told us. We haven't been able to get this close before."

That was Smith's way of telling me that the op had been worth it, as far as he was concerned.

"Do you think Amira and Clay are still alive?"

He looked me in the eyes, meeting my hard stare.

"Honestly? I don't know, but if they are, then every second is crucial in getting to them."

I let out a long breath.

"What are we waiting for?"

Smith nodded at me.

"Just making sure you're on board, buddy. Let's suit up. What do you need?"

Then a beeping sound caught his attention and he pulled a pager from his coat pocket.

"Shit! It's Larson! He's found Clay—it's not good, and he's sending the coordinates. He says he's going after Amira."

His words sent an electric shock through my entire body.

If Clay was compromised and now Larson was going after Amira, then his chances were shit. I glanced at Smith—we both knew Larson was on a Hail Mary op. We were out of time.

I stood up quickly, but then wondered what the message meant. Was Larson going after Amira to save her?

Or to kill her?

CHAPTER TWENTY-TWO

AMIRA

Rough hands grabbed me, hauling me upwards. I screamed and fought, but a man's palm cracked across my cheek so hard, I saw stars, pain shooting through my face.

"Stop fighting, Amir," came Umar's voice, soft and sibilant, whispering against my skin. "You've been chosen for a great honour. You're about to become a soldier of ISIS."

He laughed, and the sound sent fear streaking up and down my spine.

That's when I knew that I was going to die.

I kicked and screamed, fighting with everything in me, biting and lashing out, but then a fist or a boot thudded into my chest, leaving me gasping for breath. I curled into a ball, and more blows rained down on my back, hips and my arms as I tried to cover my head.

It didn't take long before I was barely conscious. Then they tied my hands tightly, the twine cutting into my flesh, and a rag was stuffed into my mouth, making me gag.

Dizzy and sick, I closed my eyes, and I prayed.

Karam, my beautiful brother, I'm sorry. I've really made a mess of things. I was so mad at you when you died, and I've been angry for a long time now. I so badly wanted to do something to help, to give meaning to your death—but there's no meaning in any of this. I'm sorry, I'm so sorry! I don't know what this will to do our parents, to Zada. This isn't how I thought it would be. I forgive you, Karam, and I hope you can forgive me.

And then for the first time since my brother's death, I prayed to God, trying to find peace within the sound of war.

I don't know if my words carried that far, but I hoped that they did.

I wished I could have seen James one last time. I'd forgiven him long ago for leaving without a word. He'd been kind when I needed kindness, and I'd forgiven him for being the wrong man at the wrong time. Maybe I could forgive myself, too.

I was dragged upwards, my arms held on both sides as they half carried, half dragged me toward a truck with blacked out windows.

Suddenly, four shots rang out and the men holding me crumpled to the ground.

Clay? Larson?

In my fear and confusion, I vaguely remembered the arms training that I'd received: the four shots had sounded like the double tap of .45 hollow point pistol, the gun that Larson used. I dropped to my knees as their blood pooled around me. Shouting and yells erupted, and then the rapid rattle of automatic gunfire and the *ping* of bullets thudding into the sheds behind me.

I managed to scramble away, heading for the forest, but I was moving slowly, so slowly.

Then Larson's huge form rose out of the copse close beside me, his face streaked with dirt and dried blood.

I tried to move faster, stones and fir cones digging into my hands and bare knees when I stumbled, but I was painfully slow, every inch of progress costing too much time. I'd almost reached him when his face hardened and the huge black pistol seemed to point right at me, but his bullets flew over my head, hitting whoever was behind me with a wet *thunk*.

"Come on!" he growled at me, frustrated with my slow speed.

And then he was flying from the thicket, his huge thighs pumping hard as he dived forward, forcing my body into the ground in a hard tackle. I felt his body jerk twice, but I could hardly breathe, suffocating as his dead weight winded me.

When he rolled off me, I tried to scream, but the rag in my throat choked the sound back.

I gagged, vomit flowing into the rag and down through my nose.

Larson was badly hurt. He lay on the dirt with blood from two bullet holes colouring his t-shirt. His eyes were open and he blinked slowly.

I watched as his eyes fluttered, the pool of blood darkening the dirt around him.

I crawled towards him and tried to grab his hand. I wanted to tell him that I was sorry I'd doubted him, sorry it had led to this moment, sorry for everything.

But then ... he just died, and I saw the moment his spirit left his body.

Umar was furious.

"Who is this? Where did he come from? Someone tell me who he is! Where are our sentries? I'll flay the skin from their backs for this!"

He lashed out, kicking Larson's corpse. I had to close my eyes when a boot smashed down on Larson's face, his nose and cheekbone splitting with a loud crack.

I don't think it was the loss of his 'soldiers' that Umar cared about, but the fact that he couldn't question Larson.

"Who is he?" he yelled into my face, spittle flying as his anger mounted.

He grabbed my shoulders brutally, shaking me until my teeth rattled.

"Who is he?"

His open palm cracked across my cheek, sending me flying backwards.

He pulled the rag from my mouth roughly and pointed his gun at me.

"Who. Is. He?"

And then I vomited again, all over his suede desert boots.

He swore and punched me in the face, and when I spat blood, one of my teeth landed on the dirt in front of me.

I was hurting and disorientated, probably had a concussion, and I wasn't telling them anything.

Umar told one of his men to put a sack over my head and then they tossed me into the back seat of a truck, my head thudding painfully against the door.

My knees were forced backwards and a man sat next to me, his rough hands stroking my leg, pinching the soft skin of my inner thigh until I cried out. That made him laugh and I recognized Munassar's harsh voice.

He pulled my panties down and thrust his fingers inside me, forcefully, painfully, enjoying the unwilling scream that broke from me, over and over again.

I cried out blindly when I felt his body over me, his thick erection pressing into my stomach.

I wanted to die.

CHAPTER TWENTY-THREE

JAMES

I stepped out of my one-room prison for the first time in nearly a month, feeling almost drunk on freedom, but fear bubbled underneath.

I had to give credit to Smith and his crew because we were on our way with full kit within thirty minutes. They were good—or Smith knew that I'd agree to help and had come equipped, which was more likely.

As we drove through the neon-lit streets of this New York suburb, Smith received a series of calls updating him with intel.

He frowned and glanced at me.

"What's changed?"

"We've heard from Clay. He's got some injuries but he's able to communicate," he paused. "He's been tortured."

"Fucking hell!"

"Yeah, that about sums it up. From what he says, they were supposed to kill him but got sloppy and let their guard down. Larson was able to take them out, but he had to leave Clay behind to go after Amira. We're taking a helo. There's no need for stealth because they were de-camping when Larson went for your girl."

"The terrorists will be long gone by now!"

He shot me a look.

"We'll bring our team home."

"You're putting a lot of faith in Larson," I said, voicing the words that had been running through my head.

"Yeah, I am."

Ten minutes later, we arrived at a private airfield where a tactical transport helo was waiting for us, along with a 12-strong Special Forces team.

I was given a set of body armour, helmet, 9mm handgun and an M4 assault rifle.

Smith shook hands with the team leader and then we were wheels up, rising rapidly as New York City faded into the night.

I could tell that Smith was worried. Clay was alive but sounded in bad shape, and there was no news of Larson or Amira.

But we had to treat this like any other live op: shut down feelings and do the job. So that's what I did. I spent the flight thinking through what I might find at the bomb factory based on the intel we'd had so far, and what steps I'd need to take to make it safe. Five more Ammo Techs like me would have been a good start.

As we flew across the countryside, the towns grew smaller and the cars on the road fewer. It wasn't long before we were rushing through the air towards dawn, just above the tree-line, when the helo suddenly dipped to the left and the order came to rappel out.

I followed the team as they surrounded a small hut but there was no resistance, and when the hut door was thrown open, I saw Clay.

"What took you guys so long?" he said weakly, but his grin was the same.

"Watching re-runs of *Airwolf*, mate," I said, crouching down next to him.

He laughed hoarsely and I passed him a bottle of water.

His hands shook, and I had to help him hold it to his cracked and bloody lips.

There were cigarette burns all over his body, and from the other burn marks on his skin, I guessed they'd been using electric shocks on him, too.

His face was bloody and beaten, his eyes nearly swollen shut, with blood from a cut in his eyebrow coating one side of his face.

"I know," he croaked, side-eyeing me through swollen slits. "You've always been jealous of my good looks."

"Yeah, jealous as hell," I laughed grimly.

He tried to smile but his face creased with pain.

"Area is secured—no tangoes," said the leader of the Special Ops team to Smith.

"Have you heard from Larson?" Clay asked hopefully, his voice gaining strength. "He was a sight for sore eyes when he stormed in here. He took out three of them with three shots. The bodies should be somewhere outside."

The team leader nodded and raised four fingers.

"Shit, four of them? Your buddy is good, Smith."

Smith gave a dry smile as he crouched next to Clay.

"Larson told me that he'd had to move camp four or five days ago—I'm not too sure how long I've been here—but it was the day that I was separated from Amira and brought here. He kept on the move, but he told me that they were using electronic counter measures to stop him from reporting in. He didn't want to head out and leave me and Amira in a bad situation." He sighed. "The terrorists only got sloppy last night when they started shipping out."

Smith nodded, then stood to listen to the team leader's report.

"Teams B and C report no activity at the first and second terrorist camp. One body—unidentified ICI male, two gunshot wounds to the chest. They're bringing the body back now. Otherwise, both camps are completely empty, sir."

Smith swore and I saw the flicker of pain in his eyes.

"You think that's Larson?"

He didn't answer my question, but stared out of the tiny window.

"We're too late," he said bitterly.

"They've got Amira?"

"Yeah, looks like. Tell us everything, Clay."

He nodded slowly.

"This is what I know: multiple targets—they're going for all the Ivy League colleges today, so there isn't much time. They raged about White privilege and institutionalized racism—definitely a big hate on those schools," and he frowned. "Teams need to look for devices that would fit in a suitcase or backpack, but bigger than a briefcase. From the way they were talking, it didn't sound like car bombs would be used —something smaller, easier to get onto campus. I don't know if it was all of the Ivy League schools, but it could be."

"On it," said Smith, speaking into his headset.

"Wait! There's more," and Clay looked at me. "They were talking about 'the woman' and I assumed they meant Amira, although they never said her name. They're going to send her into New York City with a suicide vest."

Clay met my horrified gaze.

"I know, James. I know." Then he turned to Smith. "They kept saying 'to the Square' and I took that to mean Times Square, but I could be wrong."

"When?"

He shook his head, his eyes clouding with the effort.

"Today."

I glanced at Smith.

"She won't be doing it willingly," he said, his voice sharp with certainty. "And right now, New York is about to have a big problem."

Clay nodded his agreement.

"I'll send out her description so police are on the alert," said Smith. "But I'll also tell them to be on the lookout for a woman wearing a *burqa*. It would be the perfect way to hide a suicide vest. And I'll tell them to prioritize Times Square, but also to check any other squares in the city—hell, that could be dozens." He turned to Clay. "Is there anything else, anything at all no matter how small or seemingly insignificant? If they were bragging to you, they might have been careless, mentioned something else, something you know subconsciously, a clue."

Clay closed his eyes, and we waited with barely contained impatience.

"I can't think of anything," he said at last. "I definitely heard them say Ivy League but..." he shook his head slowly. "They wanted to make a statement with their targets—it was very specific—to attack American institutions. I don't know ... maybe a museum? An art gallery? They laughed and said they'd show our Mickey Mouse government what they thought of them and..."

"Wait, say that again!"

Clay peered at me uncertainly.

"Which part?"

"About the Mickey Mouse government—did they say anything else about that?"

"Um, no?"

Smith's intense gaze turned to me.

"James, what are you thinking?"

"I don't know—nothing. It's just the way he said it."

"You have a hunch?"

"It's probably nuts..."

"Say it anyway—we're working in the dark as it is."

"I'm not sure—this might be completely wrong..."

"But?"

I took a deep breath.

"Is there a Disney store in Times Square?"

Smith's eyes widened.

"Yes, there is! Good call, James!"

CHAPTER TWENTY-FOUR

AMIRA

I drifted, far, far away, to a place where there was no fear and no pain, no war and no want. Drifting, dreaming, unsure if I was conscious or not, suspended in a place between life and death.

It was peaceful, disconnected from my body, restful, safe. There was something I was supposed to do, something I had to remember, but it was so comfortable here, so quiet. I didn't want to remember any of it.

Blue eyes.

Why did I remember blue eyes?

I swam back to consciousness, radiating pain that threatened to drown me, and my body jerked painfully, memory rushing back like a river that had burst its banks, bringing all the pain and fear crashing over me, crushing me.

Those men.

They'd used me, then left me tied up on the back seat of the truck in the dark. Every inch of me was wracked with pain, but my mind had separated from my body long ago.

I blocked out every part of that journey and what those men did to me. I didn't want to remember. But they'd made sure to leave their many marks on my body which had become a scrapbook of pain.

They'd left me naked and shivering in the darkest hours before dawn.

I lay there for a long time, waiting to die, but light was creeping back into the world, and I hated it. I wanted the darkness to consume me, because living like this, so broken, so destroyed—that would be unbearable.

Shame blossomed as I struggled to move, then saw the bites on my thighs and breasts, one nipple leaking blood. Bruises bloomed across my skin and my whole lower body howled with pain. They'd taken turns, violating me repeatedly, taking particular pleasure in making me bleed. I'd grown immune to the slaps and punches, the times they spat on me and called me a whore, but I wanted to blot out their grinning, heaving faces as they'd used my body. Abused my body.

Death would have been kinder.

It was Munassar who came for me. I stared back with dull, dead but defiant eyes. He curled his lip as if my naked body, bruised and bloodied, offended him. He grabbed my ankles to drag me out of the truck, laughing as my bare shoulders thudded onto concrete and my head bounced twice.

Blackness tinged the edges of my vision, and I was free again, floating, drifting.

I couldn't tell how long I'd been unconscious the second time, but as my body fought to stay asleep, a sharp slap across my face startled me awake.

As my eyes tried to focus, I realized that I was in a large warehouse, filled with packing cases.

I squinted, shivering with fear as I felt Umar's cold eyes watching me. He could have been staring at a rock for all the emotion or humanity I saw in those eyes.

I tried to move, but my arms and legs were still bound, and when I tried to speak, Munassar plastered heavy tape across my mouth.

I realized that I was clothed, and that surprised me. I blinked, looking down at the unfamiliar sweatpants and t-shirt that I was wearing, confused to see my own grubby, red and white Chucks on my feet.

And then with a gloating expression, Munassar carefully lowered a suicide vest over my shoulders.

My eyes widened and a long, low moan ripped from my throat as my body started to shake and tears leaked from my eyes.

"It's time to stop struggling now," said Umar, his cultured voice so calm, so controlled. "It's time to become a soldier of ISIS."

CHAPTER TWENTY-FIVE

JAMES

We raced through Manhattan and into Times Square, scattering pigeons and pedestrians as we exited the van, looking around us wildly, searching for a clue.

Up and down the entire eastern border, Special Forces teams had been deployed to each of the Ivy League universities, and every EOD operative within a 300 mile radius was being flown in.

But Times Square was ours.

"Split up," snapped Smith. "You all know what you're looking for."

People turned to stare, some taking photographs as we moved through the crowds. Smith had called for police backup—some officers from the substation were already on site and many more from all over the city were being brought in.

Frustration and fear caught in my throat as I searched every face.

It was her stillness that caught my attention. Most people aren't still—they check their phones, watch other people walking past, look at their wristwatches, scratch, twitch, itch—they move.

And when they're standing outside the Disney Store in Times Square, most people would at least glance through the windows.

This woman wasn't moving; she was utterly still.

Heavily pregnant.

And wearing a *burqa*.

But then I saw those red and white Converse shoes, and I knew it was Amira. Although she definitely wasn't nine months pregnant, which left only one reason that I could think of why she'd have a baby bump at her belly...

I started to sweat.

She hadn't seen me yet, so I radioed Smith and the team.

"I've found her. Outside the Disney store. I'm pretty sure she's wearing a suicide vest."

"Goddammit!"

"Yeah, I know. Clearing the area is going to be nearly impossible, but get the cops started. If the device is on a timer, we're fucked, but if the bomber is using his mobile phone, his cell phone, and wants to be nearby to see the results of his handiwork, there's a chance I can neutralize it first. We need to set up ECM and order e-vac."

"On it."

I wasn't a praying man, but maybe I should be. Smith's team had access to electronic countermeasures, a device that could jam remote detonation from twenty metres. A military spec device could keep Amira in the bubble for up to 100 metres.

I hoped that the police cordon wasn't going to make Umar run— we needed him to be close and stay close.

Clay stared around at the unfolding chaos.

"Umar must be here somewhere."

When Smith had tried to send Clay to hospital, he'd pointblank refused. Instead, the SEAL team medic had patched him up as best he could while we were still in the air.

"Yeah," I agreed, "he'll want to be far enough away not to risk himself, but close enough to be able to see the bomb and fire it."

Clay grimaced and stared around at the crowded intersection flanked by tall buildings.

"If he's using a cell phone to trigger the device, could the buildings block the signal?"

I shook my head.

"No, he could send a text message and the system would continue to attempt to deliver the message until it got the thinnest of signals so the device would still function."

"Shit! So as soon as he sees you approach, he'll try and fire the device."

"Yeah. I hope Smith's ECM is working."

I stared down at my hands, almost surprised to see that they weren't shaking. I started to walk towards Amira, but Clay caught my shoulder.

"It's too dangerous, brother. Wait for the cops to yellow tape the area."

"Umar will see them! I can't wait, *there's no time!*"

He grabbed my bicep and pulled me around.

"You don't think Umar will have a Plan B? We don't even know if the device is on a timer. Suit up—give yourself a chance." He gritted his teeth. "You're our best chance of saving Amira. She ... I..."

Startled, I met his gaze.

"You and Amira?"

My chest constricted.

"I care for her, brother. You know that."

I did know that, but was he in love with her? Was I?

I realized that Clay was still talking.

"You are the only one here who can neutralize this device: not me, not Smith, just you. You have to give us the best chance to stop Umar. Put on the damn bomb suit and go save our girl."

I forced myself to focus.

"Have you seen what she's wearing? If a device that size detonates, a bomb suit will be no use," I said grimly, shrugging out of his grasp.

"*If* the main charge explodes. *If*. But you have a good chance of detaching the detonator before that happens—and the bomb suit will protect you if that part functions."

"It won't save Amira," I said tightly. "And I can't wait for Smith to get the bomb suit here."

His face twisted.

"I know, brother. I know. But you're our best hope. A lot of people are counting on you." He glanced over his shoulder as an unmarked van drove toward us, startling tourists out of the way as it mounted the pavement. "Smith's guy is here now. You cool?"

I nodded and ran towards the van. I could already see police moving in to set up a barrier at the roads leading to the Times Square intersection, but there were still hundreds of people within range, maybe thousands.

Smith was already climbing into the van, dragging out the bomb suit and EOD kit with him.

It was 75 pounds worth of armour-plating inside a Kevlar suit. There were blast plates at the crotch and chest, and the helmet alone weighed ten pounds.

"Forget the suit," I shouted. "There's no time!"

Smith grabbed my arm as I opened the EOD kit bag.

"Listen to me, James! The cell is still active—you do *not* want them to see your face right now. We could need you again. You're also a Brit operating illegally in the U.S. Wear the damn suit."

Clay was already laying it out so there was no point arguing and it was easy for me to step into.

"ECM is in here," said Smith, grim faced. "It's not military grade—it's one that I use to blanket a room for meetings. It's got limited range and battery life. I'm trying to get another one here..."

He didn't need to finish the sentence, but handed me the small device. It was the size and shape of a cigarette packet.

It was a good thing I'd given up smoking—those things can kill you.

Smith looked up.

"Umar will try to trigger the explosion, so he'll stay in the area for a while, but once he has repeated failures, he'll try to get away. I'll have people looking for him."

By now, civilians were aware that something was going down. Of course, that didn't mean that they were getting out of the way—morons were stopping to take pictures. More police were pouring into the area and trying to clear as many of the pedestrians as possible, and placing road blocks across the intersections.

A news crew was already hovering nearby.

Great. If I died, it would be on national TV.

I took a deep breath and pulled on the helmet.

Immediately, my world shrunk. My own breaths were loud in my ears, like being underwater; and my peripheral vision was limited. I was detached, insulated, alone.

EOD operators called this the long walk—and it always felt longer than it really was. Always. It was the most alone I'd ever felt in my life.

Everything was about this moment: me, my skills, my ability to keep Amira alive, and to stop other people from dying. *Collateral damage*.

My senses were limited, but heightened, too. I felt remote, cut off from everything, but focused on this one task—one last task.

I stepped forward and became visible to the public. Panic broke out and I faintly heard the screams. Civilians were streaming from the intersection, stampeding, jumping over each other, crushing those who got in their way.

As I walked towards Amira, time slowed down.

I saw a piece of paper fluttering from somewhere above, and the woman whose mouth was open in an 'O' as a police officer dragged her behind the barrier. I was aware of faces at the hundreds of windows that ringed Times Square—windows that could turn into lethal glass knives and able to shred a human being if the main device functioned. I could hear the muffled sounds of a police loudhailer: *Keep back from the windows! Stay behind the barriers!* And the civilians who didn't know better, all angling for a closer look.

I saw Plan B being actioned: hastily erected blast barriers moved into place in a broad circle surrounding Amira. It would help. A little.

Amira still hadn't moved, although she must be aware of our presence by now.

What would I find when I reached her? A detonator attached to a larger device was my guess. Hopefully not a timer.

The distance between us grew shorter and the heat inside the suit began to grow. The fan that was supposed to keep the helmet cool had stopped working. I slapped the side of my head and the fan buzzed briefly, then stuttered to a halt. Bloody batteries had run out. Sweat was already beading on my forehead. I lifted the visor for some fresh air.

And slowly, her head turned towards me.

It was chilling, the way she moved with such unnatural slowness. And behind that veil I saw her eyes, those damned eyes that had haunted me night after night.

I blocked the emotion out. Emotion got in the way. Emotion got you killed.

"Amira. Tell me what we're dealing with."

Behind the veil, her eyes widened and she shook her head slightly.

"Just talk slowly. Concentrate. Tell me everything you know, what you've seen, what you've heard."

Again the widening of the eyes. Again the shake of the head.

"Amira, talk to me!"

I thought I heard her whimper, but I couldn't be sure because of the damned helmet.

Prioritise! I knew that fact that her status as an agent had most likely been compromised prior to exploitation as a suicide bomber meant that I had to expect booby-traps—probably several of them.

I tried again.

"Can you tell me anything?"

She closed her eyes and shook her head. Frustrated, I ground my teeth.

"Is the device on a timer?"

She nodded her head imperceptibly, the smallest motion. Then she shook her head. Yes and no? What the hell did that mean?

I spoke into my radio.

"Smith, it's on a timer, I think. I don't know how long I've got—the terrorists could be long gone." I turned back to Amira. "Trembler switch?"

I thought that was unlikely since she must have been driven here. Even so...

She shook her head again. More progress.

And then something occurred to me.

"Are you able to speak to me?"

A shake of the head.

"Is something physical stopping you from speaking?"

She nodded quickly, her eyes wide and filled with fear.

"Okay, this is what I'm going to do. I'm going to cut the *burqa* off you. Understand?"

Again, she nodded.

"Stay still. Don't move. It's going to be okay."

Am I lying?

I took out my knife and kneeled down with difficulty to pick up the hem of the *burqa*, then ran the blade smoothly through the cotton to cut away the robes from her body. The black material pooled at her feet, but my eyes were glued to the huge bulge strapped to her waist—a large container that I knew was filled with explosives.

The device had multiple independent circuits with obstacles to accessing and neutralizing them.

I had hardly any equipment, no X-ray, and no time.

I could see boxes, joined by tape, suspicious lumps, potted circuits that couldn't be exploited without risk.

Amira's hands and feet were cuffed together, so she couldn't have moved if she'd wanted to, and a piece of black duct tape had been placed over her mouth.

Her eyes moved frantically, and I could see fear reflected in her eyes.

A wash of anger sent a red mist over my vision but I pushed the fury away to assess the device.

I needed to be cool and calculating.

Ice cold would save our lives.

Emotions wouldn't.

Moving carefully, I inserted my knife into the container to uncover the device I had to neutralize.

Detonator. *Check.*

Explosives. *Check.*

Multiple booby-traps to stop removal of the detonator and RC. *Shit.*

At least the booby-trap hadn't been based on movement rather than removal; it would have made the job a lot harder.

More lethal.

But the detonator looked as though it had been heavily taped to the det cord, wound around numerous times with the same heavy-duty duct tape that covered Amira's mouth. Worse still, the det cord was attached to a booby-trap device. It meant that I wouldn't be able to hand the detonator to anyone to put in a special sleeve to reduce the blast and prevent it initiating the main charge, in the event that it functioned in the first place.

Fuck!

This would have to be a non-intrusive neutralization—if I could get to the detonators to cut them from the rest of the explosive, I could reduce it from a lethal device to an injury. Yes, there would still be an explosion. I'd be largely protected—although I might lose my hands—but Amira wouldn't survive.

I thought through my process and made some decisions.

First thing I had to do was cut the radio command wire. I located it easily, checked that wasn't booby-trapped and cut through it.

Amira had her eyes squeezed shut, but when I glanced up, she opened them again.

I was going to need her help to get through this.

"You're doing great. I'm going to use bolt cutters to free your hands and then I'm going to get that tape off your mouth. But listen to me—it's really important that you don't move, okay? Even though you'll feel like you want to move, *don't*. Understand?"

Her eyes widened, but she swallowed and nodded slowly.

I pulled a small pair of bolt cutters from the tools strapped to my hip and removed the handcuffs, seeing the blood and bruises around her wrists where she'd tried and failed to pull her hands free. Her arms trembled, but she didn't move.

"Good girl," I said softly, and I didn't know if she heard me.

I deliberately didn't free her feet because I couldn't risk her deciding to run. I wouldn't be able to catch her wearing 80 pounds of armoured bomb suit.

Working as gently as I could, I removed the tape from her mouth, feeling sick as she cried out.

"James! They've got a timer as well as a detonator that can be set off by a mobile phone. It's underneath the main charge. Umar hid it." Her words were breathless and laboured. "I'm so sorry!" she gasped. "I'm so sorry!"

I had to ignore her pain; I could only focus on the job I had to do.

"How long do I have?"

"I don't know! I don't know! He just laughed and said I'd meet my brother soon!"

No timescale.

"Okay, try not to think about that."

I relayed the intel to Smith.

I knew that I had to find the timer, which could be as small as an ice cube and hidden within the main charge.

"Amira, I'm going to need you to reach the RC because I can't access it, but you can. See where those wires are next to your stomach?"

"Yes ... I think ... I think ... if you can cut through some of the tape, I'll be able to reach it." Her voice dropped to a whisper. "My hands are smaller than yours."

"Okay, we'll try that, but not till I tell you."

I cut through the first layer of tape carefully, brutally aware that Amira was sweating freely and that her body heat alone could set off the detonator.

Sweat dripped down my face and I had to wipe my eyes with a piece of material from her *burqa*.

A second piece of tape dangled from the sack of explosives tied around her waist. There must be sixty pounds of HME. If it detonated, there wouldn't be enough of her body parts to put in an egg cup. And if I survived, I'd be wishing I hadn't.

"It's looser," she whispered. "I think ... I can reach the detonator ... just need to... Oh no, I think that's the timer, but..."

"Wait!"

My voice cracked out, freezing her movements.

"Booby-trap next to the detonator. Don't move."

Her body began to shake, making it difficult for me to work.

"Amira, you've got to stay calm."

I could tell that she was seconds away from full-blown panic. I was glad I'd left her ankles cuffed.

Her teeth chattered but suddenly her gaze was fixed on something behind me. I twisted around, cursing the weight of the bomb suit.

Clay! That mad bastard! He was wearing a Kevlar police vest and SWAT helmet with a pistol holstered at his side as he limped toward us.

"Jesus, what are you doing here?"

"Thought I'd see how you're doing, brother," he said, attempting a grin. Then his gaze softened. "Hey, Amira. Good to see you again, girl. You're doing great, honey. James is going to help you, so you just gotta stay calm and let the man work. You think you can do that?"

The trembling lessened and she nodded, tears hovering in her eyes.

"You look t-t-terrible," she stuttered.

"Still better looking than him though, right?" Clay chuckled.

"Keep talking to her," I said quietly. "Keep her calm."

"Will do, brother." Then he muttered out of the side of his mouth. "Smith said to check the ECM unit. He's got another on the way, eta 15 minutes."

I pulled the small box out of my pocket and showed it to him: *13 minutes.*

Shit!

I glanced at Clay, and he caught the unspoken message. I hoped Smith could pull off a miracle, and then I wondered if God had a limited number of miracles for each day—because right now we needed at least two. Three would be better.

The RC dets looked suspicious. There was a booster charge, a fist-sized knot of det-cord. I could cut most of it off, but there'd still be some attached to the detonators.

"Clay, hold the det wires away from the device."

"On it."

Would that be enough to stop an explosion? It definitely wouldn't do Clay or Amira much good.

I kept working at the tape, layer by layer, making a space where I could reach the detonator.

I found the fragmentation easily—two inch nails, probably a couple of thousand, wrapped in resin then covered in tape. It would be a hell of a job to cut through all that.

"Amira, I need you to start cutting through this tape here, while I work on the timer, okay? Just go slowly, piece by piece. Okay?"

She swallowed.

"My ... my hands are shaking."

"It's okay, you can't do any damage—just don't stab me with the knife."

Her eyes widened and she gave a jerky nod of her head as I handed her my penknife, showing her where to start cutting.

Then I handed Clay the ECM, so he could keep one eye on the time we had left, and the other on Amira.

Eleven minutes.

"What's a nice girl like you doing hanging around with this loser?" Clay said to Amira.

I couldn't see her face but a soft, strangled sound came out of her.

"Well, there's no accounting for taste. I guess I'll just have to settle for being the badass best friend. Now, when are you going to introduce me to your sister?"

"N-never," said Amira shakily, concentrating on the lump of resin and tape. "T-too good for you."

"Ooh, harsh," he said, sounding sad as he watched me cut through another layer of tape. "Crash and burn. Um, I don't mean that."

Amira laughed, her tone nearing hysteria.

Ten minutes.

"How you holding up, honey?" said Clay, trying to keep Amira concentrating on him.

"I'm trying," she said quietly. "Allah will guide me."

"Ah, right. Go straight to the top—smart move. Well, as the Big Guy said, 'We created you in pairs'."

Amira's voice was so soft, I hardly heard her.

"L-l-lucky."

But I didn't know what she meant by that.

Finally, I cut through the last layer of tape and the detonator was exposed. It was still very tight. I hoped Amira would be able to reach.

Nine minutes.

"Okay, Amira, listen to me carefully. I want you to insert your fingers here—where I'm holding open this space—and pull the detonator from the device. Slowly."

She licked her lips and nodded.

I think we were all holding our breath as she worked to remove the detonator.

"I can't reach it!" she said shakily. "I can't get to it. I can't…"

"Take your time. Look down—see that space there, on your left—work it free from there."

Finally, the detonator came loose and I could work toward getting to the next one. Amira stared at it as if it was a snake about to bite her.

"So far, so good," I breathed.

Eight minutes.

Now I'd extracted the second det, it was safer to unclip the batteries ... one glance told me that they weren't accessible.

Never a break when I needed one.

Umar had been thorough. He must have been laughing his arse off when he realized that we'd sent him the perfect plant for his plans.

I had to bypass the trap on the explosives' container. I knew that cutting in was a high stress scenario and one slip ... well, the three of us would be toast.

Thinking logically, I tried to assess the right places to target. It didn't take me long to isolate the two green wires, but then I had to strip them using my wire cutters.

Seven minutes.

We were running out of time.

"James," said Clay cautiously, "it might be a good time to take a stroll."

He was trying to tell me that time was tight without making Amira freak out.

"Working on it, buddy," I said shortly.

Suddenly Clay glanced up at the skyline.

"Shit," he said softly, gritting his teeth. "We've got snipers on the roof!"

Amira moaned and her body shook.

"Tell them not to shoot!"

Clay tapped his earpiece.

"Smith, tell the snipers not to shoot! DO NOT SHOOT! Tell them she's cooperating!"

Six minutes.

Anyone who's ever had to strip the plastic off wire knows how easy it is to cut through the wire by mistake.

And once again, that would be bad.

Finally, I manged to clear off the plastic sheath.

Five minutes.

Sweat ran down my face and I had to take precious seconds to wipe my eyes clear again.

Think! THINK!

Wires were stripped, now I had to electronically interrogate the wires by a test meter, do some maths, then shunt or cut...

Four minutes.

Shunt or cut? Shunt or cut?! I had to decide.

"James, we have three minutes, buddy."

Clay's voice was urgent.

"Oh dear Allah! Go! Leave me!" Amira's voice was shrill.

"You'd better go now, Clay," I agreed, my voice strained. "Get to a safe distance."

Amira whimpered.

"Clay, go now!" I ordered.

"Nope, not leaving you," he said, his voice quiet.

"That Kevlar vest won't protect you!"

Amira reached out, trying to push him away.

"Go!" she cried out. "Go, please! In the name of Allah, save yourself!"

"Never going to happen, honey."

Her voice shook.

"James! Make him go! Both of you! Save yourselves!"

Two minutes.

"I'm nearly there, Amira. I'm not leaving you. I'll never leave you."

"James, please! Don't die with me. Don't die for me!"

One minute.

I stared up into her soft brown eyes, so haunted with pain, and so brave.

Clay reached out and clasped her hand.

"Pray with me, Amira."

She grasped his hand as I grappled with the wire cutters, my hands slick with sweat, and Clay's voice rang out, strong and sure.

"O God, you are my Lord. There is none worthy of worship except You. I rely upon You, and You are the Great Lord of the Throne. Whatever God wills happens, and whatever He does not will does not happen. O God I seek refuge in You..."

I finally got the traction I needed to cut the wire.

"Yes! I've just got to get rid of this vest!"

I started slicing through the Velcro that held the suicide vest in place, using my knife in brisk strokes. Finally, it fell free and I turned to throw it away from us.

But I was one long second too late.

Tick, tock.

Time's up.

A ball of flames shot up as the detonator functioned, heat shearing across my shoulder, the explosion almost at grenade strength.

Instinctively, I threw myself forward across Amira, hearing the sound of shrapnel flying through the air and thudding into the bomb suit. My ears were ringing and my brain felt like jelly in my skull, but I could tell from the sound that the main charge hadn't detonated. That, and the fact that I wasn't dead.

Amira was gasping for breath, her eyes wide as I crushed her with my weight. I think she tried to speak, but I was stone deaf. Her lips moved and I saw blood pouring from a deep cut on her cheek, scorch marks across her clothes, and her hands were painted crimson as she pointed.

I turned my head, the movement sending a shocking pain through me.

And I saw Clay.

Together we'd shielded Amira from most of the blast: but I was wearing a bomb suit—and he wasn't.

Clay was lying on the ground, coated in blood. So much blood all around him. His eyes blinking rapidly, his hands clamped around the top of his thigh. And the rest of his leg was 30 meters away, still in the denim jeans he'd been wearing that morning.

As if in slow motion, I saw Smith running toward us, shouting something.

I gave him a signal to say that the main charge was safe. He kept running toward us, skidding in Clay's blood as he knelt over him.

He was saying something, but Clay's eyes were closing.

Police and paramedics followed Smith, and I remember thinking how red Clay's blood was, and how much of it was coating the pavement outside the Disney store in Times Square.

The giant windows were shattered, lethal shards of glass lying everywhere. Mickey Mouse blown sky high.

But Amira was alive.

And I was alive.

Clay was ... I didn't know.

CHAPTER TWENTY-SIX

AMIRA

When I saw the flash of light, I thought that was it. Death had come for me at last. Death had finally won.

A blow hit me solidly in the chest, knocking the air from my lungs, and heat scorched me as I was flung backwards.

I couldn't breathe, couldn't move, couldn't make my lungs work.

And I waited. Waiting for that moment when my soul would leave my body. And for a moment, I think it did. I felt weightless, light as air, and without pain.

I spiralled upwards, calm and at peace, happy. The thin thread that bound me to my battered body would break soon, and I'd be free forever.

Amira, you have to wake up now.

Karam?

Then a feeling like I'd fallen from a great height as I slammed back to earth.

I gasped as someone drove a red hot branding iron into my side. The scream caught in my throat, or maybe I screamed and couldn't hear it. My ears were ringing and my whole body was being squeezed, suffocated.

Suddenly, the weight left me, and only then I realized that James was kneeling over me. He'd taken off his helmet and he was saying something. It seemed important, but I couldn't understand him.

Then he clamped his hands against my side, hurting me so badly. I screamed and screamed and screamed ... and then I was gone, floating in blackness, floating, floating...

Someone stabbed the back of my hand and I woke up to see an IV line attached to a bag of fluids.

I was in an ambulance, strapped to a gurney, and a paramedic was pressing white hot knives into my side.

No, that wasn't right.

Her lips were moving, and her eyes kept darting to mine, but I didn't see cruelty in them, only compassion. I think she was helping me, trying to tell me something, but my brain wasn't working and I was underwater, her voice coming from far away, so far away. I tried to focus on her mouth. It was forming shapes and her eyebrows went up. Ah, a question. What was she asking me?

I tried to speak but my throat was dry and my tongue too big for my mouth. I mumbled incoherently, but that seemed to please her. She smiled reassuringly and I tried to smile back, but my lips wouldn't make the shape. I had an important question to ask her, but I couldn't remember what it was.

Something cool and soothing flowed through my veins taking the pain with it. That felt nice. But I had to remember ... something I had to remember...

The next time I woke up, pain blasted through my entire body and I groaned.

"That's it, Amira. Wake up now. You're doing great. That's it, open your eyes. I'm Dr. Walden. Do you know where you are?"

My head was pounding and my eyelids felt heavy, but I managed to peel them open, squinting at the bright lights. My eyes focussed slowly on the person standing in front of me.

This man's eyes were the wrong colour—they were brown, not blue like a lake.

"Do you know where you are?"

"Hospital?" I croaked.

"Yes, that's good. Do you remember what happened to you?"

Tears pooled in my eyes.

"Bomb."

He spoke to someone standing behind me.

"Recall seems unaffected."

"James? Where?" I mumbled. "Clay?"

And then Smith moved into view beside me.

"Hey, there. You scared the shit out of us, but you're doing okay. You're in hospital. You have a punctured lung and you've, um, got a cut on your cheek, so there'll be a small scar, a few burns—it got pretty hot out there." He cleared his throat. "James is fine, caught some frag in his hand, but he's okay. He's being debriefed now."

James. Eyes like a summer morning.

"He saved my life," I wheezed.

Smith squeezed my hand gently.

"I know. He saved a lot of people. Guy's a hero. Don't tell him I said that," and he chuckled softly.

"Clay?"

I opened my eyes again when he didn't reply.

"Clay?"

"Well, I won't lie to you—he's not doing so great. He lost a lot of blood. He's in surgery now."

Oh no.

Tears weighed me down, pulling me under.

"Sleep now, Amira."

So I did.

CHAPTER TWENTY-SEVEN

JAMES

When I opened the door to Amira's hospital room, she screamed so loudly, I nearly dropped to the floor, looking around for the danger, reaching for a weapon I didn't have. And then I realized that she was screaming at me.

The hysterical noise shut off as suddenly as it had begun and she gasped, her hand flying to her injured cheek.

"Oh ... it's you."

Not the words I'd been hoping to hear, but it was a start.

Rubbing my bruised knee, I stood up cautiously.

"How are you?" I asked carefully, keeping my distance.

Her face crumpled, and I saw her fight to hold back the tears.

"Everything is an illusion!" she cried out.

Her words were confusing. Smith hadn't said anything about a traumatic brain injury, although that was always a possibility after being caught in a bomb blast.

"What do you mean?"

I edged closer, but she turned her head to stare at the wall.

"The idea that anything will be okay. Ever."

I stayed silent, weighing her words, and finally she turned to look at me.

"I'll never be able to relax, to turn it off. My mind, my body—I have all these memories trapped inside—and it's like I'll … explode … from having them all inside me." She closed her eyes. "I dream that I'm exploding."

I sat down on the chair next to her and cautiously reached for her hand. Her fingers were cold and limp but she didn't pull away.

"I know."

She grimaced.

"That's it? *You know?* No words of wisdom for me, James?"

Her voice was sharp, knives aimed at me. I flinched.

"I wish I did."

Her shoulders slumped.

"I'm sorry. I'm a mess. I don't know what I'm saying. Half the time I don't know what I'm thinking. Oh, you're hurt!"

The white of my sling blended in with the t-shirt that Smith had found for me.

"They had to dig out a few bits of metal, but I'm okay. They don't think there's any nerve damage. I'll have to wait for the swelling to go down to be sure." I shrugged uneasily. "I'm okay."

She bit her lip as tears leaked from her eyes, but she wiped them away angrily.

"They say I'll be scarred," she announced quickly, her dark eyes darting to mine and away again. "They got a plastic surgeon to sew up my face, but…"

The bandage on her cheek was stark against her pale caramel skin, and bruises covered her face, neck and arms.

Smith told me what they'd done to her. Just thinking about how she'd been violated, sent waves of anger rushing through me with enough adrenaline so that I shuddered with rage. Evil bastards. Soulless monsters. I wanted to kill them. I wanted to stand in front of them and watch as the blood drained from their bodies.

But my anger wasn't what Amira needed right now. I wasn't even sure I could do anything to help her, everything she was going through, but I had to try.

Because I cared. About her. And through all the craziness and pain and madness, the thought of saving her, of seeing her again, of seeing her smile, maybe even relaxed and happy after we'd made love…

But it was stupid to think of that.

I'd take what I could get, even if was just shadows.

"The doc says you'll be okay..."

She didn't answer for the longest time, and it was torture to sit there and wait for her to speak, and even then she didn't give me an answer.

"Do you think everything happens for a reason?"

"What? Like ... Fate?"

"I don't know, James," she said, her voice distant. "Maybe everything does happen for a reason—God's purpose for us all, *Inshallah*."

My response was immediate and dismissive.

"You think a fanatic like Umar happens for a reason? You think Clay lost his leg because it was God's purpose?"

She frowned. Maybe it was the anger in my voice, or maybe just the volume.

My voice shook.

"You think you were raped *for a reason?*"

She nodded slowly.

"Yes, they raped me for a reason—to shame me, to belittle me; to show me that I was nothing, less than human. To show that they had all the power and I had none. There were lots of reasons." She paused. "The question is: was that God's purpose for me?"

I gaped at her.

"Amira! You can't think..."

"Because it delayed them," she said quietly. "What they did to me ... took time. And in that time, you came for me. You found me and saved all those people—hundreds, maybe thousands of people." She cocked her head on one side. "Their vanity, their need to reduce me to nothing—that led to their failure, do you see?"

I swallowed hard. Was this what she needed? To believe that her rape had been for a higher purpose? The thought sickened me, and bile rose in my throat, choking me.

"I believe," I said slowly, "that they were evil bastards—and they're the ones who deserve to die."

"We all die one day," she said tiredly, turning away and staring at the wall.

"Amira, there were mums with kids in that Disney store, did you know that? Smith's people were able to get them away from the windows and to safety in time."

She gave a small smile.

"You see? God's purpose. You saved them, James. You saved me. I haven't thanked you. What you did was incredibly brave." Then she frowned. "But ... Clay. How is he?"

"He'll live," I said bleakly. "Minus one leg. They're talking about more operations..."

"Did you speak to him?"

"Yeah," I said, softening my voice. "He asked after you."

"What did he say?"

I turned away, the words like acid on my tongue.

"He said to tell you, 'Have faith.' That's what he said."

Amira smiled.

I'd never had much faith, but now I had none. Clay's words tasted foul as I said them, but she'd asked me, and I promised myself that I'd tell her the truth if she did ask.

I didn't know what to say to her, I just knew that I didn't want to leave her. Smith had told me that she still needed to be debriefed and he'd be by to do that soon.

Suddenly, Amira's door opened, but it wasn't Smith. I didn't know these people, but I had a shrewd idea who they were.

"*Ya aynee!*"

Amira's face was blank for half a second and then a tentative smile grew wider as her eyes became glassy with tears.

"Baba! Mama! Zada! How...? When...?"

They crowded around her bed, talking in English, then rapid Arabic, then English again, words halting and broken as her mother and sister cried, and her father sat with his head bowed, tears running down his lined face, grasping one of her hands in his.

I watched for a few seconds, then turned to leave. They were her family and I was ... no one. But Amira called my name.

"James!" and she looked at her parents. "This is James."

They gazed at me, puzzled and wary.

"He saved my life."

Her father stood up slowly.

"You? You're the one."

I nodded.

He held out his hand, shaking my good hand formally, then grasping it in both of his with a surprisingly strong grip.

"Thank you," he said, his voice broken. "Thank you for saving my child."

I was uncomfortable with his thanks, and the way Amira's mother and sister gazed at me, fresh tears on their cheeks.

"You're welcome," I said stupidly. *Bloody hell, could I be more ridiculous?* "I'll, er, see you later."

Amira didn't even notice when I left.

CHAPTER TWENTY-EIGHT

AMIRA

It was comforting to have my family with me, but there were so many tears, so many truths to unpick from the myriad of lies I'd told them. They were hurt, angry, and so scared for me.

I felt like I was carrying the weight of their sadness on top of my own.

They were staying in a nearby hotel and visited every day. My parents seemed bewildered, unable to understand what I'd done and why. So they focused on my physical recovery, talking about when I'd go back to work, when I'd be in California again—anything that focused on the future.

Zada was quiet, and I knew that she was upset and angry—she didn't understand my choices at all. I saw her looking at me like she didn't know who I was anymore. I didn't blame her because I felt the same. I wasn't the woman I'd been before Karam's death, and I wasn't the woman I'd been before I met Smith. But I didn't know what this new version of Amira would be. And no one could tell me.

As soon as I was able to, I went to see Clay.

I thought he was asleep when I first saw him, and I took in the cage over the bed, keeping the sheets away from his injured leg. His eyes were covered with gauze, and I knew he had burns on his eyelids that they were treating. But then his sleepy voice made me look up.

"Hello?"

"It's Amira."

"Hey, girl!" His voice was weaker than I remembered it. "It's good to see you. Well, not see you exactly. But thanks for coming."

I smiled and sat down next to him, taking his hand in mine.

"It's good to see you, too. How are you?"

"I've been better. You?"

"Yes, I've been better, too, but I'll be okay."

We sat in silence, holding hands, with so much to say, and I didn't know where to start.

"You didn't leave me," I said, my voice shaking.

"*Ya amar*, I'd never leave you. I told you that."

"What you did, what happened to you ... I don't even know how to..."

"Don't," he said quietly. "I'd do it all over again. No regrets, Amira. I promise you. I have no regrets."

Tears began to trickle down my cheeks as he squeezed my hand.

"Thank you for saving my life," I hiccupped.

"Nah, you need to thank that crazy Brit," he said, forcing a smile. "He's the one in love with you."

His words were a sudden drenching of ice water.

"What? No!" I shook my head vehemently. "You're wrong, Clay."

"Hmm, I don't think so. Give him a chance, Amira. He's a good guy. Now, tell me about your sister. Is she single?"

I gaped at him, my brain reeling.

"Zada?"

"Yeah, she sounded cute," he grinned.

"How do you even know her?"

His expression became serious.

"She came to see me. She wanted to, you know, thank me and all that. We got talking." He smiled, his eyes glinting with mischief. "So? Is she single?"

"She's too good for you," I laughed.

"Aw, don't be jealous," he teased.

Suddenly, the door opened and James was standing there, a look of surprise on his face.

"Hi," he said quietly.

"And there's the man of the hour," grinned Clay. "Good to see you, brother."

"I'd better go," I said, standing up hurriedly. "I'll see you later, Clay."

"I'll count on it," he said.

James just watched me leave.

I couldn't think about him, I just couldn't.

I almost ran down the corridor to my room, determined to think of anything except him.

Not that I had much time for introspection, and maybe that was deliberate.

For one thing, I had to meet with Smith's people every day, whoever he worked for—I never found out—they continued the debriefing. They extracted every tiny detail of information from me about who I'd seen at the camps, what had been said, what had been done and when, any names or places that had been mentioned, what we wore, what we ate, where we slept, the toilet and washing facilities, and numerous other details that seemed inconsequential to me. Then they'd asked me to describe the methods used for making the explosives and detonators, how they were stored, packed and transported.

I had to describe Larson's death several times, which was exhausting and horrific, until it occurred to me that they were testing me for any differences in my report that might mean I was lying. That hurt, and then it made me angry. I'd nearly died trying to be some sort of super-agent, when the reality was I was just me, poor and pathetic and a terrible undercover spy. And I knew, I knew that I was responsible for Larson's death. If I'd been stronger or cleverer or more aware, I would have escaped, and then Larson would be alive.

It drove me crazy, repeating myself over and over, especially since all the information was going one way. I kept asking if they'd caught Umar, Munassar and the others, but they never answered.

I was also encouraged to have daily meetings with a therapist: some sessions were long, some short, and we talked about everything that I'd been through—not just the rapes, but the stress of the last year. She was an army doctor as well as a psychiatrist, so she had a lot of experience in combat stress. That's what she told me. It seemed odd at first to think that the nightmares I suffered were considered combat stress, but she was right. I had been in combat, I had been a soldier.

I shivered when she said that. It reminded me too much of Umar's final words to me: *Time to become a soldier of ISIS.*

They brought an *Imam* in to see me, as well. It was comforting to talk to him. He was nearing ninety years of age, calm and wise.

"You have been through much, daughter," he said, his cheeks hollow and his hands as frail as a bird's wing. "I will pray with you—but let me give you this piece of advice. I am an old man, but the years have taught me this one thing I know to be true: do not hold hatred in your heart, because hatred will destroy you. Love, daughter, love—that is the real strength in this world. As the Holy Book says, *'Stand out firmly for Allah ... and let not the enmity and hatred of others make you avoid justice. Be just, that is nearer to piety'.*"

We talked about what had happened to me and to Karam. He talked with me, prayed with me, and even cried with me. I thought I'd cried enough tears, but these were precious.

And then there was James.

He came to the hospital every day, awkward and sad, beautiful and lost, unable to say what he wanted to say, but I caught him watching me, his eyes always on me.

"Hey, Amira."

He was back again and I wasn't sure why.

I closed the book I'd been reading and for a second, he hovered uncertainly, then he pulled a chair next to my bed and sat down.

"How are you?"

I almost laughed. How could I possibly answer that question? So I gave him the simplest reply.

"I'm healing. How are you?"

He gave a small smile and gestured at the sling.

"I'll be able to get rid of this in a couple of days," then he frowned. "They'll be sending me home soon."

"Me, too."

He nodded slowly, then took a deep breath, but I spoke first.

"My parents are looking forward to me going home. They talk about 'getting back to normal' but I don't know what that is anymore."

James nodded as if he understood.

"I think we all feel like that," he said slowly, "when you've seen combat. Civilian life seems ... out of focus, somehow. Less real. I don't know how to explain it."

I thought about that and it made sense. The sheer intensity of the past few weeks was in sharp focus, so clear in my mind, all those tiny details imprinted. In comparison, my time as a nurse seemed very long ago.

"I don't know how to go back," I said simply.

"Maybe you need to do something new," he said, speaking slowly as if he was choosing his words carefully.

"Maybe, but I don't know what."

"I've been thinking a lot, while Smith had me locked up and..."

"What? Smith did what?!"

His words had taken me by surprise, and I didn't think he'd meant to tell me that because I saw his grimace.

"Um, yeah. I guess you didn't know that part."

"Why on earth would Smith lock you up?"

Colour rose in his cheeks and he looked embarrassed.

"After that last night," he cleared his throat as I looked away. "When we were together. After you said what happened to your brother, you said, 'I really hate them'."

"I remember," I said softly, painfully aware of his eyes on me.

"I, well, I thought you meant that you hated Americans, because of the bombs dropped by American drones. I was worried..."

I stared at him, comprehension dawning slowly.

"You thought I was a traitor?!"

He winced but didn't look away.

"I thought it was a possibility. And I thought Clay should know what had happened to your brother, so I tried to discuss it with Smith."

"I'm assuming it didn't go well..."

He gave a grim smile.

"You could say that. Larson put me in a choke hold until I was unconscious, then they tied me up and chucked me in the back of

Smith's truck. When I came to, I was on my way to some spook safe house in New York. They locked me in a room for the next three weeks. I didn't know what was going on. I didn't know if you were okay, if Clay was okay, if the world had ended—nothing. When Smith finally came back, it was to ask me to help with the terror attacks."

I was having difficulty absorbing everything he said.

"You came to help me even though you thought I was a double-agent?"

He shook his head at my sharp words.

"I'm sorry about that, more sorry than I can tell you. After three weeks of being locked up, I was past trusting anyone, but when I thought about you..." his voice lowered. "I thought about the night we spent together." When I didn't speak, he eventually continued. "I didn't have the full story, but Smith filled me in. Finally." He met my eyes. "I'm so sorry that I ever doubted you—I feel sick about that."

"I can't believe you thought that about me," I said, confused and upset.

"I can't believe I ever thought it either," he said, his voice pained. "After what we'd shared..."

If he meant to talk about the night I'd spent in his arms, he didn't, and I definitely wasn't going to start that conversation. It was too much right now. I couldn't carry his pain as well as my own.

"Don't, James. I can't think about that now."

He sighed and we sat in silence for several minutes.

"When are you going home?" I asked at last.

"I don't know exactly. Although there's no point leaving until I'm fully fit," and he gestured at his sling. "Soon, I guess." He looked out of the window, his gaze lost in the distance. "It'll be weird going back." Then he glanced up at me. "Maybe I could call you some time?"

I couldn't cope with this. I had to steer this conversation in a different direction.

"Maybe you could email me," I said, too brightly. "Since we're friends."

"Friends?"

He rolled the word around slowly, and I saw some of the light in his eyes fade.

"Sure," he said at last. "Friends. Yeah, I'll email you."

He left soon after that, but every morning, he was there at the hospital again. But with each day that passed, the distance between us increased.

It sometimes felt like he wanted to say more, but the words never made it past his lips, and he'd leave, sadder and more defeated.

Sometimes, I wished he would say what was really on his mind, but in other ways I shrank from him.

My therapist said I should only talk to him when I was ready. But I never was. I wasn't sure I'd ever be ready to talk about that night. Maybe if I didn't feel so ugly, so dirty…

I touched the scar on my cheek. I'd seen it in a mirror and nearly been sick. It was ugly and raw, U-shaped where a chunk of metal had torn open a flap of skin and removed some of the muscle and fat underneath. My mouth drooped slightly on one side, and my cheek was lumpy and uneven. The surgeon said that implants or collagen injections could help in the future, but first I had to heal.

I also had a gap in my bottom teeth where a tooth had been knocked out.

My body had was healing inside, too, where those monsters had ripped me apart.

I was ashamed for James to see me, and always sat with my unscarred side facing him. Stupid, I know, because he'd seen my scars, all of them, but it was hard to face him when I was so disfigured, and he was so heartbreakingly handsome.

I saw the nurses flirting with him, smiling at him, wanting those blue eyes all to themselves, but when he acknowledged them, his gaze seemed to float through them, seeking me out instead. Even now, he watched me, just like when we were at our cabin and he was training me, he watched.

But he'd risked his life to save mine, and I needed to talk to him.

Maybe tomorrow.

Or the day after.

Or next week.

Next month.

Since he mostly visited Clay in the mornings, I went in the afternoons.

"Are you avoiding him?" Clay asked me abruptly, one day. "I mean, I know he sees you, but he says you never want to really talk to him."

I didn't even bother pretending I didn't know who he meant.

"Is that obvious?"

"Pretty much. But I don't know why, and he doesn't either."

I sighed.

"It's all so complicated. I just want us to be friends."

"Hmm, well, if that's how you *really* feel," and he paused on the word for emphasis, "you should tell him that. Just be sure it's what you want."

I knew he was right. I was being unfair, but the thought of talking to James was too much to handle. I had so many thoughts and feelings whirling around in my head.

One day, Smith came to see me, and I begged him to tell me the truth, everything that had been kept from me so far.

He shrugged.

"Umar is contained, his network finished."

I stared at him and doubted.

"What does 'contained' mean? You've caught him, right? He's not going to come after me, after my family?"

He started to lay his hand on my shoulder, but I flinched away from him. I couldn't bear anyone to touch me—not even the nurses or the doctors. I was pathological about being touched.

He pulled up a chair so that he sat close to me, but not too close. Even so, I inched back on the hospital bed. I knew theoretically that I had nothing to fear from Smith, but my body didn't know that.

"I promise you, Amira. He'll never touch you again, none of them will."

"Are they in jail? Will they be tried for what they did?"

He rubbed his fingers over the scruff on his chin and it was only then I noticed how tired he looked, his expression haunted. And I remembered that Larson had been his friend. I closed my eyes—we'd all lost so much.

"I can't answer that," he said finally. "Let's just say, they'll never hurt anyone again."

I didn't know what that meant. Were they dead? In some secret prison? Being reprogrammed? Maybe even tortured?

I shuddered.

"Surely it will just make the men who follow him more desperate?"

Smith gave his usual half-answer.

"He only has power when people fear him—he no longer has power."

But that just makes his followers more dangerous, I thought. When a man has nothing to lose…

I had to accept that I'd never know the whole truth, that I'd never see justice for the men who'd raped me, who'd tried to kill me, who'd plotted to use me to kill others. But just because I couldn't see justice, it didn't mean it wasn't happening. Rightly or wrongly, foolish or not, I still trusted Smith. He said the men were 'contained', and that had to be enough for me. Maybe it was better that way. Maybe.

"Did you find the mole in your department?" I asked, wondering if he'd answer honestly. "Did they tell Umar about my brother, my real name? Is my family at risk?"

He smiled grimly.

"Because of what we've learned," and he pointed at me, "we were able to close in."

"And arrest the asshole?"

He cocked his head on one side.

"That's not the way we do things, Amira, you know that. But believe me when I say that finding who was leaking intel has been invaluable. And we'll put that knowledge to good use."

I sighed, defeated, because I did know that. If the mole could be useful, he or she would be an asset. Just like I'd been an asset.

A knock on the door interrupted my grim thoughts and my doctor walked in, tall and austere, his steel-coloured hair reassuring.

"I have good news. You're doing really well, so we're going to be sending you home soon, Amira. Now, let's take this dressing off your cheek and take a look. Yes, that's healing nicely."

Dr. Walden's words scared me. I wasn't ready to go home.

"Your punctured lung has healed well, so it's safe for you to travel by air now." He smiled kindly. "And I know your parents want you home."

I nodded, not knowing what to say, or how to express how unready I was to face life again.

Smith was watching intently, but he didn't smile. And when the doctor left, he leaned forwards, spearing me with the severity of his gaze.

"I won't tell you it's going to be okay because I know you have a lot of shit to deal with, but you *will* deal with it," he said firmly. "You're not broken, Amira. You're very far from broken, and you still have a lot of living to do."

He sounded so certain. But then again, he would, wouldn't he.

"Come on," he said, standing up and giving me a small smile. "Let's go see Clay."

I'd visited Clay many more times during the last few weeks, most days in fact, but often he was heavily medicated and in a lot of pain, so we hadn't spoken much again. I'd sat with him and held his hand because he was the one person, the one man I could touch without flinching.

But when we arrived, Clay was sitting up in bed, smiling tiredly, and the bandages covering his eyes had been removed.

He was talking to James.

"Hey, girl!" said Clay cheerfully. "You're a sight for sore eyes."

I froze on the spot, horrified by his comment, and he grimaced, his chagrin clear.

"Aw, heck. I'd say I'd put my foot in my mouth, but now I've only got one, that's not such a good idea, huh?"

I laughed abruptly, shocked out of my stupor, and Clay grinned at me.

"I got a ton of one-legged jokes. You want to hear them?"

"Not really," I answered truthfully.

But Clay ignored me and cheerfully ploughed on.

"What do you say to a one-legged hitchhiker? *Hop in!* Aw, come on, that was funny! Wait, this is better ... what's my favourite restaurant? *IHOP!* No, okay, how about this ... what do you call a sheep with no legs? A cloud!"

I started to giggle, and even though it tugged the stitches in my cheek, I couldn't stop.

"Those are so lame!" and then I clapped my hand over my mouth in horror.

Clay stared then slapped the sheets on the bed, howling with laughter.

James grinned at him, and Smith shook his head, a smile creeping across his face.

And suddenly, it was just us again, back at the cabin, the four of us, laughing at Clay being ridiculous.

As the laughter died away, Clay reached for my hand. I didn't flinch, instead accepting his warm touch.

"It's good to see you today. I was too drugged up to appreciate it much before." Then he squeezed my hand. "You look good—I didn't know you had hair. I thought you were bald like this dude," and he jerked his head at James.

I touched my hair self-consciously. For the first few days without a head-covering, I'd felt very exposed, but I was getting used to it again now, even though people stared at my scar. I'd honestly even considered wearing the *niqab* again to avoid that. But no, that wasn't who I was.

James was watching me again, and I had to turn away from the intensity of his gaze.

Clay sighed and tugged the end of my hair, bringing my attention back to him.

"It's great to see you guys."

"How are you really?" I asked tentatively.

He shrugged, his hand dropping to the sheets as if the movement had exhausted him.

"Well, my leg isn't going to grow back, but they said they'll fix me up with a new one. Something cool, like Steve Austin."

I blinked, puzzled.

"Who?"

It was James who answered.

"Pop culture reference if you're into old sh— stuff. Steve Austin was the Six Million Dollar Man, like in that TV programme from the seventies."

"Uh-huh! Mark Wahlberg is starring in the remake!" said Clay. "Current affairs, my friend!"

We all stared at him.

"What?"

It was so normal, so bizarrely normal. My heart cracked open and the tears began to flow—ugly, salty rivers turned my eyes red and made my nose run. Smith passed me a tissue.

"Aw, honey, my jokes aren't that bad," Clay said, his voice kind and sad.

"I'm sorry," I hiccupped. "I'm sorry!"

His face crumpled.

"Damn! I'd give you a hug right now but I kind of can't move. James, dude! Give the girl a hug!"

I looked away because I couldn't bear to see James' face, but then I felt his touch, light and tentative, and with a piercing wail, I fell against his chest, huge quivering sobs tearing out of me.

His good arm tightened and he murmured softly against my hair.

I couldn't hear what he was saying and I didn't care.

He was holding me, and I wasn't scared.

CHAPTER TWENTY-NINE

JAMES

It was the first real emotion I'd seen from Amira.

I held her as choking tears tore through her thin body. She'd lost a lot of weight since I'd first met her, and I could feel her ribs against my arms. I held her tighter, sharing a look of concern with Clay until he coughed and glanced away, while Smith discreetly exited the room.

It took an excruciating ten minutes of her crying her guts out and me feeling like a complete twat because I couldn't help her.

Finally, she was all cried out, her body becoming weak and limp.

I knew what she was going through—I'd been there and I still struggled with it all. The technical term was *survivors' guilt*.

Larson had been killed in front of her, and Clay was missing a leg. Other civilians had been injured by flying glass that day, and a police officer had been blinded in one eye. I knew what that felt like. A lot more people had been scared shitless and would be having years of bad dreams and therapy after seeing the detonator function, of seeing Clay being torn apart.

You don't get over it—that's not possible. You have to find a way to go on. The ones that don't are the guys who end up in their garages with a hose attached to the car exhaust.

Smith told me that Amira was seeing a shrink. I'd been offered the same help and had even tried it once; but for me, going over it again and again had never done me any favours. In fact, I'd say it made things worse. But that was me. I knew talking about it could help other people. I was wired differently.

So I held her, because sometimes human touch is the only reality left to cling to, and I'd wanted to do this for so long. Holding her calmed something inside myself, something ugly and fierce that had been screaming for blood.

Finally, she stopped crying and started to pull away from me. She looked down at my chest and grimaced. I saw that she'd left a damp patch on my t-shirt.

"Well, that was embarrassing," she said with a shaky voice as she wiped her eyes.

"Yeah, I didn't know where to look," said Clay cheerfully.

I mouthed *fuck off* while Amira's back was turned. Clay ignored it, smiling at me with a cheesy grin.

I'd sat with the bastard for hours every day since we'd all been brought to this hospital. And I knew that he was full of shit. He was putting on a great show for Amira but the guy was struggling. He didn't know what life as an amputee would mean for him. He didn't think he'd be getting much help from his family, and he was scared but trying not to show it. I didn't blame him. But I didn't know how to help him either. I couldn't help him or Amira—I couldn't even help myself.

"I didn't mean to cry all over you," she said, wiping her nose on a tissue.

"Aw, don't apologize," said Clay. "He loves being your knight in shining armour. Assuming all the salt water hasn't rusted him."

"What part of 'fuck off' don't you understand?" I groused, but he just grinned harder.

"We're Team Dare! We laugh in the face of danger. Then we eat a pint of ice cream and cry over *Call of the Wild*."

"What are you talking about?" I asked.

"Just saying that we've bonded over life experiences," he said more seriously. "So Amira cried all over you—we've known worse."

His words were sincere. Unfortunately, they made sense, too. Not that I'd tell him that.

"I love you, Clay," said Amira. "Even when you're being an asshole."

I fought off a surge of jealously while he laughed loudly.

"Girl, I just can't get used to you swearing. And having hair. It's freaking me out."

She smiled shyly, her hand flying to her scarred cheek.

"It's strange," she admitted. "I've rejected the idea of being veiled my whole life, but there was a sort of freedom with it, too. Standing out, but being anonymous, as well. It's hard to explain." She shook her head. "It did feel hot, though. But I got used to it."

"Would you wear it again?" I asked, surprised by her words.

"Not a *burqa*, no. It's too hard to see or hear. Besides, that was part of my undercover role—I'd never worn anything like it before. My sister, Zada, started wearing a *hijab* when she was fifteen. She says it's important to her—part of her identity. I never really understood, but I kind of do now." She sighed. "But I hate it, too. I hate that *those people* took everything good about Islam and twisted it out of all recognition and made it into something evil." She looked up. "But what's scarier, they really believed that they were doing the right thing, the necessary thing." She shuddered. "But I couldn't do it again. I couldn't go undercover. I'm not a very good agent."

She shook her head tiredly.

"Yeah," said Clay seriously. "It changes you. Not always in bad ways, but not always in good ways either."

We all glanced down at the space where his leg should be.

I sat there and listened to them as they talked about their time with the terror cell, and I felt again the distance between us. They'd shared something that I hadn't, couldn't—and I was on the outside again.

But later on, the talk turned to what it meant to be different from civilians, and I glanced at Amira—we were all combat vets now.

"How much longer are you going to be in town for, bro?" Clay asked me casually.

"Five days, then I ship out."

His face fell, and Amira stared at the floor. Both reactions made me feel like shit. But did it mean that she'd miss me after all?

"Smith could get the doc to tell your C.O. that you're still not fit," said Clay hopefully, gesturing to my hand. "He knows how to pull strings. Hell, he's got a PhD in being a manipulative bastard."

I glanced down at my hand, studying the raw ridge of pink skin. The scar had healed pretty well and I didn't seem to have lost any fine motor skills. That was good, because a bomb disposal officer with shaky hands was as useful as a one-legged man in an arse-kicking competition. Shit. *Sorry, Clay.*

Then Amira spoke.

"The doctor says I can go home soon, too."

We all fell silent, and it felt like another nail in the coffin of a relationship that we'd never really had.

If I stayed, what would be the point? Amira was going back to her home in California soon, and Clay was being shipped out to a veteran's hospital near his family in Ohio, whether he wanted that or not. Chances were, he'd be invalided out of the service, too.

"Nah, that's okay. But I'll hang here until my flight." I pointed at Clay. "Make sure this turnip makes it back to the boondocks."

"Is that a cultural slur?" asked Clay, arching one eyebrow.

"Nah, buddy. I'm mixed race—English and Scottish."

He laughed, then his expression sobered.

"I'm going to miss the heck out of you guys. Friends to the end."

Amira smiled sadly as she glanced at me.

"Yes, friends."

Smith returned to talk with Clay about his rehab programme, and I walked Amira back to her room so she could pack up her things.

I definitely wasn't expecting the conversation that hit me right between the eyes as she shoved clothes into a small carry-on bag.

"I want to ask you something, as my friend. It's important ... but I don't know how to say it..."

"You can ask me anything, Amira. If I can do it, I will."

"I was going to leave it longer because ... well, anyway. I guess we've run out of time."

She still wasn't looking at me, so I had no clue where this conversation was going.

"Amira, name it."

"You might change your mind ... and this isn't easy for me."

Without knowing what she wanted, I didn't know how to react.

"Just ask me."

She took a deep breath and I noticed that her hands were shaking.

"Will you sleep with me?"

"What?"

I swallowed several times, staring at her in shock. It was what I wanted, what I'd been dreaming of, but the timing was all wrong.

"Amira..."

"I want you to sleep with me, James."

"Are you serious? You can't be serious! After what those bast— after everything that happened!"

"Okay, I get it," she said softly, turning away.

I was so confused, my brain felt like it would melt.

"Get what? What is there to get? Jeez, Amira!"

Her eyes filled with tears and her voice shook.

"I understand. I get it. I'm *ugly!*"

I heard the words but they didn't compute. I stared at the back of her head as she sat heavily on the bed, her shoulders shaking.

"What? No, you're not," I said, my voice as raw as my emotions. "You're so fucking brave and beautiful. I'm half in love with you and ... you're amazing."

I cringed at my appalling choice of words.

She gave a choking laugh.

"Half in love? What does that mean? Are you in love with my pretty half?"

I swallowed and ran my hands over my head, absently noting that it was time to shave it again.

"No. I don't know," I admitted. "I've never felt this way before so I don't know what it means. But the thought of you going back to ... I don't even know where you're from!"

She still wasn't looking at me.

"Chula Vista," she said quietly. "It's a city in southern California— seven miles from San Diego and seven miles from the Mexican border."

I slumped in the chair at the side of the bed and dropped my head into my hands.

"I wish you didn't live there. I wish I didn't live where I live. I hate that you'll be 6,000 miles away from me." I heaved in a breath. "And don't talk shit saying you're ugly."

I think my words shocked her because she turned around and pointed at her scar.

"This isn't ugly?" she sneered. "I've *seen* the way people stare at me, even here in the hospital. I've *seen* the pity in their eyes."

"You haven't seen me look at you like that."

Her eyes widened.

"No," she said softly. "I haven't. Why is that?"

My answer was simple.

"I don't see it. Amira, I met you when you were wearing a *niqab* and I had no idea what you looked like. All I could see was your eyes. I like your eyes. That sounds stupid. But they haunted me. I saw them in my dreams. I'm telling the truth—I don't see your scar."

I moved to stand in front of her as I gently traced my finger down the puckered, red line.

"But I'm looking now. And I see an incredibly brave woman who was willing to give her life for her country, who nearly did. You'll always be beautiful to me."

She threw me a haughty look then turned her back.

"If I'm so *beautiful*, then why don't you want to sleep with me?"

He words were harsh and grating.

"I never said I didn't want to sleep with you."

"Don't *lie*, James!" she said fiercely.

"I'm not lying!"

"'You can't be serious!' Those were your exact words!"

I tried to hold her hand but she pulled free.

"Yeah, I said that, but it doesn't mean I don't want to—it means I feel sick at the thought of hurting you!" My voice was so loud, I was almost shouting with frustration. "Damn it, Amira! Look at me!"

She turned around slowly, her chest rising and falling quickly, and I didn't know if it was from anger or because she was going to cry again. I didn't want either.

"Then stay with me tonight," she whispered. "Smith has reserved a room at the same hotel as my parents. Stay with me."

I grimaced.

"With your parents breathing down my neck?"

She stared at me defiantly.

"Yes."

"And they'll be okay with that?"

"No."

I shook my head.

"Great."

"Please," she said quietly. "Please. I don't want my last memory of ... of being ... I don't want my last memory to be of *them*. I want ... no, I *need* to overwrite it with something good. I need to do this, and I want to do it with a friend. I need to reclaim my body. Please, James, I need this. I need *you*."

CHAPTER THIRTY

AMIRA

I was nervous as hell. I'd insisted on this, forced him into a corner, until he'd given in. And now I was sitting in an anonymous hotel room, with my parents and sister down the hall, waiting for James to knock on my door.

I caught a glimpse of myself in the mirror, and felt the burn of tears behind my eyes again as I stared at my scar. It was ugly. *I* was ugly. The bruises had faded from my body, and everything on the inside was healed—no lasting damage, the doctor said. But what the hell did he know?

And it was madness to offer my body to a man, even James. I cared for him, maybe even loved him a little if I was honest. Talking to Clay had forced me to see that James had feelings for me, real ones, and in a way, that made this all the more confusing.

If I'd had more time, I wouldn't be doing this now, tonight, but we were both leaving, travelling in different directions and the chances were I wouldn't see him again.

Even so, I was literally shaking with nerves and ready to vomit. And yet still I didn't want to change my mind either. Ideally, I'd have had longer to make this choice, but I knew in my head and my heart that I needed this with James to help me heal, to erase the horror of the men who'd raped me, to prove to myself that I was stronger, that I wasn't broken. Dented, yes; damaged, definitely; broken ... I wasn't going to let them win.

There was a knock on my door, soft and tentative.

I stood up, suddenly wishing I had something else to wear, not a pair of Zada's pajamas with candy pink stripes.

"Who is it?" I called out, peering through the spyhole, choking on the words as my mouth dried.

"James."

I slid the chain from the door, turned the lock and opened the door. He was standing there, his hands shoved in the pockets of a worn pair of jeans, a dark grey t-shirt clinging to his chest.

"Hi."

"Hi." He paused. "Do you still want me to come in or...?"

"Oh, sorry, yes!" I rambled. "Come in."

I opened the door wider and he stepped inside, hesitating near the threshold.

"Is this okay?"

I swallowed.

"I'm really nervous," I admitted. "Last time we ... well, I was too scared to care."

His face fell.

"Ugh! I didn't mean it like that. I'm just really nervous. Different nerves."

He stayed rooted to the spot.

"We don't have to do this, Amira. You don't have to do anything."

I tugged my hair back in frustration.

"I do! I just don't know if I can!"

He rocked on his heels, then nodded at the TV on the wall.

"Want to watch something?"

I blinked.

"Like what?"

"Anything."

"Oh, right. Okay, why not. Um, sit ... anywhere."

There was a hard, upright chair by the wall tucked under a small desk. He pulled it out and sat on the edge, rubbing his hands on his thighs.

"Is that comfortable?" I asked.

"Uh, not really," he said with a low chuckle.

I flipped on the TV then stared at the bed between us. It seemed enormous, looming even larger in my imagination. My mind went into freefall and I started to shake.

"Oh shit!"

I heard James' voice as if from a long way away, and then someone was holding me, and I tried to fight them off, tried to get away, but those arms held me tightly.

The scream was lost in my throat, but then I heard his voice, soft and pleading.

"Amira, baby, don't cry. It's going to be okay. God, please don't cry!"

He held me, his strong arms wrapping around me, letting the panic leak away, until I was spent and lethargic.

He carried me to the bed, letting my body rest against his chest, and we lay there, his warmth and strength soothing me.

All the anxiety bubbled under but didn't erupt again. I felt almost safe. Safer.

And I was tired of being scared, tired of feeling broken, tired of being defeated. So tired.

I woke suddenly, my body jerking awake. I couldn't remember what I'd been dreaming about, but I was left with an oppressive air, an uneasy mind.

The curtains were open, casting the room in a soft neon glow. And I wasn't alone.

With a shock of recognition, I saw that James was awake and watching me, always watching me.

"Are you okay?" he asked, his voice worried.

He was stretched out on the bed with his arm around me, my legs tangled with his. He was still wearing his sneakers, and I knew that he hadn't moved since he'd carried me to bed hours earlier.

"I'm ... I don't know what I am," I sighed wearily, and I tapped my head. "Too many thoughts."

His lips tilted upwards, but it wasn't a full smile. His expression was solemn.

"Yeah, I know what that's like."

I studied him carefully, the sadness dimming his beautiful eyes.

"Why are you here, James?"

He swallowed.

"Because you asked me and ... because I couldn't stay away."

On impulse, I kissed him.

For half a second, there was no response and I knew that I'd taken him by surprise, but then his hands reached around me carefully, and I felt the soft, warm press of his lips on mine.

He started at one side, just a gentle pressure against the corner of my mouth, light, teasing kisses along the seam until he reached the other corner, always gentle.

He paused, then leaned up on one elbow, pushing my hair out of my eyes and tucking it behind my ear.

I held my breath as he caressed my damaged cheek.

"You're beautiful," he whispered.

I jerked away, leaving his hand suspended in the air.

"Don't!" I hissed.

His hand fell to the sheets.

"I have limited vision in my right eye," he said. "Limited mobility in my right thumb, and I have six teeth that are implants—all from blast injuries."

"I didn't know," I whispered, but he continued talking.

"I have multiple scars on my right arm and a new scar on my left hand." He stared right at me. "Does any of that matter to you?"

"It matters that you were hurt, but no..."

"Then do me the courtesy of believing me when I say that you're beautiful."

He stared at me, his eyebrows pinched together, frustration reflected in his gaze.

"Oh!" I took a deep breath. "I'm sorry."

He held my hand and kissed my fingers.

"Don't be sorry, Amira. I care about you. I thought I'd never see you again. I didn't even know if I could trust you but I still cared— how crazy is that?"

"You really thought I could be that devious? Some sort of double agent?"

He shrugged and gave me a half smile.

"I have trust issues."

We both laughed miserably. What a mess.

I traced my hand along the line of his jaw and made a decision.

"No regrets," I whispered. "Make love to me, James."

"Are you sure?" he asked, and I heard the note of desperation in his voice. "We don't have to. I mean, I want to, but..."

"Ssh," I pressed my finger against his lips. "I trust you, James. And I need this."

He nodded slowly.

"Tell me what you need, Amira. Show me."

James let me make love to him.

He let me pull his t-shirt over his head, and he let me trace the hard planes of chest with my tongue. He let me unbuckle his belt and slide it from the loops, and he lifted his hips so I could tug his jeans from his body. He let me run my hands along the thick length of his shaft, his breaths faster and shallower, and he let me take him in my mouth.

His hands hovered over my pajamas and over my waist, then gently rubbing my arms.

He let me make the choices and he let me set the pace.

He let me place his hands on my breasts, squeezing gently, and then he kissed my chest, my throat, my cheeks and mouth, whispering that I was strong and beautiful and desirable. His strained voice told me how sexy I was, how hot I made him, and that he wasn't going to last much longer.

And when he stroked the insides of my thighs, he was so gentle, his touch so knowing, that it felt right, and it felt safe.

He pulled a condom from his jeans and handed it to me, holding his breath as I rolled it down his shaft.

Then I sank onto him slowly, uncertain and afraid, as we rocked steadily together. Bad memories battered at the borders of our lovemaking, but his quiet words, his touch, the sweat that broke out across my body, pushed the darkness away.

It was completely different from the first time we were in bed together. That had been about fear and need and desperation.

This, now, I needed it. I was so afraid that the last memory of being with a man would be one of pain and violence. I needed to try and wash it away. There was no one else I could ask, no one else I *would* ask, but James.

This was softer, quieter, just us, hot, but more loving, more knowing, understanding, about friendship, about love, about repair, about rebirth—not hatred, not horror.

A blistering heat roared up inside me, consuming me. My skin fizzed with electric shocks shooting up and down my body. I was hot, cold, wired, tired, a knot of jarring emotions and sensations.

It was shocking and wonderful, and it was healing.

His head tilted backwards as he came, but his eyes were fixed on mine. My mouth opened and a long sob of desire poured out of me in a wordless river of sound.

And when we lay together, our bodies cooling and calming, he held me against his body as if nothing could ever harm me again. The greyhound grace of his body was beautiful and I sighed at the thought of letting him go.

I woke abruptly, panic shooting through me.

James yelled out, making me jump and wriggle away from him. But I realized that his skin was slick with sweat, and he was fast asleep, caught in a nightmare's web.

I slid out of bed, still naked, and reached out to touch his shoulder.

He jerked and lashed out, making me squeal and fall backwards, landing on the carpet with a thud.

His eyes flew open as he sat up, the sheet falling to his waist.

Swearing softly, he jumped out of bed and reached for me, flinching as I pulled away.

"Did I hurt you?"

"No," I said nervously. "Just ... startled."

"You're shaking! God, I'm so sorry."

I let him help me up, then he strode wordlessly to the bathroom and I heard him splashing water on his face.

Eventually, he came back into the room, standing at the side of the bed, eyeing his pile of clothes as if he was about to bolt.

I patted his side of the bed, already cold. Reluctantly, he sat on the edge, facing away from me.

I hesitated to ask. Whatever he'd been dreaming about wasn't anything happy. I knew what that was like. Talking helped a little—rationalizing the fear by understanding your body's responses ... I couldn't explain why, but it took away some of the power from those memories. Maybe I could give that gift to James. If he'd let me. He'd helped me so much, more than he'd ever know, slaying the dragons that stalked through my subconsciousness—and now I wanted to help him, because that's what friends did.

"Can you tell me what it was about?" I asked tentatively.

His shoulders hunched and his head dropped into his hands.

"Bad shit," he said tersely.

I stroked the warm silky skin of his back, my fingers trailing over the tattoo that spread across his shoulders.

I hesitated, choosing my next words carefully.

"Then that makes two of us—we've both been through bad times. And we've both survived."

He turned immediately, wrapping his arms around me as if that alone could protect us from the world.

"I'm so sorry," he breathed against my flushed skin. "I wish I could have stopped them and..."

"James, that's not why I mentioned it. I have bad times, terrible nightmares, so I understand ... if you want to tell me."

He pulled a face.

"Why would you want more nasty shit in your head? I don't want you to have more."

I smiled sadly. *Still the protector.*

"Because maybe it will help you to talk about it?"

"No, I don't think so."

"Have you tried?"

He shrugged.

"Yeah. With guys who were there, who saw it happen. But you have to lock that nasty shit down—it's the only way to deal with it."

I thought about that.

"Yes, it's one way, but talking about it has helped me."

He frowned, narrowing his eyes.

"You really want to know?"

"Yes, because I think it will help you."

He sighed in defeat.

"I made a mistake and people died." He cleared his throat. "Children."

My hand flew to my mouth, shock and sympathy surging through me.

"Oh ... I didn't know..."

He looked at me with desperation.

"I tried to stop them," he said, his tone pleading.

Children. Oh no.

He reached out. I swallowed and looked at his hand gripping mine, letting my eyes rove upwards, taking in the shower of white scars on his forearm.

"Is that when this happened?"

He nodded and I touched his eyebrow, the pale scar at the edge.

"And this?"

Another nod.

"And when you lost most of the sight in your right eye?"

"Yeah."

"Tell me."

He stared unseeing, dredging the memory from the past into the present.

"One of my jobs as an Ammo Tech is to destroy captured explosives and ammo, render it safe and unusable."

"Okay?"

He looked away, his gaze lost in the past.

"I was in working with the Afghan National Army in Gereshk. It's a town in the south of Afghanistan about 120 kilometres from Kandahar. The ANA had found a Taliban arms dump, so they called me in as the nearest operator."

He grimaced.

"There were two burns pits—that's two deep pits where the explosives are put so I can detonate them but keep the blast radius contained. I had a ton and a half of HMEs, and the other pit was small arms ammo—for handguns and rifles.

"My job required laying a long fuze from the pits to a firing point, far enough so that the pits are unsighted—that's for safety. The sentries are further away but can see the pits. I'd already initiated the dems—the demolition—and was retreating from the firing point when one of the sentries saw a bunch of kids sneaking into the small ammo pit, probably to rob it.

"The sentry yelled at them, but he was even further away than me. My LCpl was with me and I told him to get clear. If I could get to the firing point and stop the fuze … but the soft bastard turned around and started running with me—because he's got kids of his own, you know? So I was trying to get to the fuze, and we were both yelling at the kids to get out.

"I sprinted to the firing point but when I got there, I knew we were too late, we weren't going to make it, and Rob was too close. He'd run right past me, shooting his rifle into the air to scare the kids away and yelling his head off. I started chasing after him, telling him to get down, but he ran closer and closer to the pits. They kids started scrambling out of the pit with whatever they'd scrounged, and it looked like they'd make it … and then … it was too late."

He stopped and grimaced.

"I was 50 metres away, so I escaped the over-pressure effects, but I was hit by frag." His voice had become a monotone. "The frag I was hit by was Rob. I still have pieces of his bone under my skin."

"Oh, James…"

"I remember lying on the ground trying to breathe, trying to get air into my lungs. I knew Rob was gone … I saw him…"

He took a deep breath as his eyes closed.

"I remember seeing some of the kids picking themselves up and running off."

"Oh … so … the children … they lived? Some of them?"

He shook his head.

"No, even though they'd survived the initial explosion, the blast over-pressure damage would have collapsed their lungs in the next day or so, and without some serious medical help they'd have died anyway."

He opened his eyes, his gaze fixed on the glow of the streetlights through the window.

"The ANA went door to door in the area, trying to find out who the kids were so they could get them medical help, but no one was going to admit to sending their kid to steal ammo. So the kids never got the help they needed—they all died.

"Humans can withstand 0.5 bar pressure without serious injury because we are squishy, but at one bar, you start to damage buildings, and people get injured more from being thrown against them."

I licked my lips as his words dried.

"James, that wasn't your fault. It was a terrible, terrible accident, but it wasn't your fault."

His voice was bleak.

"We were there to help, Amira, to make the country safer. Win hearts and minds. How much did I help that day?"

"More than you think by the sound of it," I said quietly. "A lot of munitions were taken out of the equation."

He angled a wry glance at me.

"You sound like Smith."

I shook my head.

"Really? Huh, well, he's a bad influence."

I was trying to lighten the mood, but James didn't smile.

"On a good day, I'll tell myself that. I was doing it by the book. Maybe if the sentries had seen the kids in time; maybe if the pits had been in a different place ... I don't know. Maybe those kids wouldn't have died. But I know they did. And I lit the fuze." He turned his face away. "I copped the blame anyway—I was running the dems, so ultimately it was my fault." He shrugged. "The top brass weren't saying it, but I got shuffled to a backroom job for a while after that. You can rationalize it all you want, Amira. Those kids are dead because of me."

"I'm not trying to rationalize it—I'm saying it was a terrible accident. There are so many ifs and maybes in life. Maybe if I hadn't been a nurse, Karam wouldn't have thought about going to med school. Maybe if he'd trained to be an accountant, he'd never have volunteered to go to Syria. You see? Do I think I'm to blame for Karam's death? No, but sometimes it feels like I am. On a bad day."

His eyes widened with understanding, and he pulled me against him.

"Thank you," he said softly.

CHAPTER THIRTY-ONE

JAMES

I'd never been to Arlington National Cemetery before.

I'd seen plenty of photographs, but nothing prepared me for the miles of rolling hills filled with row upon row of immaculate white headstones stretching into the distance, each one representing a soldier who had fallen, a family who had lost someone.

Not all had died from violence, but all had seen it—every one of those hundreds of thousands white headstones.

Would there ever be a time when men like me weren't needed? It seemed unlikely.

I helped Amira out of the car that Smith had sent for us. I still wasn't used to seeing her in ordinary clothes. Today, she was wearing a grey knee-length dress and a black coat. Her long, silky hair swung over her scarred cheek, and I knew that was deliberate. It was painful to see how self-conscious it made her.

Then she glanced up and gave me a sad smile.

Since our op had been denied at the highest level, I hadn't planned to come in my uniform, just thinking I'd wear something reasonably tidy, but Smith had arranged for my dress uniform to be brought over from the UK. I had no idea how he'd done it, but I'd given up wondering how he managed to do half the stuff he did—many fingers in many pies.

It might seem like a lot of effort, but wearing a uniform to the funeral of someone engaged in a denied op was making a statement—a *fuck you* to whoever had signed off on this in the first place, whoever refused to acknowledge his life ... or his death.

Amira's eyes had grown huge when I knocked on her hotel door—she hadn't seen me in my Number 2s before.

"Wow, you have a lot of medals," she whispered, her gaze sliding over my chest.

"Yeah," I breathed out as I took in the grey figure-hugging dress she was wearing. "Seen a lot of bad shit. The more shit you see, the more medals you get."

But on a denied op, there'd be no medals for me, or for Clay or Amira.

I didn't care for myself, but she deserved some recognition for what she'd gone through and what she'd achieved. The intel she and Clay had gathered meant that the police and secret services had been able to contain a significant threat level.

Resentment ate at me. The whole Times Square incident had been filmed live, and we were TV and YouTube stars, not that you could see our faces clearly enough to ID, but Press speculation had gone crazy and a lot of whackos were claiming that they'd been there. Seventeen million hits and rising was a big incentive to someone who was a fame whore.

They were welcome to it—I was very happy being anonymous, and I hoped it stayed that way for all of us. But I also hoped the Powers That Be were going to look after Amira and her family, keeping them safe from the whackos. I thought Smith would be on the case, but even with the strings he could pull, he was just one man.

If Amira asked me to stay, I would. But since that night in her hotel room, I felt her pulling away from me, inch by inch, and I didn't know what to do about it. We were running out of time—we were always running out of time.

I adjusted my Forrest Cap as the wind whipped through the cemetery scattering dead leaves over the smooth green grass. Amira slid her arm through mine as she shivered.

"My parents didn't want me to go to Karam's funeral. In their culture, women stay at home to mourn."

"Is it okay that you're here?"

Her lips tightened as she nodded.

"Larson died trying to save me. I had to come."

"Not such a tosser after all?"

She laughed softly as her eyes became glassy with emotion.

"No, he turned out not to be a tosser after all."

It sounded strange, hearing her say the word 'tosser'. Weirdly, it made me smile.

I turned to look behind me when I heard the sound of a motorcade making its way up the incline. There were also four Marines on horseback carrying the Stars and Stripes, and Larson's Regimental Colours. Six more Marines followed on foot, drumming out the slow march, and in between them was a black hearse.

I hated those cars. I'd been to too many funerals of friends.

Not that I'd really known Larson, but he'd been on our side and died tried to save Amira. That made him a damn hero as far as I was concerned.

I looked around at the rows of grave markers—too many dead heroes.

The hearse stopped when it reached us, and four of the Marines slid the coffin from the back and raised it to their shoulders.

It was all done very smoothly. They probably carried out the same ritual three or four times a day, every day, for as long as this was their current deployment. What a messed up job.

Smith stepped up next to us, and Amira gave a little jump.

"There's a reason he's called a 'spook'," I said.

She gave a shaky laugh.

"Hi, Smith."

He leaned down to kiss her cheek, then shook my hand, a forced smile on his face.

"Nice uniform, James. Glad it arrived in time. Clay says hi. He wanted to be here but the doc wouldn't sign him out. He was spitting mad."

"I bet," I said absently, looking around me. "Where's Larson's family?"

Smith's face went blank.

"You're looking at it. The Marines were the only real family he ever had. He was a tough bastard." He paused. "He saved my life. And he was my friend."

Amira rested her hand over his, and he met her gaze.

"I didn't like him much," she said softly. "He scared me a little."

"Damn," said Smith. "Just a little? He'd have been disappointed."

Amira smiled as tears glittered on her eyelashes.

"Maybe more than a little. But," and she looked down, "he tried to save me. He tried ... he could have saved himself—he could have left me, but he didn't." She looked up at Smith. "So I will never forget him, and I will pray for him always."

Smith gave a curt nod, then slid his hand from under hers and stepped away.

The coffin was ceremoniously lowered into the ground as Amira's hair blew across her face, the breeze drying the tears that slowly tracked down her cheeks. When she reached out to hold my hand, I never wanted to let go.

I was glad that we could be here. No soldier should be buried alone. I knew that Smith said Larson's family was the Marines, but it should be someone who knew him, people who cared.

"Thanks for everything, Larson," I said quietly.

As they played 'The Last Post' and the haunting sound echoed across the vast cemetery, I raised my hand in a stiff salute.

Larson deserved that, and I wanted to honour the man.

I watched as one of the Marines from the Honour guard folded the flag that had been draped over his coffin, then hesitated, clearly wondering who he should give it to.

I turned to Smith, but he'd already gone, striding into the distance, his head down.

Amira accept the folded flag and hugged it to her chest as the tree branches swayed above us.

When she climbed back into the car, the flag held tightly in her hands, she met my gaze.

"I don't ever want to go to your funeral, James."

I reached out to hold her hand because I had no words.

CHAPTER THIRTY-TWO

JAMES

Where do I go from here?

The question had been running through my head for days—and now it was my last few hours with Amira.

We were at JFK, two among thousands in the vast, white terminal.

Amira and her family were flying back to San Diego within the hour, and I had a late flight to Heathrow.

Nothing had been resolved between us, and every time I'd tried to start the *what next* question, she'd shut me down.

A wiser man would have taken the hint, but life could be short, ending suddenly, brutally—and I knew what I wanted. I knew *who* I wanted.

And now I was down to my last thirty minutes to make use of my limited charms to persuade her to agree with me.

I'd told Clay about my plans, and he'd commented that my charm offensive should be more charming than offensive. Sarcastic bastard.

Her parents were clearly uncomfortable with my presence—I definitely hadn't charmed them. They were grateful, but they didn't want me around their daughter. They definitely wouldn't want me for a son-in-law. But I had a plan...

I'd managed to persuade Amira to go for a coffee with me,

leaving her family at their flight gate, and we were sitting in a Starbucks concession. Amira was drinking some frothy iced coffee crap, and I had something that was supposed to be English tea (but wasn't).

As I reached out for my cup, wondering how to start, she caught my hand, exploring the web of scar tissue that crisscrossed my palm and wrist, interrupting the normal lines.

"So, I guess this is goodbye," she said quietly, laying my hand back on the table.

"Only for now."

She shook her head sadly.

"I don't think so, and neither do you. Not really. You said it yourself —you live 6,000 miles away. This has to be goodbye."

I studied my scarred hand, hoping I'd find the words to convince her that we had a chance.

"Well, I read the other day that they've got this crazy new invention called air travel. And email—it's like writing a letter but without having to buy a stamp—wow, magic! You should try it. And I heard telephones work across the Atlantic, as well, but that could just be a rumour."

She didn't crack a smile and she wouldn't meet my eyes.

"James, you and I don't exist in the real world—we can't. It's a lovely dream, but it's still just a dream." She shook her head. "I was so naïve—Operation Hansel and Gretel—it seemed like being in a movie at first, or a fairy tale. I'm so stupid."

Her words threw ice water over my hopes, but I wasn't going to accept that as her last word. *The game starts after you score.* I'd had those words tattooed on my back for a reason—and it meant that I needed to up my game.

I wasn't what you'd call a spiritual person, but I didn't believe that we'd been through all this shit for nothing. I was sure of that.

"It doesn't have to be a dream, Amira. We can make this work: you and me—us."

She glanced up, startled, and shifted on the hard chair.

"I don't think of you like that, James. There's too much against us."

"Like what?" I demanded belligerently.

A long sigh and she turned her eyes toward me.

"Where we live, who we are," she paused. "Our religion. We can be friends, but..."

"I don't have a religion that I practise. I have to put Church of England on my dog tags, but so what? And where we live can change. As for who we are, *you* already know that, and *I* already know that. We *fit*, Amira. We're good together."

She looked down.

"No, this is goodbye, James. It has to be."

I cupped her face in my hand so that she'd be forced to look at me. "Why?"

She blinked in surprise.

"Why? Because it just *is*."

"That doesn't make any sense," I pleaded. Her lips tightened as she frowned and pulled away from me. "We can be together," I insisted. "We just both have to want it and we can make it happen. If you want to be with me the way I want to be with you?"

I took a deep breath and held it.

When she finally spoke, it wasn't what I was expecting. At all.

"I'm going to go to Syria."

I was completely thrown by her words.

"What?"

She looked frustrated, her hands gripping her plastic cup and squeezing it too tightly.

"I want to go to Syria and complete Karam's mission. I want to work in the hospitals there and ... and *do good*." She looked away. "I need to."

"But that's crazy!"

She glared at me, clearly frustrated.

"I thought you'd say that, but I need this, James," she said forcefully. "I got it all wrong before, thinking that I could be someone I'm not—an undercover agent," and she laughed dully. "But I'm a nurse, and helping, healing—*that's* what I do, *that's* who I am. Karam would never have wanted me to do what I did, getting involved with Smith, to risk myself like that. I was so full of anger and hate that I couldn't see what was important."

"And now you can?"

I hated that I sounded so sarcastic and dismissive, but she was tearing chunks out of my heart a piece at a time. Soon, there'd be nothing left.

"James, don't."

"Don't what?"

"Don't hate me."

"I don't."

"But you will."

"Amira..."

"No, listen! *I need to do this*. Do you understand? I have to do this to be able to move on from everything that's happened. The feeling grows stronger every day. I want to go back to work. In Syria."

I stood up and started to pace, drawing the glances of people around us. I tried to get a grip and slammed down heavily into the chair.

"Jesus! Nearly dying once wasn't enough for you?" I growled at her. "You'd go to Syria, doing the very thing that got your brother killed?"

She grimaced and looked away.

"It wouldn't be like that..."

"It would be *exactly* like that! Not that much has changed in the last year. You've got Russia on one side with Putin being a mad bastard and there's no saying what he'll do. Then there's President Assad who's just as crazy and completely capable of gassing his own people again. And that's if Daesh really is beaten in Syria, which is doubtful as well, because they've just gone to ground—they're still there, everywhere, all around."

She sighed, patience and compassion in her gaze, and I knew that I was losing her.

"I know this, James. Don't talk to me like I don't know what I'm doing, like I haven't thought about this. There's so much need, so much suffering, and I can help. I know exactly what I'd be getting myself into."

"No. You think you know but you don't."

I was pretty damn certain that she had no clue, but I'd been in war zones, and I'd seen exactly how the Taliban and ISIS supporters had behaved there.

"I'll tell you what it's like," I snapped, my voice low and harsh. "Raqqa will be littered with ordnance, IEDs everywhere. The place is half rubble, which means it covers devices that haven't yet functioned but could at any moment. And as Daesh leave the city, they'll be rigging the houses that are still intact, setting timers in the kitchens, under the beds, rigging the bloody light switches. But they don't just set them to explode as soon as someone comes into the house, they set them to go three days later—when the whole family has gone back there—maximum carnage."

Her face went very still, but I continued, my voice rising.

"And the hospital itself? The one where your brother died? The building has been shelled to ruins, so you'll be working in tents and you'll be lucky if there's electricity or running water. Maybe you'll have a generator that works, but you won't be able to get diesel to run it. Not legitimately, so your team will have to buy fuel on the black market—probably from the bastards who were fighting for Daesh in the first place."

I leaned forwards letting my voice go cold.

"And if you think the last few months have been hard, you'll see far worse; you'll see things that will keep you awake at night—and you'll be seeing them for the rest of your life. Is that what you want?"

She swallowed and leaned across the table to pull my hands into her own.

"I know. And that's why I'm needed."

"Amira, you don't know!"

Her expression chilled.

"I am very aware how cruel people can be. I've lived it. I *am* living it. But I *have* to do this. I can't go forward ... I can't go forward with you or with anyone else until..."

"Until what?"

"I've paid penance."

"What does that mean?" I asked angrily.

She sighed and leaned back.

"I hardly know myself, but I *feel* it. There's something inside that's telling me to finish Karam's work. I owe it to him. I owe it to the people out there who have nothing—the people my family came from. I can help. I know I can make a difference. That's why I became a nurse in the first place."

"Then make a difference *here*," I almost shouted, remembering at the last second and dropping my voice to a hoarse whisper. "Do it somewhere you'll be safe."

We stared at each other, the divide between us wider than ever.

"James, I care about you, we're friends, good friends ... but I'll hate myself if I don't do this."

I turned away, my body stiff, unable to take the shattering pain inside. But I still had one card left to play.

"Then I'll come, too."

Silence.

I turned to face her, but she stared at me like I was the crazy one.

"You can't. That's impossible."

"Yeah? Why's that?"

"You can't follow me there!" she said, her voice rising.

"The hell I can't!"

She gave a furious laugh.

"Be serious! You think the British Army would let you do that?"

"They wouldn't have any choice ... if I was a civilian—then I can do what the hell I like."

She squinted at me as if she hadn't heard right.

"You can't leave the Army. You can't do that."

Her voice was flat.

"Yes, I can."

"But..."

"I have to give 12 months' notice, but then I'm free to go where I like, do what I want."

Her eyebrows drew together in confusion.

"And then what?"

"I'll follow you to Syria."

"But ... you can't."

"Says who?"

"James, it's just ... no! This is my journey, not yours."

"Yeah, well, you seem to think it's a good idea. If that's where you're going, Amira, that's where I want to be."

Shock spread over her face.

"You mean it!"

"Every word."

"But ... what about your career?"

"You think I give a shit about that?"

Her eyes widened.

"You'd leave the Army, give up everything?"

"I wouldn't be giving up everything—I'd be gaining everything."

For a moment, light shone in her eyes, but then it was gone again.

"I can't ask you to do that. I won't."

"You're not asking me—I'm telling you that's what I want."

She dropped her gaze to the table, and I could see the idea sinking in, but there was still a barrier in her mind, something she wasn't telling me.

"James, the last few months have been … terrifying … but I've learned a lot about myself. I thought the religion of my family meant nothing to me, but it does. Through all this madness, through all the hatred and violence, I've found my faith. I know that sounds as corny and crazy as anything else, but that's how I feel. Like God has given me a second chance. I want to explore what that means—and I want to do it through Islam."

I thumped my head down on the table, then stared up at her.

"Well, okay. If that's what you want. I don't really get it, but if it's important to you."

She shook her head furiously.

"No, not important—it's fundamental. To who I am, to what I want to be, to everything."

I scratched my ear.

"Yeah, okay. Great. Good for you—go for it."

She grimaced in frustration.

"What I'm trying to say—and making a real mess of it—is that I couldn't be with you in the way that you'd want. Ugh, don't make me say it!" She covered her face with her hands. "I couldn't be with you—sexually—because my faith wouldn't permit it."

Now, I was getting it. It burned like hell, but I got it. And I saw the obvious solution. Or at least I thought I did.

"What if we get married?"

She nearly choked.

"Married?!"

I grinned at her astonished reaction.

"Yeah, people do that. You know, when they want to spend the rest of their lives together."

She flicked my arm.

"Don't joke!"

"I'm not. Marry me, Amira. Today, tomorrow, as soon as you like. Marry me."

Her eyebrows shot up.

"You really mean it?"

"Yeah, I do. So, what's your answer?"

Her face closed down, and she took the shreds of my hope with her.

"I can't."

"Why not? You're single, I'm single, and we want to be together. At least, that's what I want. So why not?"

"I ... James, I want ... I need ... if I ever marry anyone—which is kind of a stretch for me right now—I'd want to marry a man of my own faith."

"Oh."

"You get it now?"

"Sure."

I picked up her hand again, feeling the smooth, soft skin.

"So, what do I have to do to become a Muslim?"

Her mouth dropped open and then she frowned, snatching her hand back.

"That's not funny."

"I'm not laughing. I'll convert. I'll be what you want." I sighed. "Don't you get it, Amira? You're talking about Fate, or things happening for a reason, and with all the shit that's happened, don't you think the one good thing has been *us*? If you have to give meaning to it all, isn't that it? Isn't that the miracle—that a man brought up with the Church of England fell in love with a Muslim woman who hated him and everything he stood for?"

"I ... I never hated you!"

"Yeah, you did. I saw it in your eyes."

"No ... no, I just hated ... well, everyone. My life."

"But not now."

"No. Not now." She paused. "You said you'd fallen in love with me..."

"You caught that, huh?"

"Yes, and I'm more flattered, more awed than I could ever say, but ... it won't work."

"It can!"

"James!" she yelped, her voice rising unhappily. "I can't find another way to tell you without hurting you, so I'm just going to have to say it. I'm overwhelmed that you'd consider changing your faith, marrying me, but I can't let you do that. I love you as a friend, a good friend, a special friend, but that's all."

She took a deep breath as my world fell apart.

"I can't marry you. My answer is no."

CHAPTER THIRTY-THREE

AMIRA

My heart broke for James.

I loved him. Of course I loved him. But that wasn't enough. It would have been so easy to say 'yes', to agree to everything, because then I wouldn't have to face the future alone—I'd have my best friend at my side. But that wouldn't be fair to him, to either of us.

"We can still be friends," I said weakly. "I'm being selfish, but I don't want to lose you, James. In a few years, we'll laugh about this, and you'll know you had a lucky escape."

He didn't look at me as he spoke.

"I'll never think that, Amira. I'll always love you."

I didn't know what to say, what to do to make it better, because of course I couldn't. There was no kind way to trample on someone's dreams.

I leaned toward him, taking his damaged hand in mine, wondering how I could be saying goodbye to this beautiful, kind, caring man.

Suddenly, I spotted Zada hurrying through the concourse, a frown on her face.

"Amira! They've called our flight! We have to go *now*."

James stood up, still holding my hand.

"I'll walk with you to your gate."

Zada looked at us quizzically.

As we approached my parents, I dropped his hand. He didn't argue —he simply shoved his hands in his pockets and stared at the floor, unable to meet my eyes. After all the times I'd seen him watching me, and now he couldn't even look at me. I felt like the lowest person on the planet. I'd used him to heal myself, and I'd broken his heart.

Mama and *Baba* were already freaking out about the flight, and were waiting impatiently, carry-on luggage clutched tightly.

Baba shook hands with James, thanking him one more time for saving my life, and *Mama* gave him a polite bow.

It was all so painfully awkward.

James finally glanced up, giving me an encouraging smile that didn't quite meet his eyes, and a polite kiss on the cheek, but the intensity of passion burning in his expression was far less polite. I felt a slicing sense of loss as I walked away from him.

I glanced over my shoulder and tried to smile.

But he didn't react, and a moment later, he was out of sight.

I suppressed the landslide of emotion ready to bury me—walking away from him felt so wrong.

Everything seemed different now that I'd almost died. Every minute was precious, and I needed to atone for my stupidity for the rest of my life.

"Is everything okay?" asked *Mama*, glancing at me anxiously.

"It will be," I said.

Zada gave me an odd look.

"Is James okay?"

How could I answer that?

"Oh, Zada, I've made such a mess of everything! James asked me to marry him!"

Her eyebrows shot up.

"What did you say?"

"No, of course!"

She studied me carefully.

"I thought you two were close."

"We are close. We're friends, but that's all."

She seemed skeptical.

"Just friends? Because I saw him coming out of your hotel room really early in the morning the other day. He'd stayed, hadn't he?"

I floundered with my answer, flustered and off balance.

"Yes, but ... okay, yes, he stayed. But that was different. I needed ... to stop the nightmares, Zada. And I needed it to be with a friend." I bit my lip, praying she wouldn't judge me too harshly. "Do you understand?"

She linked her arm through mine.

"I'll never understand what you went through, I can't. But if it helped, being with James, then I'm glad you were with a friend. But Amira, that man is in love with you. We all see it. Mom and Dad have been waiting for you to tell them that you were engaged or something."

I gaped at her in amazement.

"Are you kidding me?"

"No, of course not."

"And they'd have been okay with it? With me marrying him?"

She shrugged, looking uncomfortable.

"I wouldn't say 'okay' exactly, but if he was who you wanted. But ... you don't love him?"

"I do, as a friend. I'm not *in* love with him."

She looked at me thoughtfully.

"Is there someone else?" She lowered her eyes. "Is it Clay?"

"No! It's not Clay! It's not anyone! Why would you ask me that?" I stared at her as the hint of a blush bloomed on her cheeks. "Zada? Zada! No way! You and Clay?!"

She shook her head vehemently and unhooked her arm from mine.

"No, don't be silly. I like him. He's sweet and funny, cute, too."

"Oh wow! You do like him. You really like him!"

"We just talked," she said softly, blushing more deeply. "While you were seeing the therapist, I used to go talk to him. He doesn't have any family, none who cares. I smuggled in candies for him," she smiled shyly. "That boy has a sweet tooth."

I was amazed. *My little sister and Clay!* I hadn't seen that coming.

"Are you sure you don't like him?" she asked guiltily. "He's not the reason that you and James..."

"No," I said firmly. "They're both very special to me, and they always will be. But I'm not in love with either of them."

"Then what is it?" she asked puzzled. "What are you hiding?"

I took a deep breath.

"Zada, I've got so much to tell you."

CHAPTER THIRTY-FOUR

JAMES

I felt completely numb—a total absence of feeling.

The bone-crushing disappointment and humiliation ached in my chest until I was able to lock it down and throw away the damn key.

I'd offered her everything, but she didn't want it—she didn't want *me*.

Stupidly, I'd thought that when she chose me to chase away the nightmares, to sleep with me to erase the bad memories, I thought that I meant something to her. But in the end, I was just a warm body —there at the right time, and available with no strings.

I'd got it so wrong.

So I switched it all off and buried it deep. I'd had a lot of practice doing that. And right now, I hoped that I'd never remember how to feel again.

The flight home was long and boring. Unlike my flight across the pond with Smith, I was flying coach and there was no one meeting me at Heathrow. I had to get two trains and a taxi back to the base in Wiltshire.

While I'd been away, the regiment had deployed, so I'd officially been sent back to Aldershot until I was attached to a new regiment who needed EOD support. But first, I had to pick up my wheels from

Noddy, and I had the whole weekend before I had to present myself to my C.O.

I hoped like hell he had the sense not to ask me what I'd been doing in America. Officers didn't like being told 'no comment'.

I couldn't tell him about the work, where I'd been or what I'd done. And there was no one that I'd tell about Amira. Clay guessed, I think, but even he didn't know everything.

Noddy had done me a solid and looked after my Ducati like it was his firstborn. Not that he had kids—the soft bastard couldn't keep a woman interested long enough to knock her up. Not that I was doing any better.

Well, that was my opinion. Noddy said that he was too smart to get caught out. I wasn't going to argue with him when he'd looked after my wheels so well.

I slept on the couch at his place my first night back home. It was all so weird because it didn't feel like home, and I had to lie about everything. According to me, nothing of interest had happened whatsoever. Talk about irony. My YouTube video had been viewed 29 million times by now, and I had nothing to show for it—except a gaping hole in my chest where my heart used to beat.

"You missed all the action, mate," Noddy said. "You must have heard about the multiple terrorist attacks all down the east coast? They even have one of them on YouTube—suicide bomber in Times Square. You must have seen it!"

"Yeah, I saw it," I said, "but I was training down in Memphis— heat, crotch rot and mosquitoes."

Noddy yawned and scratched his vast belly.

"Sounds shite, mate. Most boring deployment ever."

I agreed, then changed the subject.

We had a few beers, ordered takeaway curry, and caught up on Noddy's life. That was a cosy twenty minutes, including scoffing the food and necking two beers each. Then we discussed Spurs' chances in the Cup.

Noddy was one of my oldest friends, and we were exchanging small talk like strangers.

The next day, I pointed the Ducati towards Aldershot.

The countryside had changed while I'd been away, and a long, hot summer had turned to Autumn. Life had moved on—mine more than most, but at the same time, nothing on the surface had changed. As I arrived at the Barracks and headed to the old accommodation block, my room was exactly the same as when I'd left it all those months earlier. Even the dust looked the same. But I'd changed so completely, I was almost surprised to recognize myself in the mirror. It was confusing and disorientating to be back here.

The world was crammed with seven billion people, and I'd never felt more alone.

CHAPTER THIRTY-FIVE

AMIRA

My phone rang and I could feel a huge smile on my face before I even answered. Clay was video-calling me. It was the first time we'd spoken since I said goodbye to him in New York, although I knew that Zada had chatted with him several times.

"Hello, sister!" he said as soon as I answered. "Oh, wait, I've been practising this: *As-Salaam-Alaikum!*"

I laughed.

"*Wa-Alaikum-Salaam.*"

Which was the traditional response to his greeting, 'Peace be unto you'.

"You look great, Amira," he said with a smile.

"Hardly!" I touched my scar self-consciously, "And I've just been for my first run in six weeks—I staggered around a three mile circuit in 920F heat—I look horrendous!"

"Nah, you look great," he grinned. "You probably smell rank though."

"Hey!"

"Just saying. Anyway, I don't care how much you smell—we shared a bed for three weeks without showering, right?"

"Ugh!" I shrieked, covering my face. "I don't want to think about how bad we both smelled. Promise me you'll never mention it again!"

He laughed.

"I promise."

Then he screwed up his face.

"Uh, so I have something to tell you ... about Zada..."

I rolled my eyes.

"Seriously, Clay? You think I don't know about you and my *little sister*. How come you didn't tell me before?"

He winced.

"I wanted to, but..."

I smiled sadly.

"It's okay, I get it. Everything has been pretty crazy. But for the record, she seems really happy, so I'm happy, too. But if you hurt her, I will hunt you down."

"Understood!" he grinned at me. Then his smile faded. "Have you heard from James? He's not answering my calls or messages."

I shook my head, guilt flaring hotly.

"No, he hasn't been in touch." *And I hadn't tried to get in touch with him.*

"Damn," he said softly. "I was hoping you guys would have spoken. Smith says James is back at barracks, but that's all he could tell me." He looked away then took a breath. "Zada told me that you turned him down when he asked you to marry him. I didn't see that coming. I mean, I know he liked you and that you two had a thing..."

I felt so guilty, and I couldn't forget the look on James' face when I said no, the moment I broke his heart.

"Oh, she told you," I said tiredly. "Yeah, it was completely out of left field. I was so shocked. I thought we were friends. We *are* friends, but ... not like that."

He sighed.

"Don't beat yourself up about it, Amira. Things can get pretty intense on an op, emotions run high."

"You think that's what it was?" I asked hopefully.

"That's part of it," he said carefully.

He didn't say anymore; he didn't need to.

Guilt squirmed in my stomach again; it was a constant nagging pain, like toothache. I could only imagine how James felt. I'd hoped that he'd talk to Clay, but apparently not.

"Give him time, Amira," he said gently. "I'm sure he'll be in touch."

I wasn't so sure. I was fairly certain that I'd never hear from James again.

"How are things at home?" he asked. "Zada said you'd told your parents about wanting to go to Syria. Damn, girl!"

I sucked my teeth.

"Yeees."

"Huh, went that well, did it?"

"They were very unhappy," I admitted, understating their shock hugely. "*Mama* cried—and they weren't happy tears—and *Baba* went to the mosque to pray. "They'll come around. They just want me to be happy. Especially after, well, everything."

He looked at me thoughtfully.

"Are you happy?"

"Getting there," I replied honestly.

"Hmm. Did Zada tell you that I'm going to convert?"

I chewed my lip.

"Yes, but will you?" I asked uncertainly, remembering that James had made the same offer to me.

"Yep," he said quickly. "I will. I'm already looking into taking instruction from the local *Imam*. Zada won't tell me what your parents think, so will you tell me?"

I groaned. I really didn't want to get between my parents and my sister, but I owed Clay. I owed him everything.

"It's a lot for them to take in," I said gingerly. "Give them time to get used to the idea."

We were silent, each contemplating the obstacles in our future.

"How are you doing really?" I asked quietly.

He pulled a face.

"The doctors say I need another operation on my stump. Maybe several more before they can even think about fitting me for a prosthetic."

"That isn't unusual," I said gently. "They'll try to make it so you'll be able to wear a prosthetic with reasonable comfort."

He nodded and sighed.

"Yeah, I know. They've explained it all to me, but the surgeon says he's worried about the integrity of the blood vessels, so..."

"You'll get through it, Clay, I know you will."

He smiled tiredly.

"So, how you feeling about having me for a brother-in-law?"

I gasped.

"Are you serious? Really? You've asked her to marry you?"

"Not yet," he said, his expression earnest. "But it's heading in that direction. She's planning to come out East so we can spend some time together while I'm in rehab. She says she wants us to get used to the idea, so we can both be sure that we know what we're doing, but I know what's real. Your sister is pretty amazing, Amira."

"So, this call, are you asking my permission to marry Zada?"

"Would you give it?" he asked nervously.

I grinned, in spite of our serious conversation.

"I couldn't be happier," I said honestly.

There was a loud banging on my door and I raised my eyes to the ceiling, regretting that I'd let my apartment go and moved back in with my parents for the next few months.

"Amira! Lunchtime! Your father is waiting!"

"Coming, *Mama*!" I yelled.

Clay chuckled.

"Sounds like it's fun living with your folks again."

I groaned.

"They treat me like I'm five years old!"

"Course they do," he said, his voice softening. "You're precious, and they're scared that you'll be leaving again one day soon." His face clouded over.

"I know, I understand. They'll come around, I just have to give them some time."

I sounded more confident that I felt.

He sighed and nodded.

"Yeah, I guess," and he gave a weak smile. "You'd better go."

"Should I give your love to Zada?"

That made him smile big, and I saluted his grinning face as I ended the call. The emptiness I felt then was hard to bear.

I jumped in the shower, washing quickly. I had a lot to do today, including going to see the HR department at the hospital and formally quitting. It wouldn't be a surprise to them since I'd been gone a year, but I needed to make it official.

My family knew the truth about my sabbatical now—but I hadn't been able to tell any of my former co-workers the truth, and I never would. My parents were devastated when I admitted that I was going to Syria. Zada cried, but I think she understood. I hoped so.

I also had to complete an application to volunteer with Médecins Sans Frontières, or as they were known in English, Doctors Without Borders. I was dreading leaving my parents again, but I was ready to move on with my life. Zada was moving on with hers, and a small part of me was jealous.

But only a small part.

Time moved slowly, but it did move. *Baba* and *Mama* gradually got used to the idea of Zada dating Clay. They'd even talked to him on Facetime, solemn and stiff, but I think his persistence was wearing them down.

She'd been out to visit him once and came back glowing with happiness.

It had taken more than three months for my paperwork for MSF to come through and for me to be approved to work in Syria. I'd had to go to several interviews, and I thought I'd have a problem with the year's gap in my résumé, but Smith had pulled some strings. Whatever else I thought of him and the work he did, he was a man of his word. Yes, a professional liar who kept his word—my life was full of contradictions.

Zada was happy for me, happy to have her sister home, but there was a distance between us that hadn't been there before. I'd hurt her when I'd left before, and now I was leaving her again.

"At least promise me this time you'll stay in touch," she said out of the blue one day.

"I promise, Zada. You know why I couldn't before."

She shrugged.

"You've explained it, but I don't think I'll ever really understand why you did what you did. Mom and Dad ... well, you can imagine," she said accusingly. Then she looked up. "But I kind of understand why you want to volunteer in Syria. I think Mom and Dad get it, too. They're worried."

"I know."

"I just wanted to tell you, to let you know, to say it out loud," she stuttered. "I'm going to miss you so much, but I love you. I love you so much."

She fell into my arms and I hugged her tightly.

"I love you, too, Zada. And I'm so happy that you and Clay are … well, I'm really happy."

"You mean that?" she asked with damp eyes.

"Of course I do. He's a great guy."

"He is!" she smiled. "He's amazing." Then her expression became serious again. "Just promise me that you'll be careful, okay?"

"I promise."

We hugged for a while longer, then I glanced at my watch.

"I'd better get going—I have to be at work in forty minutes."

While I'd been waiting for my life to start again, I'd been volunteering at the nearby free clinic. Surviving on their limited resources was good training for me, but I suspected they were still a lot better off than where I'd be going.

I had one more week before I flew to Damascus.

I was really going.

CHAPTER THIRTY-SIX

JAMES

It had been too long since I'd taken the Ducati for a spin around a racetrack, but on my day off, that's exactly what I did. It felt good. And it was a release from all the pressures weighing down on me. I couldn't race at those speeds and think about *her*.

Work had been really busy, which was a relief. Too much time to think was not a good idea for me. Crazy as it sounded, there was an EOD call-out every day of the week somewhere in the UK, and there were few enough of us trained up and ready to answer the call. So far this month, I'd been sent for because a fishing vessel's flare washed up on a south coast beach—something that was potentially dangerous to the public since the phosphorescence could cause serious burns; then there'd been two 999 calls to the police saying that local schools had explosive devices planted on the premises—both turned out to be hoaxes but it all had to be checked out—the little scrotes who'd made the calls had been caught and reprimanded, but that was two days wasted. I'd been to a house in Hounslow where TATP was being produced, and a ring of seven bomb-makers were keeping the police busy with their enquiries. And yesterday, I'd been to a building site in Guildford where a World War 2 German buzz bomb, a V1 flying bomb that had been undisturbed for 78 years, until a digger on a construction site had unearthed it.

A typical week at work.

I'd never believed in anything much before I'd met Amira, other than saluting the Queen and promising to fight for HRM until my balls were nailed to the wall. That was our pledge when we joined the Army, but in reality, we all fought for the boots on the ground, the men and women standing next to us and fighting alongside us.

Now, I wasn't sure I believed in much at all. I was going through the motions, but I wasn't living.

I tried so hard not to think about her, but I couldn't help wondering. Was she in Syria yet? Was she okay? *Was she safe?*

The Syrian government, backed by the Russians and Iranians, were saying that the war was over and encouraging the 4.6 million Syrian refugees to return. But many were afraid they'd come back to forced conscription for the men, or possibly even be detained in prison. People died in detainment. And the fact that rebel forces were still firing rockets into Aleppo and other cities made them look like lying twats, but it hadn't slowed the Syrian government's media propaganda.

Most of the Daesh fighters had been evicted from the cities, but there were still pockets of resistance, still members of ISIS who'd seeped back into society. And that mad bastard Assad was completely capable of launching more chemical weapons' attacks on his own people now he knew he could get away with it and the UN were toothless.

It made me furious, but there was nothing I could do. Maybe I even understood why Amira was there trying to help—I hated it, but I understood.

Worrying about her was something I had to live with, a constant itch under my skin that I could never reach, a sliver of pain that throbbed with each breath I took.

She'd called me once, three months after I'd arrived back. I'd stared at her name flashing up on my phone, furious and frozen, until it had gone to voicemail. It was pure torture hearing her voice saying my name, but at least I knew she was alive.

I didn't call her back. I wasn't a complete masochist.

I'd been ignoring Clay's calls, too, which was a shitty thing to do, but I couldn't face him. It was easier if I acted as though those months in America had never happened.

I left the racetrack and headed out onto the motorway. Going seventy felt slow after the speeds I'd hit on the track earlier in the day, but I kept it legal.

I parked the bike and pulled off my helmet, feeling the cooler air whip around my face. Autumn had arrived, and the long hot days of summer were just a memory.

I'd promised some of the team I worked with that I'd join them for a drink tonight. I didn't feel like going, but I'd copped a load of banter the number of times I'd cancelled over the last few months.

We went to a local pub and had a few pints, ignoring the fact that there was a gang of single women smiling at us in the corner.

When four Guinnesses had taken the edge off, and I'd had enough of hanging out and talking crap with the guys, I'd gone back to my room.

Alone.

CHAPTER THIRTY-SEVEN

AMIRA

Life in Raqqa was hard in ways that I hadn't anticipated. Just day to day living was a struggle, and my job was incredibly pressured.

Weekly video-chats with Clay kept me going.

I saw him try to smile as his face appeared on my laptop screen, but I could tell that he was worried. I knew he had every reason to be concerned, but danger had become just another fact of life. I didn't take stupid risks, but I didn't want to feel suffocated by his concerns either because there was nothing either of us could do about it. Except for me to leave—and I wasn't ready to do that yet.

Even so, I was still looking over my shoulder every five minutes, certain that I was being watched, certain that I wouldn't make it to the end of the day. Panic attacks left me paralyzed, and my doctor wanted me to take anti-anxiety meds to take the edge off. I wasn't keen on the idea but I was seriously considering it because I needed to be able to function.

I was one of thousands who lived with PTSD and survivors' guilt—all the patients we saw and most of the staff had experienced some level of trauma. We all understood the price we were paying.

And I missed my family. I missed them so much it was like losing a part of myself.

We talked most weeks, but the long and irregular hours I worked didn't always make it easy. Talking to Clay helped. He'd been deployed to war zones more than once—he understood, so that made it easier.

I was so happy that he and my sister were trying to make their long-distance relationship work.

"How was work today?" Clay asked, his voice concerned.

"Bad day," I admitted, rubbing my bloodshot eyes. "Two gunshot wounds and a teenager with blast injuries. One of the GSWs had a collapsed lung, too. I was the only medic available, so I had to puncture his chest with a needle to let the air escape. It should have been done by a doctor following an ultrasound or X-ray, but there wasn't one available, and I knew that if I didn't do something, he'd die."

"Did he make it?"

"Holding on, but it's doubtful. He'd lost a lot of blood before I saw him." It was just the way things were. I shrugged. "But now the main fighting has stopped, I'm seeing a lot of children with malnutrition— nine with rickets in two days. Sometimes there's just so much suffering and so little we can do. We're seeing 400 people a day in our outpatient department suffering from basic things like diarrhoea, coughs, and non-communicable diseases. It doesn't sound like much, but because they haven't been treated for months, sometimes for years, chronic conditions like these become serious, even life-threatening. It's like trying to plug a hole in a dam, knowing that at any moment the water could come rushing down in a flood. It's scary, but then you get used to it, too, the adrenaline. You know? But it's why I came here."

He nodded. If anyone understood about the way being in a constant state of alert wore on your nerves, it was Clay.

"Anyway, I have to go get ready now. I'm dying for another falafel sandwich."

Clay frowned.

"You sure it's a good idea you going out at night, even in a group?"

"I told you things are changing here—we have two new bars and yes, the falafel restaurant. It's so good, we're going again. We'll have security with us, I promise."

He didn't look happy about it.

"You're being careful, right? Not using the same routes or the same cars—you've got to keep mixing things up. Don't get into a routine— you don't know who's watching. It's not a good idea to go back to the same place this soon."

His nagging tone annoyed me, but it was only because it came from a place of love and concern that I tolerated it.

"Clay, I promise you. We're taking all precautions. Look, I have to go now because Janice will be knocking on my door in a minute."

He tried to smile.

"I'll talk to you on Saturday—I have an afternoon off. Tell Zada I love her—and you're not too bad either."

"Yeah, back at you."

I raised my eyebrows and blew a kiss at him.

I turned off my laptop and started getting ready. Dressing to go out didn't mean much more than showering and putting on a little eye makeup before I went out. I always dressed conservatively here, with loose clothes that covered my arms and legs, and I wore a *hijab*, too. Many women still wore *niqabs* and a few still wore *burqas*, but more and more were dressing in western clothes, even though most still kept their hair covered.

Syria was changing. The poor country was battered and bruised, down but not out. I was proud of the work we were doing here and I loved it. The optimism of the people, the desire to get back to normal, the Mediterranean climate—I was falling in love with the country of my birth.

There was a knock on the door and my friend Janice called out.

"Come on, Amira! I'm starving! Let's go!"

Laughing, I tucked my hair into my *hijab*, then grabbed my wallet and shoved it my jeans, before heading out. Janice was from Dallas and an ER nurse like me. The rest of the group consisted of Neil from Toronto who was a doctor, Michelle from Belfast who was a nurse specializing in paediatrics, Nazar who was from London and a dentist. Plus, of course, Yaman who was our local Mr. Fixit and bodyguard.

Raqqa was a city of ruins. It was always a sobering sight to drive through the bomb-damaged streets and see the burnt-out shells of buildings, abandoned cars riddled with bullet holes, the roads full of craters. Sometimes it felt like a sinister ghost town with rubble-filled streets.

But it was changing. People were trying to find a new normalcy.

So, tonight we were going to *King Falafel's Café* to order the renowned falafel sandwiches made by the owner Zain. Sooo good! Really spicy, just how I liked them—they reminded me of *Mama*'s cooking.

We pulled our plastic chairs around a small table, sipping water as we waited for our order to arrive.

"I'm so hungry I could eat a donkey," groaned Nazar.

"Don't look too closely at the meat," Michelle said with a grimace. "It probably is donkey."

I shuddered.

"I'm going to stick with my regular..."

"Falafel sandwiches again?" asked Neil, raising his eyebrows.

"You betcha! I've been dreaming about these since last week!"

"As much as you've been dreaming about your hunky soldier?" asked Michelle slyly.

I shook my head, ignoring the slice of pain inside me as I pointed a finger at her.

"You know that Clay is one of my best friends *and* my sister's boyfriend!"

"Aw come on! He's a hottie! You've got to tell us *something*—we're your friends. Be kind to us lesser mortals who don't have video-calls from hot guys."

She was so animated, she sent her plastic silverware flying to the floor, and she had to crawl under the tiny table to look for it.

At the same time, the food arrived, saving me from having to say too much.

"Well, I will tell you one thing," I said as I picked up my sandwich, "Clay is totally●●●●

CHAPTER THIRTY-EIGHT

JAMES

I'd had a busy and boring morning of filling in paperwork. Every call-out came with pages of reports to file. Tedious, but necessary. I was swamped with the damn stuff, and I only had another twenty minutes before a meeting with my C.O. to be briefed about next week's training exercise in the Brecon Beacons, so I was trying to stay awake as I typed more forms.

When my phone rang a few minutes later on that Tuesday afternoon, I was glad of the distraction. But when I pulled it out of my pocket, I saw that the number had a California area code.

"Hello?"

"James Spears?" came the heavily accented voice.

"Yes, who's this?"

"James, this is Ammar Soliman, Amira's father."

A strange twitch started behind my right eye.

"Yes, sir. It's good to hear from you. How are..."

"Forgive my impatience, but her mother is very concerned. We haven't heard from Amira in a while, five days, in fact."

My chest started to ache and the twitch behind my eye intensified.

I'd been ignoring Clay's calls, as usual, and I hadn't listened to his voice messages either. How long had he been trying to contact me?

I walked past Captain Hammond's office where I was due for the briefing, and stood outside in the cool air.

"Has my daughter been in touch with you?" he asked, a note of desperation leaking into his voice.

"No, sir, I haven't heard from her. Maybe it's a comms ... communications problem."

He hesitated.

"Maybe, yes," but his voice sounded doubtful.

"Mr. Soliman, is there a specific reason that you're worried?" *Apart from the fact that your daughter is working in one of the most dangerous cities in the world.*

"It's probably as you say," he began, "but my cousin in Damascus says that rebels launched a rocket attack when the government's troops moved against them—that was on Wednesday. Official Syrian news channels report that the rebels were pushed back, but my cousin says some of the rockets landed near the hospital." His voice trembled. "Amira's not answering her cell phone and the phone number at the temporary hospital in Raqqa doesn't work." His voice cracked. "And there are more reports on Syrian internet news sites that there have been several car bombings in the city, as well. The government is trying to deny it, but I'm afraid it's likely to be true."

I stopped breathing.

"We can't find out anything about Amira," he said, his voice growing desperate. "I used the emergency MSF number that Amira gave me but they've lost contact with the team in Raqqa. They told me they're sending help from Damascus, but that could take days and we can't wait that long. Not again! I can't ... her mother ... but Clay said you could help—you have contacts! You can find out! Please, James, for our daughter's sake, please find out what has happened to her!"

I had zero contacts in Syria other than Amira herself, but Smith would know people.

"I'll find out what I can, sir."

That was the only promise I could make him.

"Thank you, James. I ... thank you."

He hung up and I dialled Smith's number immediately, swearing when it went to voice mail.

"Smith, Amira's not answering her phone, and I'm hearing reports about a Daesh RPG attack on her hospital and car bombs in the city. If you can find out *anything*, I need to know … yeah … thanks."

I went back to my room and listened to Clay's messages about Amira, begging me to call him and to speak to Smith, each of them more desperate. I shot him a text to say that I'd been in touch with Smith, and then I waited.

I'd forgotten that I was supposed to be talking to my C.O. He could sod off. I'd never liked him anyway.

It was midnight before Smith returned my call.

"Have you found her?" I blurted out.

The long pause told me everything.

"It's pretty bad out there right now," said Smith. "Clay called me last night and I've been putting out some feelers, trying to get intel. I've got some Special Forces contacts who are working with SDF in the city, a final push to force the rebels out. The new temporary hospital was badly damaged during the attack—it's non-operational, so she won't be there. The UN is trying to find out where the medical staff have been sent, but they have zero leverage."

My mouth was dry.

"Casualties?" I asked, the tension in my voice giving me away.

"Multiple," Smith said quietly. "There's no way to get names right now."

"Did the RPGs take out mobile phone towers, too?"

"Some, yeah. My contacts have sat phones."

Of course they did.

"And the car bombs? Do you know what part of the city they were in?"

"All over, from what I'm hearing. Multiple strikes coordinated with the RPG attacks. Bastards were making a last stand."

"I thought Daesh were supposed to be long gone?"

His voice was flat.

"That's what the Syrian Press reports, but those are run by Assad's people." He sighed. "It's bad in Raqqa, buddy. You need to go there … bring our girl home."

I wasn't sure I'd heard him right.

"James, I'm serious. Even I don't have the power to divert a Special Ops unit to go look for her, but if you can reach Cyprus, I can get you into the country and give you a contact name." His voice became determined. "I've emailed you a ticket for a flight to Paphos that leaves from Heathrow in four hours. I'll have a contact meet you at the harbour resort and get you on a boat to the Syrian coast. Then it's 280 miles overland to Raqqa. I'll arrange documentation that says you're an oilfield worker. They're trying to reopen the oil wells in central Syria, the nearest one is 50 clicks from Amira—that's your cover. My contact is doing this for U.S. dollars so don't tell him more than you have to—stick with the cover story. He's going to arrange transport, fuel and a weapon. But he's not willing to go with you, so once you're on Syrian soil, you're on your own. Go there, find Amira, and bring her home. We owe her that. And James..."

"What?"

"I'll deny ever having this conversation with you."

He hung up, and I was left staring at my phone, blood thundering in my ears.

What I was about to do was career-ending and bordering on suicidal. Not that my career mattered to me anymore, but if I was caught or when I came back to the UK, I'd be arrested and it would probably mean a court-martial, maybe even jail time in the Glasshouse, Colchester's military prison. That was best case scenario. Worst case, I'd be arrested as a spy in Syria. And shot.

I didn't even have to think about it.

I packed a small bag, stuffed my passport in my back pocket and snatched up the keys to my Ducati.

The sentry at the guardhouse gave me an odd look as I headed out at 2am, but he had no reason to stop me, no orders that prevented me leaving; he just lifted the barrier and watched me ride away.

I'd never forget that night, racing the sunrise as I headed to London and Heathrow Airport. The urge to twist the throttle as far as it would go was fierce, but the last thing I needed was to get caught by the police for speeding.

A million thoughts buzzed through my brain, each worse than the next as desperation drove me mad.

My mind tortured me with a thousand scenarios of what could have happened. It could just be comms problems, but then why would Smith have told me to get over there? Did he know something I didn't?

Had Umar's network reached her there somehow? How well could I trust Smith's contact, especially if he was working for the money? Then I thought guiltily of Larson: I hadn't trusted him at one time. Or Amira.

I prayed that she was okay, hopeful even that there'd be a message on my phone by the time I got to the airport, and I'd just have to turn around and face a bollocking from my C.O.

But then I imagined her hurt and alone, lost and in pain, unable to call for help. My stomach clenched as I pushed the panic away.

Amira didn't need a friend now—she needed the soldier in me.

I reached inside myself for that coolness, that emotional blackout that would see me through this. One by one, I locked my emotions down, focusing only on the task ahead, the op.

The temperature rose slowly as the sky turned from grey to gold, the cold air snapping at my jeans and leather jacket.

In theory, I could make the drive to Raqqa in one night, but I knew there would be numerous checkpoints along the way. I planned to get as much money as I could out of ATMs at the airport and change it into U.S. dollars, the currency of choice in a lot of bad places. I'd need the bribe money if I was going to get through.

And I'd need a lot of luck.

Amira, hang on. I'm coming.

When I arrived at the airport, I called Clay, and he answered on the first ring.

"James, thank God. Where are you, brother?"

"Heathrow. I'm planning to be in Raqqa this time tomorrow."

There was a long silence at the end of the line and when he spoke again, his voice was hoarse.

"I can't thank you enough for doing this, James. I know that it's been tough for you. What you're doing for Amira, for her family ... words will never be enough."

"It's fine," I said gruffly.

He sighed.

"She cares about you," he said softly. "She's just afraid to show it. She's been through a lot. And now ... just bring her home, James. Bring her home."

I ended the call even more agitated. For weeks I'd been living with the belief that Amira didn't want anything to do with me, now I wasn't sure.

I wasn't sure about anything—except the need to find her.

The flight to Paphos was full of holidaymakers. I stood out like a giraffe in Oxford Street, my black mood sending out very distinct *fuck off* vibes.

It was annoying the piss out of me to be around all that bloody *joy*. I buggered off to a quiet corner and stared morosely at the spectacular gold clouds bleeding into the dawn.

Anxiety ran through me like a low-level electrical current. I wouldn't let it take over, but it was there, humming beneath my skin.

Needing something to do, I pulled out my phone and dialled Amira's number. Maybe she'd answer, maybe she was okay...

Her voicemail clicked on, but at least I could hear her speaking. I left another message.

"It's James. Your dad called me—your parents are really worried. The news coming out of Raqqa isn't great and we need to know that you're safe." I took a deep breath. "I just need to hear your voice, okay?"

I pulled the phone away from my ear and swore, corralling my swirling thoughts before I made an even bigger tit of myself.

"Look, I've called in some favours from our favourite spook, and I'm coming to get you. I can't say more over this line, but you know what it means. I'm on my way. Whatever it takes, Amira. Whatever it costs. I'm coming. So just hold on for me. Just hold on and I'll be with you really soon." *I love you.*

I ended the call and shoved the phone in my back pocket. I rubbed my eyes and scraped my hands over my face, feeling the stubble under my fingers.

I thought about calling her parents, but with no news, it wouldn't help them.

The four hour flight to Cyprus was going to feel very slow.

It was another two hours until I was supposed to report for duty, and I wondered how long after that they'd start to look for me. Probably they'd ask around first, try my mates, see if anyone knew something. The first 24 hours is 'absent from place of work'. Still no word after that, and I'm officially AWOL. My C.O. would get the

Regimental Second in Command or the Adjutant to leave a message on my phone first. When I didn't respond, they might even start calling around the hospitals to see if I'd had an accident.

When that didn't give them a lead, the RMP would hand it over to the civilian police, and I'd be on put on the police PNC national database. Eventually, they'd trace my bike to Heathrow...

With luck on my side, I'd be in Raqqa before anyone back at the barracks started to worry.

CHAPTER THIRTY-NINE

JAMES

I turned off my phone's airplane mode immediately after landing, before the plane had finished taxiing to a stop on the runway at Paphos. I had some pathetic hope that Amira would have returned my message, and we'd laugh about what a mess I'd been waiting to hear from her.

But when my phone was active again, there were no messages. None. Not even from my C.O. or any of my mates at work.

And there was me worrying about being stopped at Heathrow.

The truth was, no one gave a shit.

As soon as the aeroplane's doors were opened, I was up and out of my seat, rudely pushing past everyone, ignoring their annoyed stares and muttered comments.

Going through immigration took a few seconds as I waved my British passport at them, and then I was out in the main concourse, looking for the taxi rank.

The heat was already in the high eighties and was forecast to go much higher. I ignored the brilliant sun and the perfect cloudless sky. All around me happy holidaymakers were clutching their luggage, ready to enjoy a week of doing nothing except eating and sitting in the sun.

Something about the normality of it, their sheer innocence gave me hope. But at the same time, I wanted to shove the war in their faces. They were so close to the Middle East's madness, but they could have been on Brighton Pier, if it wasn't for the fact that the sun was shining.

The taxi driver was chatty. I wanted to shoot him before we'd gone a hundred yards. Didn't he know that there was a war going on?

Bloody civilians. They preferred to live in denial. It was the same when I'd come back from Afghanistan the first time—reverse culture shock. It took days to get over how casual people in the UK were about wasting water: twenty minute showers, washing their cars, watering their stupid lawns. Where I'd been posted in Helmand province, water was flown in along with food supplies. Nothing was wasted and I didn't shower for months.

And then I got back to England, with Afghan dust on my boots and in my clothes, and no one wanted to talk about a war 3,000 miles away. No one wanted to know that IEDs were killing 19 year-old squaddies. No one cared.

Just like here. A war on their doorstep. Don't talk about it. Don't acknowledge it. And maybe it won't be true.

Don't want to scare the tourists.

But it felt like the world should be as worried as me. Carrying your cares by yourself was lonely.

I thought about calling Smith again, but he'd made it very clear that wasn't an option. I didn't want to call Clay either—not until I had news. The man was still in hospital, facing further surgeries and months of rehab before he could walk again.

The taxi driver was relentless, telling me in tedious detail about his brother's restaurant where I should definitely go for dinner. *Fat chance*.

Bored of his upbeat sales pitch, I interrupted.

"Got many Syrian refugees on the island?"

He snorted and changed the subject.

I already knew that Cyprus took a tough stance on Syrian refugees. *Bastards*.

He dropped me at a resort on the eastern-most tip of the island, muttering under his breath as he snatched the money from my hand.

I wandered into the resort, trying to look like a tourist enjoying a stroll, ordering a bottle of beer from the bar, before heading out to the pool area, my aviators shading my eyes.

Heat bounced up from the white concrete, but it still enticed some sunbathers intent on turning their skin into bacon. Instead, I found a place where I could watch the entrances and exits without being obvious.

My contact arrived an hour later, just as I was on my last nerve, and wondering how far I'd get without help.

He sauntered through the pool area, ogling women in bikinis, before casually nodding at me.

I waited 20 seconds then followed him to the secluded balcony as he pretended to look at the view over the calm, blue Mediterranean Sea.

"You have money, friend?"

"I was told it was all arranged, that you'd have my documents, transport and ... protection."

He snorted impatiently.

"Whoever told you that was wrong. I have overheads."

Great. A shakedown.

"How much?"

"Two thousand American dollars."

I glanced across, seeing his smug expression.

"Sure."

He grinned, surprised it had been so easy.

"I'll pay you when I get back."

His smile slipped, replaced by annoyance.

"No, no! You must pay now! This is very dangerous and I am a businessman."

I leaned against the railings, staring out to sea.

"How about you give me what was agreed, and I don't throw you over the balcony? Those rocks don't look like they'd be a comfortable landing."

His mouth dropped open and he tried to move away from me, but I clamped my hand on his wrist, drawing him close as he stared down at the razor sharp reef skimming the water beneath.

"Listen, *friend*," I said pleasantly. "I've had a really bad day. But yours will be a lot worse unless you do what you were contracted to do.

But if I come back alive, you'll get your two thousand dollar bonus—and you'll get to live a long and happy life." I pulled him closer. "Piss me off, and you'll be dead within the next thirty seconds. Your choice."

I didn't get any arguments after that, but I probably hadn't made a friend for life either.

He led me out to his car and gave me the travel documents that Smith had arranged for, then we drove south to a small, isolated beach, where a greasy-looking dude was waiting with a beaten up fishing boat.

Then he showed me the arsenal he'd acquired for me: a Russian AK-74 assault rifle that was older than I was, and a Makarov pistol, probably from the 1950s but still used by the Russian military—it looked prehistoric.

"Do these even work?"

I didn't need a misfire when my life was depending on it.

"Yes!" he said, indignantly. "Best quality!"

I pointed the pistol at him and started to pull the trigger. From the way sweat broke out on his forehead, I concluded the arms were probably adequate.

I nodded and accepted four clips of ammo—hardly enough if I got caught in a fire fight. Christ, I hoped that didn't happen.

And then I was on my way with the fisherman who clearly wasn't happy to have me as a passenger.

The boat chugged away across the Mediterranean, skimming the Syrian coastline until the sun began to set and stars appeared in the sky. Then he cut the engine, and we ghosted onto a silent beach where an ancient American Jeep was sitting on the sand. My skin prickled with the sensation that I was being watched, but the lack of moonlight meant that I couldn't see far. Good for me to stay hidden—bad if I wanted to know what was coming for me.

I waded the last twenty feet to the beach, but the boat had already turned and headed back to Cyprus by the time I made it to shore.

Being abandoned in Syria without transport was not what I needed right now. I prayed that the Jeep was fuelled, and almost cheered when it started on the second try.

It coughed and wheezed, then throatily roared to life. I cringed, ducking down to avoid imaginary bullets, but none came. Cautiously, I pulled out my phone and brought up the route to Raqqa. I'd already memorized it, but checking helped me to calm down. It wasn't the most direct road, but Smith had said it had the fewest checkpoints.

Driving at night was hazardous to say the least. The road was pockmarked with craters, and burnt-out cars and tanks littered the ditches. I saw the neon glow of towns in the distance, but stuck to my route, zigzagging through the ridge of mountains that followed the coastline. There were more cultivated fields than I was expecting, but as I drove east, the desert crept forward to meet me, flat and arid, stretching in all directions.

According to the map I'd studied, a narrow green belt ran through the centre of Syria, following the path of the Euphrates River. Raqqa was built on the north side of the river, two hundred miles inland.

The first hour and the last hour of driving would be the most hazardous because I would be closest to populated areas. I was concerned about meeting patrols, especially since a curfew was still in place. It was risky.

But then again, everything about this mission was risky. And I didn't care. The mission had one aim, one outcome that mattered.

I drove through the night, twice having to turn off my headlights and drive cross-country when I saw headlights from a patrol, then looping back to the main road. I doubted that they'd give me a chance to explain—they'd be more likely to shoot first.

But if I blew out a tyre by driving over a rock, I was fucked.

The first patrol, I avoided easily, but the second one was persistent, and I had to lay up for over an hour while they searched the desert for me. It was sheer luck that I wasn't caught. But every soldier needs luck.

As I left the well-irrigated cotton and wheat fields behind, driving towards Raqqa, I hit my first checkpoint at dawn when the city was in sight. This time there was no way around.

Armed soldiers manned the barrier and ordered me out of the Jeep. I gave them my story about being an oil worker, but they studied my papers minutely, arguing amongst themselves, probably wondering how far I'd driven when the curfew had only been lifted an hour ago.

The fact that I was armed didn't bother them, but seeing that my Jeep had spare fuel, that was enough to make me very interesting.

Despite some of the oil wells near Raqqa coming back on line, there was still a lot of work to do, a lot of engineering to be repaired. Smith had chosen a good cover story for me. But petrol that had been refined was still at a premium and worth a lot of money on the thriving black market.

The soldiers eyed the fuel cans enviously, clearly wondering whether I was worth the risk of fleecing, or whether I'd make trouble for them. In the end, I made it easy, and handed over $200 and a ten gallon can of petrol.

I hoped I wouldn't have to make that sacrifice at every checkpoint, because I was going to need the fuel to get back, or even make a run for the Turkish border, although that was only 60 miles away.

Silently, they watched me drive off, and I let out a long breath when they were finally out of sight.

Two more checkpoints later, and down $500 and four more petrol cans, I drove slowly through the bomb-blasted city, skirting craters and bullet-marked buildings that looked as though they were about to collapse. Raqqa had been reduced to rubble, and yet there were signs of life returning: a few people going about their business as dawn rose quickly in the east; cafes opening, offering strong, sweet coffee; several motorbikes on the road, but very few cars. A pack of stray dogs roamed the streets, skinny and feral, they bared their teeth as my Jeep rattled past.

I wore sunglasses in the half-light to hide my blue eyes, and I'd wound a scarf around my head so I didn't stand out as much. I thought of what Amira would say if she saw me now—and the irony wasn't lost on me.

I knew that the Jeep was drawing attention, as well. Unfortunately, I needed to have wheels. I was prepared to shoot any bastard who decided they wanted to try and take the Jeep from me.

I followed the GPS to the location of Amira's temporary hospital, but when I got there, my heart sank—it had been completely obliterated with only a stark ruin, black against the sky and a few tattered tents. I'd hoped that there might be administrative offices, something still there so I could ask around. But the place was deserted and only the ghosts remained.

I cut the engine and climbed out, careful to tuck my sidearm into the waistband of my jeans, and slung the rifle over my shoulder.

"Amira, where are you?" I whispered.

A young boy was watching me, his expression scared and defiant.

"*Mustashfaa?*" I asked, jerking my head at the rubble, using the Arabic word for 'hospital'.

He stared at me blankly, then pointed into the distance and shouted something I didn't understand.

"Hey, wait!" I called, but he was already gone, diving behind an abandoned building.

I had no choice but to drive in the direction he'd indicated and hope I'd get lucky. Besides, he might decide to tell someone about the stranger who couldn't speak his language, so waiting here on the off-chance that I'd find someone from the hospital wasn't an option. People had been killed for a lot less than the cans of petrol I was carrying.

I drove slowly, keeping my eyes open for a makeshift hospital, a sign, or someone I could ask.

After ten minutes of driving in circles, I saw a tattered flag fluttering in the wind, and I felt my heart leap with relief. The flag was green with a white star and crescent, and the letters 'MSF' printed boldly below. As I turned the corner, I saw several large canvas tents the size of marquees, and I knew that I'd found the new base of the temporary hospital.

More soldiers guarded the perimeter of the canvas buildings, and I saw ambulances parked nearby—several looked like they'd been strafed by machine guns. My dormant anger was reawakened, flashing into fury in seconds. *Who fires on an ambulance?*

The soldiers stared me down as I approached, but I didn't drop my weapons. I didn't point them at the armed guards either—I was desperate, not suicidal. Getting killed this close to finding Amira was not part of the plan.

"*Salaam-Alaikum,*" I said cautiously. "*Al'iinjlizia?*"

I asked if anyone spoke English, and hoped like hell that someone did.

One of the soldiers nodded.

"Little English. What you want?"

"I'm looking for Amira Soliman. She's a nurse at the hospital. You know, a nurse? Medic? Doctor?" I stumbled on as he stared at me. "Her parents are worried about her and asked me to look for her. Do you know where I can find her?"

He scowled, and I knew that he was wondering about our relationship—Muslim women weren't supposed to be friends with a man they weren't related to, not if they were devout, not in this part of the world.

I tried again.

"Amira Soliman. Nurse—a medic. Her parents haven't heard from her since the bombing. They're concerned. Her father sent me. Can you help me find her?"

They muttered amongst themselves, gesturing with their rifles, which was somewhat disturbing. It was clear that the man who said he spoke English didn't understand most of what I was saying.

I stood helpless and impatient as they argued amongst themselves.

Their conversation grew more animated by the second, and then one of them gestured for me to go with him. I wasn't happy leaving the Jeep and cans of petrol with them, but if he was going to take me to Amira, that was all that mattered.

I took a step forward to follow him, but one of the soldiers who'd been doing the most shouting blocked my path, clearly wanting to take my rifle, too. I was *not* happy about that. In the end, it seemed like a deal breaker, so I gave it to him reluctantly. He didn't try to pat me down—amateur—so he didn't know that I still had a pistol tucked in the waistband of my jeans.

The first soldier was waiting impatiently for me to follow, and strode off at a fast pace until we were in the centre of the canvas city.

He pointed at a spot near the entrance to the largest tent, indicating that I should wait outside.

Excitement and anticipation ballooned inside me, and I could already feel the smile hovering on my face, thinking of Amira's surprise when she saw me. I'd probably get a weapons-grade bollocking from her, too, but damn if the thought didn't make me smile.

I waited with increasing impatience.

Ten minutes passed, and annoyance turned to frustration.

A thin drizzle began, turning the tents gunmetal grey, and frustration turned to a fear that churned in my gut.

After half an hour of clawing desperation, a thin woman with pale

skin and blue eyes walked towards me. Her hair was covered with a
hijab, but her eyebrows were blonde.

It wasn't who I wanted to see, but I sensed that she'd be able to tell
me something.

"Yes?" she asked warily, glancing at the soldier who'd escorted her.

"I'm looking for Amira Soliman. I'm a friend of her parents."

"Do you have a name, friend?"

She had a Northern Irish accent and a glare that reminded me of
my first drill sergeant. And I realized how dodgy this much look, so I
tucked my sunglasses into my pocket and pulled the scarf from my
head.

"My name is James Spears. I'm a friend of hers. I, um, met her in
America last summer. Maybe she mentioned me?"

The woman shook her head, her eyes narrowing.

"I met her parents and her sister, Zada," I hurried on. "Her dad's
name is Ammar." *What else?* "We have a mutual friend, a guy called
Clay, maybe she mentioned him?"

She gasped, her hand flying to her throat.

"Clay? Amira's Clay?"

That wasn't what I was expecting to hear, and jealousy uncoiled
restlessly inside me.

"Yeah, I know Clay. So is she here? I've been going crazy when I
couldn't get through to her. I thought her phone must be out of action,
and her parents are really worried. Clay asked me to come here and
find her."

She didn't smile back.

"How did you get here?"

My smile fell as I sensed her evasion.

"It wasn't easy," I admitted.

"No, I'd imagine not."

"So, is she here?"

She sighed and rattled something in rapid Arabic to my guard who
gave me a disdainful look, then ambled off.

"You'd better come inside," she said, ducking back into the tent.
"We're doing the best we can, but it's chaos. I'm Michelle, by the way."

I nodded, even though I was walking behind her and she couldn't
see me.

Unease prickled under my skin.

"Not trying to be rude here, Michelle, but what aren't you telling me? Is Amira hurt? Was she in the hospital when it was shelled?"

"No," she said hurriedly.

"No, she wasn't hurt or no she wasn't in the hospital?"

My voice rose, and I saw her wring her hands.

Finally, she led me to a corner of the tent where a couple of medics were writing up notes on what looked like a picnic table. Their faces were etched with exhaustion, their eyes red, their scrubs stained with blood. I turned away and studied Michelle.

She sat down, composing herself, but her hands were shaking. Then she looked up at me with tears in her eyes, and wretched certainty filled me as I saw my future spinning into nothing.

"I'm sorry, James. I'm so terribly, terribly sorry. Amira was hurt in a car bombing. She's not here anymore—she's being repatriated to a military hospital in Germany. An ambulance took her to the airport earlier this morning. I'm so sorry, but you've missed her."

CHAPTER FORTY

JAMES

I closed my eyes, trying to take in what I was being told. Amira was hurt, but at least she was on her way out of here.

"How bad is she hurt?" I asked harshly, winding my emotions back tightly.

Michelle sighed and shook her head.

"She's well enough to fly, so that's positive, but she needs another blood transfusion and we simply don't have enough." She hesitated. "We suspect there's internal bleeding somewhere, but we can't be sure without the correct equipment. We have to risk moving her now."

Michelle held my hands, painting a vivid picture.

They'd been out to a small café to eat. They were laughing. Amira was happy. They were all happy, relaxing after a long shift.

Michelle dropped her fork and had been under the table when the car bomb detonated. Being clumsy had saved her life. Four of the others had been killed by flying glass. Dead. Men and women who'd volunteered in this shithole because they wanted to make the world a better place. Dead.

Michelle had held Amira's hand as her blood pooled around them.

"So much blood," Michelle said softly. "We managed to get her stabilized for now, but we don't have the resources to help her here.

The phone towers were damaged, too, and MSF Headquarters only managed to send an email to her parents last night."

I nodded, trying to take it all in.

"When was her flight?"

She gave me a tired look.

"Who knows? Flights don't happen on time around here. When's it's safe, I suppose," and she shrugged. "I'm sorry, James, but that's all I can tell you. It's possible her flight hasn't even left yet. If you leave for the airport now, you might make it in time to see her."

I thanked her and stood up quickly.

"If you don't make it in time," she called after me as I strode away, "would you come back and donate some blood—we sorely need it."

I promised that I would, but I was already running and I don't know if she heard me.

The hospital's armed guard was very reluctant to let me take the Jeep, and it was only when I pointed my pistol at the leader's face that I was allowed to drive away. I had to leave the rifle.

I kept expecting to hear the sharp crack of a bullet behind me, but nothing happened.

I grabbed my phone, cursing when I saw it was nearly out of juice. I just hoped that it could direct me to the airport before it died.

I'd never been to Raqqa before but as it turned out, it wasn't that difficult to find the airport. I followed a line of trucks bearing the logo of various charities, all heading in the same direction I was travelling, and I figured they were going to the airport, too. But when I arrived, I didn't have the correct papers, and the perimeter was circled with barbed wire—all very well guarded.

It took the rest of my petrol cans and almost all of the cash I had with me to bribe my way inside.

I could see a large American transport plane parked close to the main runway. If I'd had any spare cash, I would have bet that this was the plane Amira was on.

I growled with frustration as the bureaucrats and administrative staff refused to let me know if she was on the plane or not. In the end, I used the last of my precious dollars to be able to see inside.

The whole plane was filled with MSF staff and charity workers being evacuated. Several of them looked in critical condition, and all of them had wounds of one kind or another. My eyes skipped desperately as I prowled between the rows, searching for Amira.

Until finally, near the rear of the plane, I found her.

Her eyes were closed and there were streaks of blood on her face. She looked so pale and still, I was almost afraid to touch her.

"Amira," I said softly. "Amira..."

Her eyelids flickered and she opened her eyes slowly, her expression bewildered.

"Ja... James?"

"Yeah! I'm here, thank God."

"What are you doing here?" she asked faintly.

"Your dad called me—he was worried because he hadn't heard from you. Comms are down all over the city and the news was bad."

She nodded slowly.

"But ... how did you find me?"

"I ran into your Irish friend, Michelle. She told me you were being flown out. That's good, really good." My gaze dropped to her bandaged hands. "You're okay though, yeah?"

She blinked wearily.

"You shouldn't have come."

Her words were so intensely painful that I couldn't breathe.

I swallowed twice.

"Your parents were worried ... Clay was worried, I was worried..."

A ghost of a smile hovered on her lips.

"Always worrying about other people, James." Then she sighed as her eyes began to close, and I could tell that she was heavily sedated. "I can't believe you're here. I can't even imagine how you managed it, that you put yourself in such danger. But it's so good to see you. Are you really here? I'm not dreaming this?"

I took her hand and it lay limply in mine.

"I'm really here. There's nowhere else I want to be."

"I'm so sorry about what I said last time, when we were at JFK. So many times I wanted to contact you, but I was scared. That seems so stupid now. I'm so sorry..."

"It's okay," I said, my heart lurching. "We can talk about it later. You're going to be okay and..."

"Hey, dude," called a man in the uniform of a U.S. Marine. "You gotta get off—we're going wheels up in ten."

"Can I stay with her?" I asked desperately, and he shot me an incredulous look.

"We're not a taxi service, buddy! We're overloaded as it is—we're not taking anyone who can walk on by themselves."

I turned to Amira, crouching down next to her, still holding her small hand in mine.

"There are so many things I want to tell you," I said, my voice breaking. "I love you. And I know that the timing is terrible ... but I've missed you. These months without you have been shit. I'd do anything for you, you know that, right? Anything. I'd give you the world, if I could, and every star in the sky."

Her eyes opened briefly and she brought her bandaged hand up to my cheek.

"Sweet James. I don't deserve you..."

Her eyes closed again and I carefully placed her hand in her lap, reluctant to leave, desperate to stay.

The Marine glared at me and I knew it was time to go. The sands of time had finally run out. I'd played my final hand, and I'd lost.

But at least Amira would be safe.

I stood up stiffly, surprised to find that my face was wet with tears.

"Please," Amira said suddenly, staring up at the Marine as she grabbed my hand to stop me from leaving. "Please let him stay. I need him. Please!"

"Ma'am, I can't authorize..."

"Please! Please!"

"Damn it," he swore softly. "Okay, he can stay," and he turned to me, "but don't get in anyone's way."

"I won't. Thank you!"

He stalked away mumbling to himself and shaking his head.

CHAPTER FORTY-ONE

JAMES

There was nowhere for me to sit except on the floor next to Amira. Every time someone needed to get past, I had to squeeze out of the way. Being here was probably breaking a hundred rules, but I didn't care.

I held Amira's hand and talked to her, but I was seriously worried how weak her pulse felt and her skin was cool and clammy. I couldn't tell if she was sleeping or dipping in and out of consciousness. I wasn't a trained medic, but even I could tell that she was fading.

The overworked doctors on board, did what they could for all the injured, but I saw one man die in front of me. I didn't tell Amira when she asked me; I told her the guy was sleeping.

"Maybe we can try and get to see Clay when you're better," I said, squeezing her hand.

There was the slightest uplift of her lips.

"He's a great guy," she said, her words so soft that I had to strain to hear her over the plane's engines.

I had a lot of time for Clay, but I felt a surge of jealousy when Amira talked about him.

"He's going to marry Zada," she said.

"Your sister? Seriously? I didn't know! That's great."

"He tried to tell you," she whispered, her quiet words blasting me with guilt.

"I should have replied to him," I said stiffly.

"I know why you didn't, and I'm sorry. So sorry. All my fault."

I held her hand in mine carefully.

"Well, you're not getting rid of me now. Maybe you could come and see me in England, or I'll come and visit you."

"Sounds nice," she said weakly. "So tired."

"Don't try and talk, Amira. Save your strength. We can talk when you're home."

"So tired. James…"

"Yes?"

But she was asleep. I held her hand as the miles passed, but she was so cold.

"Hey," I asked one of the crew, "can I get her another blanket? She's really cold."

She frowned at me, then leaned over, pressing her fingers to Amira's neck. Then she lifted one of her eyelids, before glancing at me quickly.

"I'm sorry. She's gone."

My world spun.

"What?"

"I'm sorry, her injuries were too bad. She didn't make it."

"But … that can't be right! I've been sitting right here."

She laid her hand on my shoulder.

"I'm sorry. She has no pulse, and her pupils are fixed and dilated. There's nothing you could have done."

Even after we arrived in Germany, I sat with her until they took her away.

I didn't remember leaving the plane. A wrenching sensation scoured my chest as if someone was pulling my ribs out one by one.

I was outside, on my knees, retching my guts out.

My fingers sank into the mud as vomit spattered the dirt in front of me. My stomach heaved again, but there was nothing left, and it was with a bizarre sense of surprise that I realised I was crying.

The last time I'd cried, I'd been taken into foster care. I'd promised myself then that nothing would ever hurt me again.

But here I was, covered in mud and puke, and crying like a damn baby.

Everything was gone: my hope, my future, the love of my life. My shitty, stupid, pointless life. I'd come charging over here to save her, but I wasn't needed and I couldn't help. It was a cosmic joke, and I was the punchline.

"Why?!" I raged at the sky. "Why? Why did you take her away?" I screamed. "You're a bastard, God! A devious, lying fraud! You're nothing but a sideshow trick! You're the greatest con of all! You're a cheap suit, God, with your holy words and your promises! You're a dammed liar! You can go to Hell! Because I'm already there!"

I screamed again, rage and despair tearing my throat.

My hands shook as I pulled the old Russian pistol from my waistband, my hands slick with mud. I put the gun against the side of my head, staring up accusingly at the rain-racked sky.

"FUCK YOU, GOD!"

I pulled the trigger, waiting for the bullet that would end my life.

But all I heard was a dry click.

I pulled the trigger again and again and again, but nothing happened.

"Useless piece of Russian shit!" I yelled, dropping it in the mud.

I started to laugh as rain and tears poured down my face, and I collapsed into the dirt, lying on my back, my eyes closed.

Even death didn't want me.

I waited for something, anything, but nothing happened.

No one came.

No one spoke to me.

No one cared that a man had lost his sanity in front of them.

The rain came down more heavily, pelting my face, saturating my clothes. Cold seeped into my body, a welcome numbness.

But the world kept turning, and the sun would rise and set.

Eventually, I sat up, scrubbing my hands over my face, smearing more mud and snot across my skin.

Two U.S. Marines came running across the grass next to the plane, their rifles pointed at me.

"Move away from your weapon! Hands on your head!"

Maybe I could get them to shoot me to put me out of my misery. I reached for the pistol that was still in the mud nearby, but the one behind me didn't shoot me. Instead, he smashed his rifle butt into my face, sending blood gushing from my nose.

Like I said, death didn't want me.

I began to laugh again, tasting my own blood as it flowed down my face and into my mouth. I licked my lips, wet with salty blood, and I laughed.

The other Marine grabbed the pistol and handcuffed me, hauling me to my feet.

I'd promised Amira's parents that I'd find her and bring her home. I'd failed.

I'd failed at everything.

Failed at this game of life.

The next thing I remember was staring up a short, tanned Major in the British Army.

"Get up, you piece of filth!" he yelled.

Huh. I was still alive. What a kick in the balls.

Confused and in pain, I sat up slowly. I'd been lying on a metal cot in some sort of cell. Whether it was at the airport or the local police station, I couldn't say.

I rubbed my eyes, then spat at his feet, a gob of spittle landing on his shiny black boots.

He jumped back and swore.

"Spears, you piece of shit! You're under arrest for desertion. You'll be transferred back to the UK to face a court-martial. Understand? Understand!"

I just stared at him, watching his face turn crimson, matching the red cap that marked him as Military Police.

And then I started to laugh. And laugh and laugh.

I laughed so hard that I crashed to my knees, laughing so hard my ribs might crack. I laughed so hard it brought tears to my eyes.

I knelt in the dust of a German jail, laughing and crying, losing my mind, while a Royal Military Police bastard clamped handcuffs around my wrists and hauled me away under arrest.

My career was over.

Amira was gone.

And there was no point in living anymore.

EPILOGUE

THREE MONTHS LATER

The buzzing grew louder and despite the anaesthetic, pain flared through my numb body.

Breathing helped. Yeah, that's what I had to do—keep breathing. *Breathe or die*.

I wasn't sure it was much of a choice.

The tattoo artist paused, pulling the needle from my body, surveying his work. He glanced up.

"Doing alright there, mate?"

The skin on my chest was red and inflamed, tiny droplets of blood oozing through the stain of ink, the design beginning to make sense. As much as anything could in the shithole that was my life.

I grunted, and he went back to work.

I welcomed the pressure of the needle, enjoyed the pain piercing the numbness that I'd carried for months.

Amira was dead. So it had all been for nothing. Everything we'd been through. So much nothing.

After my arrest, I'd faced a court martial for being AWOL and I'd served time in Colchester, the Military Corrective Training Centre—

prison in all but name. Each day was the same: PT, breakfast, drill, PT, lunch, PT, evening meal, PT, drill, room inspection, show parade every hour till 5am, then PT, breakfast... it tortured the body and numbed the mind. It was supposed to break you and remodel you as a perfect soldier.

But I was already broken—there was nothing more they could do to me.

They tried to threaten me with the charge of desertion which carried a ten-year sentence. But my defence counsel pointed out that my commander had sent me on a training task to the U.S. that turned out to be an illegal op—which was tantamount to kidnapping—and wouldn't they rather the whole thing didn't make the newspapers. He even suggested that I should be expecting a promotion, a medal and a posting of my choosing.

He'd made his point.

I suspected the hand of Smith in the fact that I only served a few weeks of the six month sentence that I'd received, but I didn't know for sure because I never heard from him again.

My career was over and my exit had been fast-tracked—administrative discharge they called it. No one wanted to work with me, and no C.O. wanted me under his command.

Yesterday, I'd been in prison, now I was out—not quite a dishonourable discharge, and I was a civilian again.

I didn't care. I didn't care about anything.

My phone vibrated in my pocket and the tattoo artist paused again.

"You want to take it?"

Clay calling.

He was persistent, I'd give him credit for that. But just like all the other times he'd tried to talk to me, I ignored it. I'd ignored dozens of texts, emails and calls. The guy wasn't getting the message.

I turned off my phone and threw it on top of the pile of clothes next to me.

The tattoo artist shrugged and went back to work. Maybe he had a lot of fucked up customers.

An hour later, he'd finished.

On the skin above my heart was inked a set of claw marks, deep and red and raw, blood dripping from them.

Having Amria's name tattooed on my chest would have been too small, too ordinary for what I felt. Her absence, the finality of our last minutes together, it had ripped my beating heart from my body. I should be dead, but my flesh continued to live and I didn't understand how that was possible. A man shouldn't live when his heart has been torn from his body.

But I did.

And every day I had to find a reason to keep on living.

I was pretty sure that one day soon, I'd run out of reasons.

And then I'd find peace.

Inshallah.

TO BE CONTINUED...

ARE YOU READY FOR MORE?

Please don't be angry with me for ending James' and Amira's journey like that. I'm sorry, I am. But this is a story about love and loss and learning, growth and strength and change.

Everything has changed for James. And although it's the end of Amira's story, James will go on...

PROLOGUE

JAMES

The first time I tried to kill myself, I failed.

Obviously.

The gun misfired. I kept pulling the trigger and nothing happened, just empty clicks and a cosmic frustration.

But next time, I'll do it right, no mistakes. I have it all planned out. There's a bottle of 25 year old Irish whiskey with my name on it, a handful of sleeping pills, and a plastic bag over my head. It will be a quiet end, peaceful. Which is ironic really, and nothing like the way I've lived my life.

So with everything in place, the last thing I want is to find a reason for living.

CHAPTER ONE

JAMES

I lay on my mattress, eyes dry and head aching.

I hadn't slept, I'd just sobered up slowly during a long night of too many thoughts and all the painful memories stirred up by seeing Clay.

What was the point of anything? I hated what I was, who I'd become. And I hated that I didn't have the guts to finish it either. Each day when I woke, I thought today would be the day. But by the time I collapsed at night onto the filthy mattress in this shitty doss house, I'd lived another day. Not that anyone would call it living: I was existing.

Like I said, what was the point?

I reached for the bottle by the side of the mattress, but it was empty. I must have finished it during the night. I couldn't remember.

Rolling to my hands and knees, I clawed my way upright using the wall to support me, then staggered to the disgusting shared bathroom. It hadn't been cleaned in years, possibly decades, but I didn't care. It was a toss up which smelled worse: the bog, the scummy shower, or me.

My piss was the colour of rust which meant I was dehydrated. There was grim satisfaction in the thought that I was slowly killing myself with drink. Faster would be better.

A heavy pounding on the front door bruised my brain, but despite all the grey cells I'd been assassinating steadily over the last 15 months, I had a shrewd idea who was making all the racket, so I ignored it.

When the front door was flung open with sound of the wooden frame splintering, I sighed and shuffled back to my room to lie on my mattress, waiting for the inevitable.

I heard Clay's heavy footsteps clomping up the stairs, noting a slight unevenness to his gait. I closed my eyes, remembering again the moment I saw the explosion rip through him, the blood on my hands, my ears ringing. I could see the panic on her face, taste her fear, feel the futility boil inside me as time ran out, the inevitability of the seconds counting down—then flames and noise, the stench of burning, flying through the air and...

He kicked open two other doors before mine was slammed into the wall, sending chips of paint flaking from the ceiling, and my mind skittered and lurched back to the present.

"This place is a frickin' dump, James."

"Yeah, it suits me," I said tiredly, depressed that I hadn't been able to find another bottle of whiskey to sink into. "Well, you found me. What next?"

He didn't answer, but I heard him stomping around my room, so I cracked an eye, watching without interest as he tossed the few clothes I had into my old Army kitbag, emptying drawers and...

"Don't touch that!" I said sharply, sitting upright, suddenly very awake and very sober.

He paused, his hand hovering over a shoebox that I kept hidden at the back of the wardrobe.

"Make me stop," he said with a challenge in his voice.

Fury exploded inside me, piercing through the shield of numbness, and I launched myself at him. He stumbled, my weight knocking him backwards, but then he recovered his balance and put me down with one punch.

I lay on the floor winded, my jaw howling in agony as I felt my cheek start to swell.

"Aw, damn," said Clay, leaning over me to offer his hand.

I ignored his outstretched arm and scrambled to my knees, pulling the precious shoebox toward me as I hunched over it protectively. I didn't care about much, but no one touched that box.

I pulled off the lid, just to check, just to see, and stared down at the small square of folded silk. My fingers shook as I stroked it, taking the smallest solace from the feel of it, knowing it was safe.

"That hers?" Clay asked softly.

I nodded, my throat closing as I choked down emotion.

I touched the folded material once more before I replaced the lid, wiping angrily at my eyes.

Clay touched my shoulder.

"Come on, brother. Amira wouldn't have wanted this for you."

Hearing her name sent tremors racing through my battered body and broken mind. But Clay hadn't finished.

"She wouldn't want you living like this." He hesitated. "Look, Zada's in London with me and she'd really like to see you."

I shook my head. I wasn't in a position to see anyone, especially the woman who should have been my sister-in-law.

I glanced at Clay's hand resting on my shoulder and paused. He was wearing a platinum wedding ring.

"You and Zada?"

He smiled and nodded.

"You were invited to the wedding."

I hadn't known, hadn't checked my emails in months.

"Congratulations," I said dully. "She's a great girl. She's ... great."

His eyes lit up.

"Yeah, she is. I'm a lucky bastard."

Then he picked up my kitbag and snatched my shoebox, tucking it under his arm.

"Hey!" I yelled, stumbling to my feet. "HEY!"

He was already out the door and halfway down the stairs when I came pounding after him. I tripped the last three stairs and landed on my hands and knees at the bottom, winded and pissed off.

"Give me my fucking box!" I yelled after him as Clay strode down the street.

"Come and get it!" he called over his shoulder.

Furious, I picked myself up and limped down the road after him, wheezing like an old and knackered sixty-a-day smoker.

After a few hundred yards when it became clear that I couldn't keep up with him, he took pity on me.

My head pounded and my whole body ached. Everyone else on the pavement was giving me a wide berth, avoiding the scary-looking homeless guy they saw.

When we hit the main road, Clay hailed a Black Cab, leaving the door open for me as he clambered in. The driver didn't look too happy about having me as a passenger, too, but Clay didn't give a shit, just throwing a hard stare until the man turned back to his steering wheel.

Hesitating, I held onto the door, out of breath and hurting, eyeing the shoebox on the seat next to Clay.

"Where are you going?"

"Do you care?"

I licked my cracked lips, then climbed in.

Feeling like shit, I tried to touch the box, but Clay moved it nearer towards him, a warning in his expression. So I slumped against the vinyl seat, closing my eyes. Clay didn't speak either, and I was nearly asleep by the time we arrived outside a large, budget hotel.

Clay paid the driver as I stood looking warily at the glass and concrete exterior. I didn't belong here with decent people. But Clay hustled me inside, stepping quickly past the frowning receptionist and into the lift.

Swiping his key card, we rose to the twelfth floor and Clay marched me along the corridor, opening the door to a small single room.

He tossed my kitbag on the bed, then carefully placed my shoebox next to it. I touched it quickly, avoiding Clay's eyes. Touching it helped.

"Get cleaned up," he said, then closed the door.

I sank down on the bed, too exhausted to hold onto my anger. I had two choices: pack up my shit and leave right now, knowing that Clay wouldn't come after me again. Or, I could stay.

I wanted to leave. The weight of Clay's hope was too heavy, his expectations too unmanageable, but I was tired of my own thoughts. Just so damn tired. And the bed was soft, the room clean and bright.

Then I noticed that there were two plastic carrier bags on the bed. I opened one gingerly and saw a pair of men's jeans, two shirts and several t-shirts. The other bag contained socks and underwear, a pack of disposable razors, other toiletries and a toothbrush.

I ran my tongue over my teeth, cringing at the furry gunkiness, and wondering how bad I smelled. I'd grown immune to it a long time ago, but something about the brightness of this hotel shamed me.

Pulling off my boots, I stepped into the tiny bathroom. Weakening further, I turned on the shower, marvelling at the hot water that came pouring out.

Making the decision to stay wasn't too hard after that. Bought for the price of a hot shower—I was a cheap date.

I stripped off all my clothes and stood under the water, and if tears mingled with that steady stream, no one would ever know.

When I finally climbed out, I cringed at the ring of grey scum that had settled at the bottom. Then with renewed energy, I filled the tub with water and poured in a healthy amount of shampoo, dumping all my dirty clothes and those from my kitbag in it. I couldn't remember the last time I'd done any laundry.

Or the last time I'd cared.

Wiping the steam from the mirror, I shaved off the bushy beard, then ran the razor over my scalp.

I looked gaunt, and even through the haze of steam, I saw the emptiness in my eyes. My body was too thin, and I could see my ribs well enough to count them. But from beneath the grime and hopelessness, I began to recognize myself.

I brushed my teeth four times, surprised to find pleasure in being clean.

When I turned to see how the laundry was doing, the bathwater was grey with accumulated filth. I scrubbed the clothes hard, and it took three lots of rinsing before the water ran clean. It was a huge effort to hang the dripping clothes over the shower rail, and by then I was completely knackered and collapsed onto the bathroom floor, out of breath and sweating alcohol.

My hands were shaking, too. This was the longest I'd been without a drink in months. Acknowledging that desperate craving ramped the need higher. I drank some tap water, but threw it up almost immediately.

My stomach hurt and my head felt like a road gang were drilling through it.

But Clay had thought of that, too, and I found a box of dry crackers and a packet of Ibuprofen in the goodies on my bed.

I swallowed four pills and managed to eat some crackers, as well.

I lay down on top of the bed, staring up at the ceiling that swirled and spun.

Going cold turkey was going to suck donkey balls.

Funny, it never occurred to me to go and find a drink.

If Clay thought I was worth saving, maybe I wasn't a lost cause. The question was: did I want to be saved?

It took three days for the alcohol to be purged from my body. Three days of shits, shakes and sweats, itching skin, racing heart and hallucinations that scared the crap out of me. I dreamed that I was back in our cabin in the woods, breathing in the scent of pine trees and our sweat in the humid summer. Those dreams were good until the ending, always the same ending, her blood on my hands and me screaming until I puked.

Clay came and went, bringing food that was left untouched, more Ibuprofen for the blistering headaches that made me think my brain was melting.

But on the fourth day, I woke up with a little more clarity, a trace more humanity. My head ached with a dull throb, but I was definitely feeling like my old self, which was not necessarily a good thing. Clarity brought back painful memories, and without the numbness to cope, I was a confused and anxious mess.

I couldn't explain why I kept going, kept trying to detox and get clean. I didn't understand my own motivation. Maybe because Clay wanted this; maybe because Zada was waiting to see me, and I knew I couldn't have let her see me as I was.

The hotel door opened and Clay walked in, a huge smile on his face.

"It walks, it talks, it's nearly human!"

"Fuck off," I grumbled without much heat.

"You're looking a whole lot better, brother. Think you can face some breakfast?"

I gave him a wry look.

"Not a full English, but maybe some dry toast and coffee."

He nodded.

"And Zada? Are you ready to see her?"

I sucked in a long breath, my jaw clamping.

"I want to see her," I said slowly. "But I'm dreading it, too. No offence."

He sighed.

"None taken. I get it. But she really wants to see you. You're important to her. She wants to feel this connection with you—for Amira's sake."

Searing pain throbbed inside my chest as Clay said her name. Grief and guilt, and the endless emptiness of knowing that she was dead—that I hadn't stopped her, hadn't saved her.

Clay rested his hand on my shoulder.

"Is it so bad that you can't even bear to hear her name?"

"It's just been a while," I murmured.

He hesitated, his lips pressed together.

"Do you want to talk about it?"

I shook my head, swallowing hard.

"James, brother ... she cared about you, you know that, right? She wouldn't want *this* for you."

"I'll be fine. I just ... I'll be fine."

He let me live with the lie and didn't comment further.

I showered and shaved as quickly as I could, given that my hands still shook slightly, and wore the new jeans and one of the shirts that Clay had bought for me. The only footwear was my old Army boots, but I cleaned them up as best I could and gave them a spit polish.

Clay laughed.

"Man, I haven't done that since Boot Camp. My old Drill Sergeant could spot a speck of dust from a thousand paces. He was a mean son of a gun."

I glanced up, amused.

" 'Son of a gun'? Harsh language, Clay."

He laughed.

"Yep, I'm trying to swear off cussing along with drink. Living clean these days, buddy. You should try it."

There was a long pause and then I nodded.

"Maybe I will."

He held out his hand, pulling me up from the bed and into a tight hug.

"I've missed you, James. Promise you won't disappear on us again."

I tried to say something funny or stupid—tell him he was a damn pussy—but I couldn't do it. Sincerity gave his words power, and I felt them.

"I can't promise," I said, at last. "But I will try."

"Good enough for now," he said with a faint smile.

Then for the first time in four days, I left the hotel room.

Zada was waiting for us at a breakfast table. She looked exactly the same except she was wearing glasses while reading a newspaper.

And God, she looked so much like her sister, so much like Amira. The same beautiful dark eyes, the same caramel skin, the same slender hands. But it was the sight of her *hijab* that stopped me in my tracks.

It was the same.

It was the same colours, the same pattern, the same as the square of silk that I kept folded up in my shoebox.

I froze, mid-step.

"Ah, man," Clay said quietly. "I should have thought of that."

Zada's welcoming smile dropped and her hands flew to her headscarf.

"This? Oh James, I'm so sorry! I should have thought—my mother gave us one each. I wear it all the time to feel close to Amira, but I didn't think…"

My heart jolted painfully, but I bullied a weak smile onto my face.

"It's okay, it's fine … it's good to see you, Zada." I was lying. It hurt like hell. "And, um, congratulations. On the wedding."

Her eyes darted nervously to Clay, and he held her hand.

"Thank you," she whispered.

After the most awkward greeting ever, we sat down and even Clay seemed lost for words.

I could have kissed the waitress when she arrived with the menus.

Clay and Amira both ordered the full vegetarian breakfast.

"Only toast, please, and coffee."

The waitress left with our order and we all sat looking at each other.

Zada's smile twisted.

"Did you know that Amira tried out to be a cheerleader once?"

I shook my head. There were so many things I didn't know.

Zada gave a hollow laugh.

"Dear Allah, what a disaster! She was such a klutz, you know? She knocked over a pyramid of six cheerleaders when her cartwheel went wonky. Complete high school fail. She never lived it down."

Her words caused a sharp stab of pain in my chest as I remembered Amira tripping in her *burqa*, and I'd picked her up, arranging her small body against mine. The pain of that memory was intense and unconsciously I rubbed the tattoo over my heart, my private memorial to her.

I looked up to see Clay and Zada watching me with concerned eyes.

"Maybe I shouldn't have said anything..." Zada began, her voice dropping to a whisper.

"No," I disagreed at once. "Tell me everything. I want to know."

And so she did—the good things, the sad things, the funny things —all those small moments that make up a life. All the moments that I hadn't been there for.

The pain of loss ripped me apart again. It should have been Amira telling me her high school stories, Amira making me laugh over her awkward attempt to be a cheerleader, but we never had the chance.

We never had the time.

And now, we never would.

It occurred to me that I'd never known Zada's Amira, the one who'd laughed openly. It hurt to think that I'd never known her light-hearted or free of the sadness that weighed her down. Our relationship had been forged in doubt and hardened in fire. Had we ever had a chance?

"She loved working in the ER," said Zada, her voice stronger now. "She loved the challenge, the adrenaline of never knowing what was going to happen, the rush."

She looked at me directly.

"That's something you both have ... had ... in common. Maybe that's why she ... you know ... volunteered in the first place. Maybe that's why she went to Syria." Her tone softened with uncertainty, questions in her voice. "Maybe she was addicted ... to the intensity."

Was that true? Was that what we'd seen in each other?

We sat in silence, the coffee cooling in front of me.

It was Zada who spoke first. There was no preamble—she just dived in, saying what she'd clearly been waiting to say.

"I want you to take this job with Clay. I want you to keep him safe."

"Zada..." Clay began. "Let the man drink his coffee first."

"I'm sorry," she said, looking at me then back at him. "But it's been on my mind for weeks. You say James is the best, then no one else will do. I can't lose you, too, Clay. I love you."

His expression softened as he gazed at his wife, and I had to look away. Seeing their love so obvious, so easy, it ripped me open. I even glanced down at my chest, half-expecting to see blood oozing through my shirt.

But no, my worst wounds were on the inside.

Zada's words soaked through me and I found myself speaking firmly.

"I'll do it," I said. "I'll go with Clay. I'll keep him safe—or die trying."

Clay laughed uneasily.

"Hopefully, it won't come to that."

"Thank you," said Zada earnestly.

Then she leaned across the table and squeezed my hand. I nodded uncomfortably and slid my hand under the table.

There was a long, tension-filled pause. I swallowed and cleared my throat.

"So, what's the plan?"

Clay's expression cleared, and Zada leaned back in her seat.

"What do you know about Nagorno Karabakh?"

I searched through my memories but came up blank.

"Georgia?" I guessed. "Ukraine?"

It definitely sounded like somewhere in the former Soviet bloc.

"Close," replied Clay. "It's a disputed territory on the western side of Azerbaijan, mostly mountainous or forested areas: Russia to the north, Iran to the South. They've had nearly three decades of fighting since even before independence from the Soviet Union in 1991. The territory has been treated like a bone between a pack of dogs, with soldiers from Armenia, Azerbaijan, Georgia and Chechnya all joining in. Throw in some Kurd mercenaries and Mujahideen, and well, you can imagine."

"Jesus." I glanced at Zada. "Um, sorry."

"Yeah, I know," said Clay, ignoring my verbal stumble. "The Halo Trust has been working there on and off since 2000 de-mining tens of thousands of hectares, but Nagorno still has one of the highest per capita incidences of landmine and unexploded ordnance accidents in the world. James, a quarter of the victims are children."

His lips thinned as he quoted that statistic, and Zada was visibly upset.

I held back a sigh.

Clay was a good guy, a great guy, but he was also an idealist. And how he managed that after 11 years in the U.S. Marines, I'd never know. He thought he'd be flying out there to make the world a safer place, and maybe he would, but I knew ex-ATOs who had taken these non-governmental organisation jobs and found out that they were under-resourced with a fairly hazardous approach to health and safety. Hopefully, not this one.

Clay needed me more than he knew. And I didn't have anything better to do with my life.

I didn't have anything at all.

"When do we leave?"

BOMBSHELL is available now!

REVIEWS

Reviews are love :)

Honestly, they are! But it also helps other people to make an informed decision before buying this book.

So I'd really appreciate if you took a few seconds to do just that by leaving a review.

Thank you!

MORE ABOUT JHB

"Love all, trust a few, do wrong to none"—this is one of my favourite sayings. Oh, and 'Be Nice!' That's another. Or maybe, 'Where's the chocolate?'

I get asked where my ideas come from—they come from everywhere. From walks with my dog on the beach, from listening to conversations in pubs and shops, where I lurk unnoticed with my notebook. And of course, ideas come from things I've seen or read, places I've been and people I meet.

If you've seen me at any book signings you'll know that I support these military charities:

www.felixfund.org.uk – the UK Bomb Disposal Charity

www.eodwarrriorfoundation.org – the US Bomb Disposal Charity

www.nowzad.com – helping servicemen and women rescue stray and abandoned animals in former and current war zones

This story has heavily featured the work of the Halo Trust, but my information on de-mining around the world comes from two sources, neither of whom want to be named, but I thank them both unreservedly.

If you want to find out more about the work of the Halo Trust (Hazardous Area Life-support Organization), go to www.halotrust.org

ACKNOWLEDGMENTS

This story is personal to me in many ways. I have friends amongst the EOD community, so it's important to me because of that. I've tried really hard to get the details right, although I have no military background myself. Yes, I did have people I could go to ask for further information. **But any mistakes are mine, and mine alone, as is any creative licence with the story.**

Wanting to write, being a writer, it's a lifelong lesson, and one that I'm still learning. But there are a number of people who have helped guide and sculpt *this* book. So I'll start with these women, all amazing in their own rights, all different, all supportive.

To J and Justin. Again. To Danny C.

To Krista Webster, for stepping in to help when I needed it, and for sorting out those pesky timeline issues.

To cover model Gergo Jonas, who is so much more than a handsome man, and has become a good friend, too.

To cover model Ellie Ruewell, whose good humour and big smiles made the photoshoot the *best* fun.

To the real Alan Clayton Williams who asked me to give him an awesome death, but became a hero instead.

To Sharon Tómas for my gorgeous website, kindness and support

To Tonya 'Maverick' Allen, travel buddy and my own personal cheerleader.

To Sheena Lumsden and Lynda Throsby for many things, including their friendship and wicked organisational skills.

To the real Rose Hogg, who is standing in for James's 'first time', the lucky lass.

To all the bloggers who give up their time for their passion of reading and reviewing books—thank you for your support.

And to my readers. Not only do you have great taste, but you rock!

GLOSSARY

Burqa – an enveloping outer garment worn by women in some Islamic traditions to cover themselves in public, which covers the body and the face

Daesh/ISIS – Islamic State

Didashah – traditional men's garment in Syria

Hijab – a veil worn by some Muslim women which usually covers the hair and neck

Imam – the title of a worship leader of a mosque

Inshallah – as God wills it

Mashallah – as God willed it

Niqab – a garment of clothing that covers the face

Pbuh – 'peace be upon him' is a conventionally complimentary phrase attached to the names of the prophets in Islam

Quran – the central religious text of Islam

Salat-al-zuhr – noon prayer

Military Terms

AT – Ammunition Technician: bomb disposal officer (UK)

AWOL – Absent Without Leave

Dems – demolitions (destroying ammunition or explosives)

C.O. – Commanding Officer

Det cord – detonation cord

EOD – Explosive Ordnance Disposal / bomb disposal

Go dark – off the grid/without communications

HMEs – homemade explosives

IED – improvised explosive device

LCpl – Lance Corporal

MREs – Meals Ready to Eat: U.S. military rations

PNC – Police National Computer (UK)

PT – Physical Training

RC – Remote control

RMP – Royal Military Police

RPG – Rocket Propelled Grenade

Sat Phone – Satellite Phone

Scrote – low life

SDF – Syrian Defence Forces

Squaddie – low rank soldier

UN – United Nations

Weapons-grade – a British Army term that means serious, harsh or large-scale

REVIEWS

Reviews are love! Honestly, they are! But it also helps other people to make an informed decision before buying my book.

So I'd really appreciate if you took a few seconds to do that.

Thank you!

MORE BOOKS BY JHB

Series Titles
*The Education Series
An epic love story spanning the years, through war zones and more...
*The Education of Sebastian (Education series #1)
*The Education of Caroline (Education series #2)
*The Education of Sebastian & Caroline (combined edition, books 1 & 2)
Semper Fi: The Education of Caroline (Education series #3)

*The Traveling Series
All the fun of the fair ... and two worlds collide
*The Traveling Man (Traveling series #1)
*The Traveling Woman (Traveling series #2)
*Roustabout (Traveling series #3)
*Carnival (Traveling series #4)
*Gypsy (Traveling series #5)

The Justin Trainer Series
The bodyguard and the billionaire
Guarding the Billionaire (Justin Trainer series #1)
Saving the Billionaire (Justin Trainer series #2)

The EOD Series
Blood, bombs and heartbreak
*Tick Tock (EOD series #1)
* Bombshell (EOD series #2)

The Rhythm Series
Blood, sweat, tears and dance
*Slave to the Rhythm (Rhythm series #1)
*Luka (Rhythm series #2)

Standalone Titles
Contemporary Romance
The Lilac Cadillac
Battle Scars
One Careful Owner
*Lifers
At Your Beck & Call
The New Samurai
Exposure

New Adult
*Dangerous to Know & Love
Dazzled
Summer of Seventeen

Paranormal
*The Dark Detective: Venator (Book #1)
*The Dark Detective: Paukúnnum (Book #2)

Novellas
Playing in the Rain
*Behind the Walls

Anthologies of Short Stories
*The Year Book Volume 1
*The Year Book Volume 2
*The Year Book Volume 3

Audio Books
One Careful Owner
(narrated by Seth Clayton)

On the Stage
Later, After: Playscript
Trailer

With Alana Albertson
Father Figure

* These titles are published in languages other than English. Please check Jane's website for details—and receive **a free short story every month** when you sign up for her newsletter :)

QR code for Jane's website

ROMANCE WITH STUART REARDON

Books written with my lovely co-author

Two book series - contemporary romance
*Undefeated
*Model Boyfriend

Three book series - romcom
*Gym Or Chocolate?
*The World According to Vince
*The Baby Game

Standalone
Survivor Love Island *(romcom)*
*Touch My Soul *(novella)*

WRITING AS BERRICK FORD

Police Thrillers, UK

Dead Water
Dead Man's Dive
Dead Reckoning
Dead Shore

www.berrickford.com

www.ingramcontent.com/pod-product-compliance
Lightning Source LLC
Chambersburg PA
CBHW071105250626
47159CB00002B/607